THE MARK OF SALVATION

CAROL UMBERGER

INTEGRITY®

PUBLISHERS

Nashville

DEDICATION

To Daniel and David, beloved gifts from God.

ACKNOWLEDGMENTS

I AM DEEPLY INDEBTED to many people for their love, support, and encouragement:

Pastor Ken Hohag and his wife Melanie, for inspiring me with their thirst for the Word of the Lord and for showing my family and me what it means to live a life of service.

Lillian Monson, proud member of Clan Campbell, who shared her love and knowledge of weaving, tartans, and textiles with me. What a joy it was to spend those hours learning from you. If there are errors in the manuscript, they are mine alone.

Dawn and Grace Wexler for asking the questions I didn't think of. Thank you, Dawn, for journeying with me as we seek to learn what it means to be women of faith.

Lori, Diane, and Angel for countless cups of coffee and sharing the ups and downs of writing for publication.

Khrys Williams, indispensable critique partner and cheerleader. I couldn't have done this without you!

Lisa Tawn Bergren, editor, mentor, and friend who trudged through a less than perfect manuscript despite a brand new baby and once again, deftly made my story shine. Thank you so much.

And last but certainly not least, my wonderful husband and sons who have come to recognize "the stare" that means I'm lost somewhere with my characters again.

Author's Notes

THERE IS ONLY CONJECTURE and circumstantial evidence to suggest that Templar Knights gave aid to Robert the Bruce at Bannockburn. However, the idea caught my imagination and thus Ceallach came to life. I have barely touched on the Bruces' incursion into Ireland. Edward Bruce was crowned king of Ireland in 1316 and was killed two years later in battle there. The succession to the Scottish throne was then settled on Marjory's son Robert Stewart, thus beginning the line of the Stewart kings. In 1324, Elizabeth Bruce gave birth to a male heir, David.

For a list of resources I relied upon, please visit my website at www.carolumberger.com. I enjoy hearing from readers and you can reach me at carol@carolumberger.com or write to me in care of Integrity Publishers.

May God bless you as abundantly as he has blessed me.

PROLOGUE

"Brothers will refrain from boasting of
past prowess or brave deeds."

—from the Rule of the Templar Knights

Are you sure we can cross here?" Marcus asked his foster
brother. He stared at the fast-moving creek that flowed along
the edge of the stone castle.

"What, are you afraid? You don't trust me?" Robert
taunted.

"Sure, I trust you. But trusting you got our seats whipped
for swinging from the barn roof."

"We did it, though, didn't we?" Robert smiled in glee.
"That's worth a certain measure."

Marcus grinned back. Impossible, that this boy would
someday be the king of Scotland. They were all doomed. "Aye,
but my seat is still sore."

"Then the water will feel good."

"Until the current knocks us down and carries us to our
deaths."

"Be bold, Marcus. I'll go first and measure the water's
depth with a stick."

"Our clothes will get wet." Marcus didn't want to seem
afraid. He wasn't—not really.

1

"Take them off if you're so worried."

"I can't do that. We'll be in enough trouble if we are caught with our clothes on let alone without them."

"Then follow me!" commanded Robert, as he plunged into the stream.

Do you remember that day by the stream, Robert? Or the time we explored the caves in the nearby hills? I would've followed you anywhere then. I'm still following you, but the consequences are far more daunting than a session with your father's strap. The fate of a kingdom rests on your broad shoulders. If I still believed in God I would pray for your success.

—from the private journal of Ceallach of Dunstruan

Scotland 1307

CONCEALED BEHIND THE TREES AND ROCKS on the hillside overlooking the main road to Cumnock, Robert the Bruce, king of Scotland, watched as the English Earl of Pembroke and his troops paraded down the narrow mountain road. Pembroke had acted dishonorably at Methven, attacking Bruce after giving his word as a knight that he would not fight until the agreed-upon time.

The Scottish army had been decimated and Bruce ached to take revenge on Pembroke.

He turned to his natural son, Bryan. "What do you make of it?"

"There aren't many of them," Bryan said. "We could take them at the pass."

"But?" At nearly seventeen years of age, the boy was wise beyond his years and an accomplished swordsman. Robert often tested him thus, and Bryan rarely disappointed him with his grasp of tactics.

2

"Pembroke is making no effort to surprise us. It's as if he wants us to know he's here."

"Aye, you're right not to trust him," Bruce said. "Still, we may be able to defeat him if we use the land to our advantage." They quickly mapped out a plan and called the other officers to them. But before Bruce could give the order to move out, a breathless sentry raced up to them.

"What is it lad?" Bruce asked in alarm.

"My laird, make haste. 'Tis a trap. John of Lorne and his highlanders are coming through the woods behind us."

Just months before, John of Lorne had nearly captured Bruce at Dalry Pass. Bruce's wife, sisters, and daughter had been with him. To assure the women's safety, Bruce had given all his horses to them and the men who protected them and sent them north out of harm's way. He and his army, such as it was, had been on foot ever since. Fortunately, Lorne and his highlanders would likely be on foot as well.

With brisk efficiency born of countless such close encounters, Bruce issued orders. "James, divide the men into three groups. You escort one east, my brother will take one to the west, and Bryan and I will lead the rest and head south. Circle around and we'll meet at the old cottage at Loch Dee."

Edward Bruce nodded. "I know the one. God go with you, brother."

"And with you. Now go!"

Bruce watched as his orders were carried out, but the sound of a baying hound soon sent him and his band of twenty men running. Their pursuers crashed through the brush behind them and it soon became apparent that, for some reason, only Bruce's party was being followed.

Waving his arms, he indicated that his men should scatter and try to diffuse their pursuers. He ran, Bryan beside him, dodging branches and rocks. The sounds of pursuit continued and the hound sounded closer now, obviously excited. Bruce stopped and listened. Could it be? Breath coming in gasps he said to Bryan, "The dog . . . I recognize his voice. He was once mine. Lost him at Dalry."

"He knows your scent then," Bryan said. His expression showed that he, too, realized the peril they were in.

"Aye, and a more loyal animal never lived. He'll stop at nothing to be reunited. He'll bring Lorne straight to us."

"Then we best run faster."

From the corner of his eye Bruce caught movement. Five men, fleeter than the others, were closing in rapidly. "Look to the right!"

Bruce drew his sword and Bryan did the same. "There!" Bruce pointed to a large rock and they ran and put their backs to it just as the men caught up to them. Three came after Bruce; the other two took on Bryan. With a mighty swing Bruce dealt a blow that sheared through one man's ear and cheek and into his neck. The man went down hard. His two companions retreated.

With a moment's reprieve, Bruce went to Bryan's aid and with a sideways slash of his sword took off the head of one of the attackers. The first two returned to the fray, their anger renewed. Bruce met them, cutting through one's arm while Bryan finished off his man. Bruce killed the remaining attacker and for the moment, they were safe.

Panting, drenched in sweat, they leaned on their swords until the sound of the baying hound sent them running again. Nearing exhaustion, knowing they couldn't keep up this pace, Bruce cried out when they stumbled upon a small stream. "Blessed be our God!" Bruce rushed forward, into the cold water. "That dog's loyalty threatens to be the death of us. We'll use this stream to lose my scent."

"Aye," Bryan said as he jumped in, close on Bruce's heels. Within minutes the dog's barking faded until finally they could no longer hear it. They left the stream, boots sloshing with water but they dared not stop to empty them. They walked on, determined to make Loch Dee yet this night.

Just after moonrise they came to the edge of the woods and glimpsed what had been an abandoned cottage the last time they'd come through Loch Dee. But tonight smoke arose from the chimney. None of Bruce's men were camped outside, so the occupants were strangers—enemies until proven otherwise.

Bryan laid a hand on Bruce's arm. "You stay in the cover of the trees, my laird, while I see who is here."

He stepped into the clearing, sword drawn. "Hallo the cottage," Bryan called.

After a moment, a man answered. "Who goes there?"

"Weary travelers in need of shelter for the night."

There was silence and Bruce quietly withdrew his sword. The whisper of metal on metal was like a reassuring friend's hand upon a shoulder. He held his breath, waiting.

"All travelers be welcome so long as they are loyal to our king, Robert the Bruce. If not, be gone with you."

Bruce breathed a sigh of relief at those words. He couldn't go on much farther. He sheathed his sword and joined Bryan as the door of the cottage opened, casting warm light upon the clearing.

Bryan stood aside, sword in hand but lowered. "Then welcome your rightful king."

With a look of astonishment the man opened the door wider. Bruce entered and noticed a young woman to his right, dressed in men's clothing. A sword hung at her belt and she carried herself in the way of a fighter. Even more curious, the men with her seemed to defer to her, as if she were the leader. The woman boldly strode into the firelight and he noted that she was but a year or two older than Bryan. She stood before Bruce and bowed. "Your Majesty. I am Morrigan Macnab."

A clanswoman of his enemy, John of Lorne. Bruce placed his hand on the hilt of his sword and Bryan raised his.

Her men stepped forward but she waved them off, holding her hands outstretched, palms up in front of her. "We mean you no harm, King Robert. In fact, we offer our swords to your cause, if you'll have us."

"The Macnabs are for England." Bryan said, his sword still at the ready.

"Aye, my Uncle Angus serves John of Lorne and the king of England. But we do not."

Robert studied the girl. Her men stood around her, protective, yet Bruce sensed she could well defend herself. "I would like to hear your reasons," Bruce said.

"And so you shall." She motioned toward the warm fire and pan of something cooking. "You look tired and hungry, my king. Come, eat and rest and I'll tell you my story."

Bruce looked to Bryan and the boy lowered his sword, although he did not sheath it. The smell of the food and the invitation to rest both appealed greatly. "I am grateful for your hospitality, Morrigan Macnab."

As Robert and Bryan ate roasted hen and oatcakes, Morrigan spoke without hesitation. "My father and I fought against you at Methven, my laird. We were with Prince Edward's troops."

Bruce eyed her warily, unsure even now if they'd been lulled into sharing food with one who meant them harm. Robert exchanged glances with his son but neither made a move for their weapons. "Go on, lass."

"The Earl of Pembroke's treachery was the least of it that day. The prince and his knights rode through the countryside, killing indiscriminately. Women and children were cut down in their villages for no reason other than that they were Scots."

"You participated in such evil?" Bryan asked, barely holding his temper in check.

Bruce felt his own anger rise, but he and Bryan were outnumbered. Though they'd fared well earlier today against overwhelming odds, Bruce didn't care to test fate, or God, again so soon. He would hear this woman out. There was something in her deep blue eyes that made him want to trust her.

"We did not take part in the massacre of innocents. The prince's behavior sickened me, and I aided the people the best I could after Edward and the others left."

Bruce nodded. "Aye, he so dishonored the vows of chivalry that even his father, the Hammer of the Scots, chastised him."

Morrigan stared into the fire, and Bruce saw her shudder. The sight of people slaughtered in battle could unnerve the most seasoned of warriors, had unnerved him at times. Obviously young Morrigan still suffered the effects of her experience.

"I will never fight for the English again," she said. "Nor will those here with me."

"It matters not which side of the battle you're on, war is terrible," he said gently.

"Aye, it is. But I must ask you directly—would you slaughter women and children?"

"I would never sink so low, not even if their men were my enemies."

With a determined nod of her head she said, "Then my offer to join you stands."

Morrigan was but four or five years older than Bruce's own daughter. Robert would spare them both the horrors of war if he could. "Your men are few in number, and you are . . . female."

Bryan stifled a laugh and she gave him a withering look. "Come the morrow, I will show you what a mere female can do."

Early the next morning, Bruce's men had not yet arrived. Their routes would undoubtedly take longer than the one he and Bryan had stumbled upon. Rested and well fed, Bruce and Bryan joined Morrigan and her men on the hillside above the cottage.

Morrigan pointed. "Do you see those crows perched in yonder tree?"

"Aye." Bruce smiled at her bravado. "But that is nearly beyond the range of my most skilled archers."

"Remember you said that. You'll be dining on those birds." There was no boasting in her voice, only confidence. And just a touch of irritation at his disbelief.

Morrigan placed an arrow on her bow, notched it, and slowly pulled back on the string. Taking careful aim, she released the arrow and Bruce watched in awe as it pierced two birds at once.

Suitably impressed, Bruce said, "Well done! Tell me, are your men as skilled as you?"

One of the men stepped forward. "Morrigan is by far the best archer among us, but we are all veteran fighters, Your Majesty."

Bruce stroked his beard as he considered how he might make the best use of this offer of help. Morrigan and her men drew close to him, standing in a half-circle before him. To a man, they looked eager to join his fight. "I have no doubt you would be useful to me in battle. My army is pitifully small. But I also have need of people who can move about the countryside and listen for rumors and watch for troop movements. Perhaps even spread false information for me."

They didn't hesitate. The one who had spoken earlier nodded and Morrigan answered, "That we can gladly do."

"Good. I'll send messengers from time to time. Come to me if you learn anything I should know."

BRUCE AND HIS WARRIORS headed south the next day, to be nearer the plentiful game in Galloway. They set up camp in the high, rocky valley of Glen Trool. The way into the little valley was so strewn with boulders it was inaccessible by horseback, thus preventing a frontal attack by a mounted enemy. His army would be relatively safe here. Once the tents were in place, Bruce sent many of his men—who still barely numbered three hundred—out to hunt for venison. Aye, this was a good camp, a safe haven. Here his men could stay for a while, recuperating, tending to wounds, preparing for the battle that lay ahead.

These past months had been difficult for them all, but Robert felt the burden deeper than any. Three of his five brothers had been killed fighting against the English. His effort to safeguard his wife, daughter, and other womenfolk by sending them north had failed. All had been captured and taken to England as prisoners. If only that cursed Edward would acquiesce and give him what was rightfully his!

The hunters rode out again and he and Bryan stayed in camp, enjoying a chance to sit in the relative quiet. But a sentry's shout soon interrupted them. He and Bryan hurried toward the man, who was apparently wrestling with a newcomer. But Bruce smiled when he saw his sentry holding fast to a familiar young woman.

"Let her go, Will."

"Her?"

Laughing at Will's confusion, Bryan said, "Hello, Morrigan. I see you are still wearing trews."

She cast a scowl his way. "Well I can't very well run through the heather and bracken—much less ride a horse—in a skirt, now can I?"

Bruce nodded to Will and he released her. "Morrigan, it is good to see you," the king said. "But you don't look pleased to see us."

"My laird, 'tis always a pleasure to visit with you and your *charming* son. But I didn't come on a social call. Pembroke is headed this way, my laird, with fifteen hundred troops. They mean to catch you by surprise."

Bruce walked over to look out over the valley and the others followed. "Where are they, Morrigan?"

She pointed to a forested hillside several miles away.

Robert thought for a few minutes then said, "We are greatly outnumbered but the terrain will be to our advantage. He can't make a frontal cavalry charge over these boulders, and the pass behind us is easily defended. Pembroke's men will have to come on foot, which might have worked if we weren't aware of the attack."

He looked at Bryan and Morrigan and both nodded their agreement with his evaluation. "Then let him come. We'll be waiting, thanks to you. Well done, Morrigan."

Quietly Bruce ordered his men to send a scout for the hunters to return to camp and arm themselves. The Scots would hold their high ground.

They barely had time to form up and take position when the English raced out of the woods and across the field of boulders. Morrigan let loose an arrow and caught the leader of the charge in the throat.

"Good shot!" Bruce exclaimed.

The English, alarmed to find the Scots armed and waiting for them instead of unaware, halted their charge. That hesitation proved fatal to their attack. Bruce cried, "Upon them now!" and the three hundred Scots rushed forward. The English fled back the way they had come.

Relieved at the quick victory, Bruce solemnly laid his hand on Morrigan's arm. "One day I will repay you, Morrigan Macnab."

"Unite our country, my laird, and oust the English. That will be reward enough."

February 1308, The Hills of Carrick

CEALLACH KNELT BEFORE HIS FOSTER BROTHER, the king of Scotland, not on the marble floor of a stately palace, but on the dirt floor of a small stone cottage in the hills where they'd been children together. No trappings of office surrounded the royal personage, for Robert's clothing was nearly as threadbare as Ceallach's own.

The months of hard travel, of hiding and fear, of bone deep weariness, threatened to overcome Ceallach. He knew that Bruce had also known treachery, deceit, and physical deprivation this past year, and knowing that had given Ceallach hope of sanctuary. Raising his head, he prayed his eyes would not betray his desperation. Robert was his only chance for anything resembling a normal life.

Robert smiled. "Rise, Marcus of—"

"Nay, sire." Glancing at the three men standing nearby, Ceallach pulled Bruce close to whisper, "Please, Your Majesty. I go by the name of Ceallach."

Bruce studied him a moment before saying, "I understand. Rise then, Ceallach."

Ceallach stood as the king waved away the others. They moved to the other end of the cottage, giving the king privacy.

Robert laid his hand on Ceallach's shoulder. "All right. How can I be of help?"

Ceallach managed not to flinch from the touch; he simply moved away so Robert had to remove his hand. His wounds were barely healed and even an innocent touch could cause the skin to break open and ooze. "I think we can help one another, my laird. I have need of sanctuary. You have need of weapons and money."

Ceallach had nothing to lose. Either Robert accepted him and gave him refuge, or Ceallach's life would end here in the wilds of Carrick. No sense mincing words. "I have no home, Robert. I am not safe in any country in all of Europe, save possibly for Scotland. All I held dear was stripped from me, and I'm lucky I escaped with my life."

Robert's expression turned bleak, and suddenly Ceallach feared Robert would banish him, since his very presence endangered anyone that harbored him. Hoping to forestall such a possibility, Ceallach confessed. "I would pledge myself to your cause, Robert."

"You would fight for Scotland's freedom?"

"I am a warrior. 'Tis the only life I know."

"This is no holy war, Ceallach, fought to uphold the Church."

Ceallach laughed. "No war is holy, Robert. To think otherwise is a fool's game, and I'm done with being a fool."

"But you would fight for freedom?"

"If that is your cause, then, yes. I would do so willingly, for I have no home, no country, not even a church to pray in."

"Nowhere else to turn." A gleam came into Robert's eye, and Ceallach relaxed. "Then join with me. We shall be free men once more."

Ceallach the Warrior, weary, desperate, at his strength's end, wiped tears from his eyes and followed his king into the night.

ONE

When not engaged in military duties
brothers shall lead the life of a monk.

—from the Rule of the Templar Knights

I *woke from a nightmare again last night. As I'm sharing Robert's tent, I awakened him with my shouts for the third time this week.*

This morning he offered me a bundle of precious parchment, a quill, and some ink. "If you won't talk about it, then you should write it down."

"I'm not sure I can." I don't want to revisit my past—the dreams are bad enough.

"I think you must tell the story before your nightmares consume you."

Maybe he's right. It's been eight years and still I cannot sleep without . . . no, I cannot begin with those visions, yet I need to understand what happened. And why. Perhaps if I start with the hopes and dreams of my youth I will eventually be able to write down the events that have scarred me as an adult.

As a child I listened with awe to my foster father's stories of going on crusade to the Holy Land, especially his tales about the Templar Knights. Their bravery in battle and devotion to

13

God stirred my imagination, and by the time I was but ten years old, I felt called to become such a religious warrior.

At the age of sixteen I earned the golden spurs of knighthood and took vows of poverty, chastity, and obedience as a Templar Knight. At that age, a young man's blood runs hot, but I learned to cool mine with prayer and fasting. I was determined to honor Christ and myself by keeping my vows.

Ah, the idealism of youth.

Let it simply be said that all I've ever wanted is to serve God and use my skills as a warrior to win souls for him. As a man of the sword, Robert understands that desire better than anyone. He, too, longs to go on Crusade and to devote his warrior's skills—gifts from God—to the defense of the faith. That is a laudable aspiration, but I applaud his decision to see Scotland freed from tyranny before taking on such a quest. Perhaps one day we will ride to the Holy Land together.

June 23, 1314, Bannockburn

THE NIGHTS WERE SHORT THIS FAR NORTH and dawn broke especially early this Midsummer's Day, or so it seemed to Countess Orelia Radbourne. Once again she had accompanied her husband, the Earl of Radbourne, to the site of a battle. She studied their tent's walls, glowing with the early light of a warm summer sun, something that usually pleased her. But this time, for reasons she could not explain, she desperately wished they were back home and safe at Radbourne Hall.

They shared a pallet of sheepskins, and John stirred in his sleep. Awakening, he stretched like a cat as he had every morning of their marriage. She smiled, fighting the urge to cling to him and beg him to take her home, take himself from danger. But she did not embarrass either of them by such an unseemly display. It would have done no good. He was pledged to fight and must do so.

John sat up, instantly alert in the way of a soldier. He leaned on one arm, staring down at her. "I can see by that frown on your face that you are already worrying."

"Yes. And don't tell me not to. It won't do any good."

He kissed her cheek and stood up. "I know. But I'll say it anyway—don't worry." As he donned his clothes, he continued. "We outnumber the Scots four to one. Our supply train stretches nearly twenty miles long. We will make short work of Bruce and his rabble."

She stood also and began to dress. "That's what you've been saying, and yet look at what happened to Henry yesterday."

"Yes. Well. Bruce is a notable warrior. I've never before seen anyone stand in the stirrups and deliver such a blow as Bruce dealt Henry."

Orelia shuddered. Henry de Bohun was—had been—young and somewhat rash, but he'd been their friend. Now he was dead at the hand of the Scottish king himself. The first of many, she feared.

Apparently aware of her apprehension, John continued his attempt to reassure her. "Fortunately, few of Bruce's men are trained in the art of war. Most are simple highlanders with crude weapons and insufferable tempers."

"John, how can you speak so about your fellowman?"

"They aren't my fellowman, Orelia. They are England's enemies. The sooner we subdue them and civilize them the better."

The heat in his voice warned Orelia not to press further. She didn't approve of such disparagement but did not want to send him off to battle with angry words between them.

He struggled with the fasteners on his chain mail. "Call my squire to help with this."

"Nonsense. I don't want to share our time together with young George. Here, let me."

He bent his knees to accommodate her shorter stature and she tied the leather bindings. John was a good man and a worthy husband. Their marriage had not been a love match but they had found love together. When she finished the task she stepped around him and finding her boots, sat on a chest to put them on.

"Thank you," he said.

"You're welcome." She frowned at her tangled bootlaces.

"You're frowning again." He bent and stilled her hands with his. "Today will be better, love. England will be victorious and then we shall take our share of the spoils. We can stay in Scotland on our new estate and create a home in peace."

Orelia had come north with John to help him establish their new home and to escape her brother-in-law's wife and her increasingly hostile behavior toward Orelia. Alice and Richard had already produced a daughter, and the woman never passed an opportunity to remind Orelia of her own childless state.

Orelia shook her head. She would not waste time thinking of that woman. Orelia was here to begin anew with John, to begin a new chapter in their marriage. One that did not include Alice.

A number of other men had brought their wives and household goods to Stirling. They were so sure of victory that they didn't want to waste time returning home before taking over the promised Scottish estates.

She and John had come together as man and wife again last night, no longer in hope of creating a child. After seven years of marriage they had no children and were resigned that there would be none.

Still, like Hannah of the Bible, Orelia petitioned the Lord daily, hoping that he would hear her prayers and promising to raise the child for God's work if only he would bless her with a son. But John had suffered a serious fever as a child, and the healer had warned him that he might not father children as a result.

John tipped her chin up. "The battle won't last long; I'll be back for supper. Make plans for furnishing Dunstruan and leave your worries to God. What will be, will be."

She closed her eyes and swallowed. "And if you should die?"

He touched her cheek and she opened her eyes. His gentle smile should have eased her anxiety, but it didn't. "If that should be God's will, Orelia, then I will see you again in eternity. Don't lose faith. No matter what happens you will not be alone."

She threw her arms around him and clung to him. He allowed it briefly, then gently put her aside and finished donning his armor. With a quick kiss and a confident dip of his head, he left her.

CEALLACH'S HORSE SHIFTED BENEATH HIM, dancing sideways until Ceallach nudged it with his lower leg. With trembling hands he patted the horse's neck, trying to soothe them both. The clamor of battle truly surrounded him. He tried to concentrate and not slip from the present into memories of a battle from long ago. But Ceallach was as helpless now to stop the pain as he'd been eight years ago in a French prison.

Sweat dripped into his eyes—the white hood he wore to hide his identity only added to the heat of this warm summer day. But he would have perspired if it had been an icy January night.

The English let loose a barrage of arrows, some of them flame tipped. None reached as far as where he sat astride his horse, but Ceallach's heart pounded. Terror and fear swept through him. His limbs froze, just as they had when his torturer had drawn near . . . torch light dancing in his eyes . . . Ceallach's trembling hands clutched the reins as if they alone held him in this time and this place.

Still he did not retreat. Years of training would not allow it and he sat in the middle of this battle wrestling with his painful recollections. Someday he would let the memories return, put them on paper and take away their sting once and for all. But here on the battlefield he would release fury instead—only holding himself in check enough to ensure that his wrath came down on English, not Scottish, soldiers. That much he could do, he was fairly certain.

With a cry he sent the horse forward into the fray, battle-axe swinging, blood lust flooding through him, crazing him, conversely easing him. Now the trembling stopped, and the sweat was the result of effort, not fear. He drove his horse toward the English standard and the king who rode beneath it.

THE EARL OF PEMBROKE on Edward's left and Sir Giles d'Argentan on his right each seized a rein of Edward's horse. "You must leave, Your Majesty. You must not be captured, or the day is truly lost."

"No, I won't leave the field." Edward yanked the reins from them and tried to move forward.

His compatriots held him fast, gesturing toward the fields in which his troops were clearly languishing. Then came the final blow. Upon the hill to his right was a sight that would cower the bravest man. Six knights in white surcoats emblazoned with the red cross of the Templars raced their horses down the hill with several thousand reinforcements close behind, clearly headed for Edward's standard. The day was surely lost.

The Scots—sensing victory—pressed forward, steadily advancing.

"Flee!" Pembroke screamed.

Pembroke and d'Argentan and some five hundred English knights, pushed and barged through the ranks, fighting off determined Scots who tried to get to the king. As Edward and his protectors fought their way through the press, Edward's shield bearer was captured along with the royal shield and seal.

Edward kept the Scots that reached him at bay with his mace, flailing it until his muscles screamed with pain. His knights battled furiously to free him. Again and again their horses were trapped, surrounded by furious Scots determined to unhorse the English king. Edward lost count of the number of his knights who were dragged to the ground as they desperately fought to reach the road where they could flee to Stirling.

CEALLACH DODGED THE MACE and nearly got close enough to unhorse Edward before being driven off again by English knights. When the road to Stirling suddenly opened up, the English turned and fled the battlefield.

Good. Let Edward run. Let him taste the fear that daily lived in Ceallach. Fear of recognition; fear of capture; fear of imprisonment in a cold, dark cell. And the even greater fear that he would be taken from that cell to the chamber of horrors too great to think on. Ceallach would follow closely behind, feeding Edward's demons.

The hood covering Ceallach's face had slipped in the melee, blocking his view as the holes cut for his eyes shifted sideways. He pulled the hood off, looking for his fellow Templars. Instead he came eye to eye with a young English squire frantically gathering his master's weapons and horse to flee the field.

Ceallach raised his battle-axe to strike, but the fear evident on the boy's face pierced Ceallach's consciousness. Ceallach hesitated, and the young man scrambled aboard the horse and took off after his king. Ceallach pulled his mask in place and gave chase, hounding him halfway to Stirling Castle.

At the edge of the carse, Ceallach reined in his mount and headed west. Having accomplished what he'd set out to do, he raced to the rendezvous behind Gillies Hill where he was to meet up with the others who'd worn the red crosses. He and his comrades hurriedly removed their surcoats.

As he laid the tattered cloth into the chest in a hole in the ground, Ceallach mourned the loss like a death. How proudly he'd worn this mark of honor from the very first day it was bestowed upon him. And now that mark could cause his death. Shaking off the melancholy he hurriedly slammed the lid. Quickly they filled the hole with dirt and covered the chest, then scattered leaves and twigs until the spot looked quite natural.

The others mounted their horses and fled. Three of them planned to sail together to Norway. Another would return to his family deep in the northern highlands of Scotland, far from King Edward, far from France. The fifth man's plans were undecided, but they all had agreed not to contact one another. Their good-byes had long been said, this last mission together their homage to the past, what had once been right and true and good.

Ceallach did not watch them ride away. But he couldn't leave without marking the spot. He picked up a large rock and placed it on top of the chest's resting place. Using his knife, he carved a cross on the side of the stone to mark it.

Perhaps one day he would return to this spot and retrieve what he had lost.

CEALLACH REJOINED BRUCE. For eight years Bruce had avoided such a fight, ever since the defeat at Methven. The Scottish army was relatively small and ill-equipped for a pitched fight and yet they'd just defeated the might of England in precisely such a battle. From the insane promise to relieve Stirling that Bruce's brother Edward had made a year ago had come the greatest victory in Scotland's history.

Bruce got down on his knees and prayed aloud in gratitude for this deliverance. Ceallach did not join him.

When the king stood up, he gave Ceallach a questioning look. But he simply looked away from his brother. Ceallach had stopped praying years ago—when God had turned away from him in his time of need.

Ceallach surveyed the battlefield once more, watching as the English foot soldiers madly dispersed in all directions. "The commanders have deserted the field."

"Aye. The few who remain are making no effort to organize or lead their troops."

Ceallach shook his head. As a result of the lack of leadership, many of the English foot soldiers had already been swept away and drowned in the swift current of the Firth of Forth or were sucked into the swamps surrounding the river. Others seemed to be making their way to Stirling Castle, trudging up the narrow road to huddle under the mighty crags surrounding the fortress.

"The field is ours, Your Majesty. We've won the day."

"Aye, it would seem so. But the English may very well reform and launch an attack from the castle."

Just then James Douglas rode up to them, pulling his horse to a quick stop. "My laird, let me go after Edward. He can't take refuge in Stirling; he'll have to keep riding, and I can crown the day with his capture."

"Granted," Bruce said. "But you may take only sixty of our cavalry. The rest must remain close at hand—they are not to follow Edward under any circumstances. I will need them if Edward launches an attack from Stirling."

"Aye. Then I'm off," Douglas declared as he spurred his horse into a canter.

Bruce turned to Ceallach. "Go and tell our commanders to keep their men in formation and to brace for a possible attack from the castle."

TWO

Meat will be served three times a week except during active campaigning when it may be served once each day.

—from the Rule of the Templar Knights

Today's successful fight against the English reminded me of my early years as a warrior. By the time I joined the Order, Acre—the last Christian outpost in the Holy Land—had fallen three years before. Few of us were sent to Outremer after that, though we all hoped that another Crusade would be mounted against the Saracens. We trained for war, but as a practical matter, we also learned more domestic skills. While I could see the need to learn such skills to help provide for the Order, still I chafed at the lack of military action.

I apprenticed as a weaver with a man named Peter, a master weaver and fellow Templar. The years went by and Peter taught me everything he knew about weaving and creating patterns with the loom. My tapestries and cloth were much in demand. Opportunities to sell my work were numerous—commissions from wealthy Parisians were plentiful, and the Templar treasury benefited from my craft.

Perhaps I took too much pride in my skill and that is why God took it all away.

EDWARD AND HIS KNIGHTS raced to the gates of Stirling Castle, the great fortress that overlooked the countryside in every direction. Edward ordered his men to pound on the closed gates until they were opened. Anxiously he watched the road behind them lest Bruce attempt to attack while they waited to gain entrance.

Finally the commander of the castle, Sir Philip Mowbray, stood above them on the parapets.

"Open for the king," Pembroke demanded. "The battle is lost and we must take refuge here."

Ignoring Pembroke, Mowbray addressed Edward. "Your Majesty, I regret that I can't give you sanctuary."

"Are you mad?" Edward screamed. "Let me in!"

"May I remind you, my lord, of the terms of your agreement with Bruce? If he should win the battle, Stirling must be turned over to him. If you are found inside the gates, you will be his prisoner."

Edward slumped in his saddle and stared at Pembroke. Shaken by the realization that Mowbray was right, Edward said, "We must ride for the nearest English held castle, then." Wheeling his horse about, Edward gave the order to ride out.

Having fought most of the day with little sleep the night before, Edward and his retainers wearily fled east toward Dunbar. A small force of Scots led by James Douglas dogged their heels the whole way. They could not stop nor rest, and any who did were captured or killed by the Scots. When at last they reached Dunbar, the Scots followed so close that the castle guards dared not open the gate wide enough for the horses for fear the Scots would ride in as well. Edward had to fling himself from his horse and rush on foot through the barely open gate, leaving the poor beast behind.

Pacing the parapets of Dunbar Castle, Edward watched with impotent fury as the Scots gathered his horse and those of his men and led them away. Would the Scots take the horses and return to

Stirling, or would they lay in wait for Edward to leave Dunbar so they could capture him?

He stopped beside Pembroke and said, "Thank God my father isn't alive to see this day."

Pembroke said nothing and Edward cursed. "The battle could have been won. In another hour the Scottish lines would have broken, I know it. We were holding our own, were winning! Where did Bruce get the reinforcements? Why didn't I know about them?"

"They and the Templars turned the tide against us," Pembroke agreed.

"Yes, they did." Edward pounded his fist into his palm. "I want those six men found and brought to me—dead or alive."

"As you wish, Your Majesty."

Late that evening the defeated king of England sneaked out of Dunbar Castle like a lowly thief. He boarded a boat that took him safely to Berwick. He left behind a defeated army, a train of supplies twenty miles long, his royal shield and seal, and any hope of returning to London as a conquering hero.

ORELIA AND SEVERAL OTHER WIVES remained with the baggage train about a mile away from the battlefield. The sounds of fighting, muted by distance, could be heard as a murmur in the background. Close by, insects droned in the dazzling sunshine. Orelia and two other wives found shelter from the sun beneath the branches of a willow tree growing on the banks of a nearby creek. By late afternoon Orelia feared the battle would not be over as swiftly as John had predicted.

They were preparing to light a fire to cook the evening meal when a horse and rider raced up to them. Jumping down from his horse, the man shouted at his wife, "Grab your belongings—just the saddlebag—and be quick about it!"

One of Orelia's companions dashed to the wagon that held her things. Orelia watched, concerned by the man's haste. "What is happening?" she asked him. "Where are you going?"

His wife returned and the man quickly attached her saddlebag to his saddle and was about to remount when Orelia grabbed his surcoat. Fighting panic she demanded, "Tell me why you are fleeing the battle, or I will report you as a deserter."

Those words secured his full attention. "*I* am not deserting. 'Tis King Edward who has fled the field. The battle is lost and I'm not waiting for the Scots to finish me off." He yanked his clothing from Orelia's hand.

How could the English have lost? Orelia held fast to the horse's bridle. The man must be lying, though why he should do so she didn't know. "Why aren't you waiting for the army?"

"All is chaos, my lady. There is no one in command to tell me different, so I'm riding for the border. You would be wise to do so as well." He grabbed the saddle to mount his horse.

"Wait!" Orelia cried. He turned back to her and she gestured to her remaining companion. "What shall we do?"

"If you want to leave with us," the soldier ground out, obviously reaching for patience, "unhitch a couple of the cart horses. But hurry."

Orelia looked at her companion. Lady Angela Heathrow, young but decidedly plump, said, "I should wait for my husband—I'm not much of a horsewoman and I definitely can't ride without a saddle."

Orelia sensed the man's losing patience. But Orelia wasn't at all sure the carthorses were even trained to carry riders—most were not. Mounting one without a saddle might be more dangerous than taking their chances with the Scots. "Are you sure, Angela?"

Angela nodded her head and looked terrified at the very thought of mounting one of the beasts.

Orelia looked back at the man, who by now had pulled his wife up behind him on the horse. "Can't you wait with us until our husbands return?" she beseeched him.

"I'm not waiting for the Scots to find this supply train. Mount up or stay, but make up your mind."

Furious with the man's impatience and lack of chivalry, Orelia wondered just how well he would treat them if she did manage to get Angela on a horse that didn't buck her off.

With as much dignity as she could muster, Orelia said, "Perhaps it would be best if we stayed here together, then. Our husbands will no doubt come for us soon and they might wonder where we are."

With obvious relief the man said, "I'm sure you're right. God be with you, ladies. Hang on, love!" Steadying his wife with a hand on her thigh he spun the horse about and raced south.

Daylight faded and still no one, English or Scottish, came for the women. Angela looked to Orelia for leadership, and she kept her busy searching for firewood and rummaging for foodstuffs in the wagons. As a precaution, she urged Angela to arm herself with a knife. But from Angela's clumsy attempts to find a place to wear it, Orelia could tell Angela was more likely to wound herself than an enemy. Still, Orelia insisted.

As night fell, Orelia knew that John should have come for her by now. Something was terribly wrong. Obviously she was going to have to spend the better part of the night here with Angela. Orelia made room inside one of the wagons that was covered with an oiled cloth. When they'd finished supper and doused the fire, the tired, frightened women crawled into the wagon for a miserable night's sleep.

THAT NIGHT CEALLACH AND THE OTHERS CELEBRATED—the feared renewed attack had never materialized and Edward of England was running for his life. Ceallach celebrated as he knew he shouldn't—with ale and even some *uisgebeatha*. More than was necessary. Much more. But the fiery liquid calmed his tattered heart, made it stop racing, drove away the fear and the memories. Aye, he became a normal man when the whiskey dulled his feelings. A man without demons running through his very veins.

But if the whiskey loosened his fear, it never loosened his tongue. After years of living in near silence, he'd long ago lost the ability to make idle chatter. He rarely spoke and then only when asked a direct question. Alone at the edge of the crowd, Ceallach slowly and quite deliberately became drunk.

One of the camp women came and sat beside him. She'd sat with him before and unlike so many of her kind, she didn't press him to make conversation. But the invitation was there all the same, in the way she brushed her breast against his arm when she reached for the flask of whiskey. Or in the wise smile she gave him when he jerked away from the touch.

He knew nothing of women and their ways after so many years of monastic life. But even Ceallach could read the invitation in her eyes and the lift of her brow.

Hating himself, knowing it was wrong but powerless to stop, he drank until the last of his inhibitions slipped away. When she reached out a hand to him, he went with her. He was damned anyway; might as well seal his doom in the arms of a willing woman.

When he disrobed, she gasped at a gash on his thigh. He must have been wounded in the fray, but he'd not felt the blow or any pain. Nor did he feel any when she poured whiskey into the wound and bound it. This wasn't the first time he'd been hurt and hadn't noticed it.

The next morning Ceallach awoke to an empty bed and a head full of hammer beats with each pulse of his heart. He was glad the woman was gone—didn't want to have to talk to her or anyone else until the whiskey had worked itself out of his system. But long before that had a chance to happen, Bruce sent him to inspect the English supply train. Although Ceallach's head stopped pounding by the time he mounted his horse, pain still lingered behind his eyes.

He rode down the line of wagons until he came to a deserted campsite with a still-warm fire. Quietly he dismounted, tied his horse to a wagon, and crept into the camp. He shook his head. He couldn't see anyone, but he heard the murmuring of conversation. Female voices? His head was in worse shape than he thought.

ORELIA AWOKE, not sure of the time or what had awakened her. Angela still slept and Orelia wondered if her companion's sleep had been as fitful as her own. She'd lain awake for hours listening for John's return. Long after midnight she'd gotten up and left the wagon to look at the stars and to listen. All was quiet then, just as it was now.

She'd finally fallen into an exhausted sleep a few hours before sunrise. Cautiously she stretched cramped muscles. Her movements awakened Angela.

"Is it morning?" the woman asked.

Orelia straightened her clothing. "Yes, it is. Did you sleep well?"

"Not really." Angela sat up. "Has someone come to retrieve us?"

"No, no one is here. We are quite alone."

Angela said, "Maybe they are sleeping in the camp—they wouldn't want to wake us."

"If anyone had ridden into the camp, I would have heard them." Orelia assured her.

After all of John's brave predictions that the English army would be victorious, here she was, alone, perhaps at the mercy of her enemies. Orelia hoped she'd made the right decision in staying with the wagons. What foolishness. Of course it was the right decision. Even if the Scots had won, John and the others would eventually return for the supply train.

She fingered the small dagger strapped to her leg in the special sheath John had made. He had shown her how to use the weapon, had made her practice until he was satisfied that she could defend herself. He'd insisted on this when she'd decided to accompany him.

Where was he? Why hadn't he come for her? The knife felt reassuring there beneath the folds of her dress but she'd feel better if she knew the answers to her questions. Cautiously, she moved to the opening at the end of the wagon.

Pulling aside the oilcloth just slightly, she blinked at the early morning light. All she could hear were the restless movements of the horses, still fastened in their traces. Poor beasts were probably as hungry and thirsty as she was.

Dare she leave the relative safety of the wagon? How could she not? She pulled back the opening wide enough to slip through it, stuck her head outside, and shrieked with terror at the sight before her.

A tall, dark-haired, kilt-wearing knight stood not five feet away with his hands over his ears, groaning as if in pain. She stopped screaming and reached for her knife. The feel of it in her palm calmed her and she held it in front of her.

The man removed his hands from his head and reached for her.

"Stay back!" She jabbed the knife toward him and he yanked his hand back, moving quickly for such a large man.

"I mean you no harm, lady." The lilt of his voice was not as pronounced as other Scots she'd listened to.

"Then leave at once. Before my husband returns," she added. Perhaps he would think her man had only left to relieve himself and would soon be back. She could sense her companion coming up alongside her, and Orelia pushed at her, willing her to remain hidden. Apparently Angela understood because she made no further move toward the opening.

"Is your man a Scot?" the warrior asked.

Puzzled she said, "Of course not. He's the Earl of Radbourne."

"Well, unless he's turned traitor to England, he'll not be coming back here any time soon. Now come out of the wagon and I'll see you safe—"

A muffled sneeze from inside the wagon gave away the fact that Orelia was not alone, destroying any hope of persuading him to simply walk away.

He withdrew his sword from its scabbard. "Get out of the wagon, lady. And if your husband is wise, he'll follow you."

"My husband isn't here, you barbarian."

"Get out, now!"

The cold steel in his voice told her he was not to be trifled with, and Orelia spoke to Angela. "Come. We must do as he says."

Reluctantly they crawled out of the wagon and stood in front of the warrior.

CEALLACH'S HEAD FELT MORE THAN A BIT FUZZY and his soul was burdened from his night of forbidden activity. His punishment for such behavior crawled out of this supply wagon—two hostile women. Englishwomen. The one with the knife might just know how to use it; she held it as if she meant to do him harm. "What are you doing here?" he asked.

"Waiting for our husbands to return for us," the one with the knife answered. The other one nodded, clearly terrified.

To assure himself that the wagon was now empty, he waved the women aside with his sword. They backed up and he poked the blade into the opening then cut the material away. Aside from some baggage, the wagon appeared empty.

He sheathed his sword and looked again at his prisoners. The one he'd first encountered was a woman of no more than twenty-five years. Her golden hair hung in a disheveled braid and she wore a beautifully woven shawl of a distinctive blend of colors. The other woman, plump and anxious looking, had dark brown hair and appeared to be quite young.

The Earl of Radbourne's lady said, "Is it true that the English army has been vanquished?"

"'Tis true, lady."

She drew herself up. "Will you help us find our husbands?"

Find their husbands? He had no idea how to locate lost husbands. "All the English who were able have fled. Looks like your men have deserted you or . . ." He decided against finishing the sentence. Better to let them come to their own conclusions. He gestured to the other wagons. "Are there more women with you?"

"There were a few others, but their men came for them."

"You should have left with them."

She looked at him as if he'd said something particularly absurd. "I assure you, sir, our husbands have not deserted us. They must have been detained."

"It doesn't bode well that your men haven't returned for you." What the devil should he do with them? Just leave them here? Somehow that didn't seem wise. "Come with me."

Straight-backed and haughty, Lady Radbourne asked, "Just who are you and where are you taking Lady Heathrow and me?"

Ceallach was just a little too groggy and far too inexperienced in conversing with women. The woman last night had not demanded that from him . . .

"Sir? I said where are you taking us?" Lady Radbourne's tone of voice and condescending manner were wearing very thin. He'd never dealt with female prisoners. But he guessed the best course was to take them to the Scottish camp.

He untied his horse and mounted. "My name is Ceallach, and I'm the king's foster brother. Now, gather what you can carry and let's go."

Lady Radbourne scowled.

Now what? The woman stalked off to the wagon. From where he sat atop his horse he heard a great deal of muttering and banging about inside the cart before she finally climbed back out. Empty-handed. Both of them stood there, arms across their chests. The blond woman's eyes flashed icy blue. "I wonder if we might take the cart?"

Ceallach thought on it. "All right. Can you drive it?"

"Yes."

Her answer surprised him. *She* surprised him. "Well, then let's be off."

Ceallach reined his horse around and set off for Bruce's camp. Belatedly he glanced behind and saw the women clamber aboard. Lady Radbourne took the reins and got the beasts moving, no small feat since the animals were no doubt tired and hungry.

Now and again he looked back to make sure they were following him. Not entirely sure he could trust the woman, he dropped back and rode beside the lead horse. When they reached the camp, Ceallach gestured for her to pull up and she did so. He looked over his shoulder at the two women, and the fear he saw on their faces pierced him.

A temporary stockade constructed of logs and boards stood in front of them. Inside, several dozen men sat on the ground or wandered aimlessly. Sentries walked the outside perimeter. To his dismay, Ceallach watched as one of the prisoners relieved himself in full view of anyone glancing in his direction.

Ceallach decided then and there that he would not leave these women here—enemies or no—unless their husbands were among the prisoners and could protect them. "Wait here," he said.

Searching about in the confusion, Ceallach saw a knight nearby saddling his horse. Ceallach rode over to him but did not dismount. The man looked up from his task and Ceallach motioned to the women. "I need to find their husbands. Who's in charge here?"

The man pointed to a knight standing off to one side. "Mactavish."

"Thanks." Pleased that he'd found the warden so easily and that he would soon be able to turn over his prisoners, he dismounted and walked over to the man in charge of the prison. He told him who he was looking for and Mactavish checked his list.

"Nay, neither of them's here."

The men were probably dead and though they were enemies, Ceallach regretted their deaths and what it would mean to the two women.

Mactavish stared at the women, and Ceallach didn't care for the expression on the man's face. "I'm sure we can find a place for them here," Mactavish said.

Not a place suitable for the genteel. "Can you tell me where to find King Robert?"

"Last I heard he was inspecting the morgue at St. Ninian's."

Ceallach hesitated to take the women to the kirk. The gruesome task of burying the dead would be even worse to observe than the prison. Ceallach glanced at his prisoners, huddled together on the seat of the cart. A number of soldiers had gathered around them, taunting them and making crude references, reinforcing Ceallach's suspicion that the ladies would not be safe here. He supposed they would have to stay with him for now.

Unhappy but resigned, Ceallach turned back to the warden. "I think it would be best if I take them to the king."

He shrugged. "Suit yourself."

Ceallach returned to the wagon and tied his horse to the back. Seeing Lady Radbourne's pale face and trembling hands, he said, "Your husbands aren't here, and this is no place for you." Conscious that men were still gathering to stare and taunt the women he shouted, "Stand aside! These women are prisoners of war, and I am taking them to the king."

Ceallach climbed aboard the wagon and took over the reins with one hand, keeping the other one near his sword hilt as he made his way through. He breathed easier when they had left the crowd of men behind. Though the women certainly continued to draw attention as Ceallach drove the wagon through camp, they reached the kirk without further incident.

The place was busy with graves being dug and wagons coming and going, bringing in more dead. Rows of bodies lay in the warm sun and Ceallach halted well away from the sight and smell.

Ceallach addressed Lady Radbourne. "I will inquire about your husbands while I search for the king."

Her face grew even whiter. "You think they are here?"

Until now Ceallach hadn't realized that while he assumed her husband was dead, Lady Radbourne still obviously assumed the man was alive. He considered her question and then quietly answered, "I think it is likely, my lady."

She drew a deep breath and said, "How will you know if . . . if our husbands are here? Will you, or anyone else, recognize their coat of arms?"

Ceallach shook his head.

Lady Radbourne straightened her spine. "Then I think we shall have to search for them ourselves. Angela?"

The other woman nodded reluctantly.

Ceallach tried to imagine his mother or sister facing such a task. Though they'd both died a dozen years ago, he still remembered his sister's aversion to dead things. And he knew only too well the damage a sword or battle-axe could do to the human body. "Are you sure? It won't be a pleasant task."

"We didn't expect it to be," Lady Radbourne snapped.

"Very well." There had been a time in his life when Ceallach would have asked God to comfort the women. Looking at their grim, fear-laden faces, he wished he still could. But since he no longer trusted in God's intervention, Ceallach sought another means of encouragement.

He motioned to a knight standing nearby. When the man walked over, Ceallach explained the situation, and the knight joined them, taking Lady Heathrow's arm.

Lady Radbourne accepted Ceallach's offer and laid her hand upon his arm.

They walked along the rows of dead. Lady Heathrow and her escort worked their way quickly and were soon a distance away. But Lady Radbourne paused at each man, as if she mourned each one's passing. Though her back remained stiff, she swiped at tears more than once. Gently Ceallach urged her forward.

When she nearly tripped over a carelessly discarded weapon, Ceallach pulled her close. "Careful, my lady." She did not pull away as he expected her to, and Ceallach stood still, allowing her to gather her composure. He admired her strength, for it took nearly all his will to glance at the maimed bodies. And she must search the faces, looking for a beloved face and no doubt praying that it wasn't there.

They turned up the next row, and halfway along she cried out. Pressing her hand to her mouth she moaned, "No, dear God. No!"

Her other hand grasped his so tightly it was if her pain became his. She swayed and he held her upright as her moans tore at his heart. He felt helpless. Useless. Abandoned. Just as he had when Peter died. And just as it had been then, God was nowhere to be found when Ceallach needed him.

ORELIA STOOD IN MUTE CONFUSION as she stared at John's body. His face seemed at peace, giving her hope that he had not suffered too much before death claimed him. Tears raced down her cheeks and she let go of her companion's hand and sank to her knees beside her husband's body.

The man named Ceallach knelt beside her. "Is this your husband?"

She nodded, and once again grasped the big Scot's hand, needing to draw strength from the living so she could face the dead. With her other hand she touched John's face, recoiling at the coldness, at the proof that this was not a nightmare from which she would soon awake.

"Would you like me to search him for valuables?"

Revulsion at the thought of this man handling John hit her. "No! Don't touch him!" She snatched her hand away from his, the Scotsman's closeness no longer a comfort but rather a reminder that he and his kind had killed John.

Wordlessly she searched for John's crucifix, praying that the necklace had not been lost. Of all the things she wanted to remember of her husband, his steadfast faith was the one thing she felt sure she would need to cling to in the difficult days to come.

She sobbed as she found the silver chain beneath John's surcoat. Gently she lifted his head, removed the precious cross and wrapped her fingers tightly around it. Orelia clung to it, held it to her own chest as she fought waves of despair and anger at John for leaving her like this. She clenched the cross until the pain from it dug into her flesh and brought her back to the present.

A shadow fell across Orelia as Angela Heathrow knelt beside her and folded her into an embrace. "I'm so sorry, Orelia."

"Did you find—"

Angela shook her head. "Nigel may be wounded, at the hospital. This knight is going to take me to search for him."

Orelia nodded. "I'm glad for you." Glad that Angela might be spared this pain and grief.

"I'll stay with you until . . . the burial."

"Oh, you mustn't. Go to your husband. It will be days until the funeral at Radbourne."

Angela looked at her sadly. "You won't be allowed to take him home, Orelia. The dead are being buried here."

Frantically, Orelia sought the man who'd brought her here. Seeing he was still beside her, she jumped to her feet and demanded, "Is it true? I won't be allowed to take my husband home to be buried?"

He rose to his feet. His expression showed compassion but his words gave no solace. "Aye, it's true. You will be detained until Bruce arranges your ransom. You will not be allowed to leave until then, and it is better that we bury your man here and now."

Orelia's shoulders sagged. John was dead. Truly gone. And rather than burial at home in Radbourne Hall's graveyard, he would be forever kept from her in this foreign land.

THREE

All daughters of Eve are banned from the order's properties in their entirety.

—from the Rule of the Templar Knights

L*ady Orelia is lovely, even with a tear-stained face. Her grief tugs at my heart. She seems to take comfort from prayer, and I envy her that solace.*

But Lady Orelia is a distraction from my purpose with these pages.

Namely, to rid myself of the memories which haunt me.

The Templar rules governed every aspect of my life. Despite the restrictive nature of living as a monk, I found some measure of security in knowing the appropriate response for any situation. Expectations for behavior were clear, and those few times when I acted rashly, my infractions were dealt with justly.

The one thing I found most difficult to accept was not being able to see my mother or sister. On their rare visits to my cloister near Paris, I was forbidden to hug them or kiss their cheeks in greeting. I longed for the simple pleasure of embracing my dear mother. When she died within a week of my sister from a lung ailment, I wasn't allowed to travel home for their funerals. How I struggled with my grief! Only Peter's assurance that I would be reunited with them in heaven kept me from total despair.

After their deaths I reconciled myself to the lack of female company and indeed became quite used to the society and friendship of men. After so many years of cloistered life, I fear I've quite forgotten how to relate to the fairer gender.

LADY ORELIA'S TEARS were more than Ceallach could take, and he hurried off to see to the burial. He found the man in charge and arranged for the English nobleman to be buried within the hour. *Take care of this last obligation and she'll be off your hands,* he told himself. *Robert must see to her welfare as a prisoner of war.*

When Ceallach returned with the priest, Lady Radbourne's eyes were dry, her face reddened from crying. Ceallach stood across the open, shallow grave from her. The simple, hurried ceremony left little time for meditation or farewells. All about them, men toiled over more graves. The priest apologized for the brevity of the service before rushing off to attend to another burial.

The two women hugged, then Lady Heathrow left with the knight who would escort her to the hospital and a possible reunion with her wounded husband. Head bowed, Lady Radbourne stared down as the grave diggers shoveled dirt on top of the crude casket. Covertly, Ceallach stared at her. With her blond hair and delicate features, she was a beauty, undoubtedly bred to be a lady of some stature. He'd seen color high in her cheeks himself at the campsite; now she looked weary and peaked. Saints above, the lass wouldn't faint now, would she?

Her fingers absently stroked the cross he'd seen her take from Radbourne's neck . . . "John," she whispered. Her blue eyes stared into the grave upon the nearly covered box . . . She swayed and Ceallach hurried to her side.

Before he reached her she'd sunk to her knees and Ceallach had to pull her to her feet and back from the edge before the ground gave way. He held her arms, gently urging her away from the quickly filling hole.

"Let me go!" She struggled out of his grasp, striking her fists on his chest and keening her husband's name. "John! Why did you leave me? *John!*"

Ceallach tried to calm her hands, tried to offer comfort, but she was beyond consolation. As the final shovels of dirt landed on the mounded grave, she stopped hitting Ceallach and once again knelt down. This time, Ceallach let her go, stood beside her, helpless in the midst of such obvious grief.

Over and over again she picked up handfuls of dirt and let them sift through her fingers. Her lips moved, and Ceallach realized she was praying, the words unintelligible to all but her and her God. He hoped she found solace from her prayer.

Did she have children and family waiting for her back in England? He had to get this lady to Bruce so that she could return home and mourn with her own people, where she belonged. She certainly didn't belong here. With her enemies.

Lady Radbourne stood up looking composed despite the tear tracks on her cheeks. "What now?" she asked in a dull sounding voice.

Ceallach gazed at the cloudy skies, away from her troubled gaze, to the late afternoon mist rolling in from the nearby sea. What was to become of her? Would she languish in prison as Bruce's own wife had languished for years? "I don't really know. I will take you to the king—perhaps your ransom can be arranged with speed so that you may return home."

"Home."

There was no joy or even anticipation in her voice or expression. But why should he care? Ceallach couldn't afford to become entangled in the woman's problems. He walked her back to where his horse was tied. While they'd waited for the priest, Ceallach had removed her things from the wagon and seen that the horses were cared for. The lady's two baskets hung from his saddle.

"You may ride, lady. I shall walk." She didn't argue. He helped her mount and led the horse to the makeshift camp behind Gillies Hill. He hoped to find Black Bryan Mackintosh or one of the king's other lieutenants.

He found Sir Bryan with the king amidst a grouping of tents. And more women. Bryan saw him and strode toward him. Bryan, who had become an accomplished knight since Ceallach had first met him seven years ago, had a nasty scrape on the side of his face and a purple bruise colored the skin all around it. "What happened to you?" Ceallach asked.

"I got knocked on the head yesterday." He made a dismissive gesture with his hand. "'Tis nothing. Come, you are just in time. The king and I are about to honor my foster brother, Adam, and Fergus Cookson."

Ceallach raised his eyebrows in question and Bryan said, "I don't know what the king has in mind for Adam, but Fergus is to be knighted."

Ceallach remembered his own knighting ceremony—the day of fasting and the night of prayer before taking the solemn vows. But his vows had meant choosing a way of life, vows that bound him not to a human lord but to God and his Son. Vows that had governed his life for fifteen years and had ended in . . . Ceallach gave himself a mental shake. *Stay out of the past.*

"I need to speak to the king about this woman."

Bryan glanced back at Lady Radbourne, sitting stiffly on Ceallach's horse. "From the looks of her clothes I'd guess she's English."

"Aye." Ceallach tugged the reins and kept walking, wanting to reach the king, make his explanation and be done. The day had become heavy with mist. Flags drooped from their poles and the tents sagged under the weight of the damp air. But the people gathered in the little clearing were in high spirits.

Before he reached his fellow Scots he tied the horse to a tree branch and spoke to his prisoner. "Wait here. I shall return shortly." Without waiting for a response, he walked over to Bruce, who welcomed him.

Bryan rejoined the group and made introductions. "Ceallach, you never did get a chance to visit with us at Homelea before the battle. This is my wife, Lady Kathryn, and her cook, Anna. That sprite Kathryn is holding is . . . our daughter, Isobel." Lady Kathryn said hello but her shining eyes were on her husband as if he'd said something truly amazing. *Women. Who could understand them?* Bryan was newly wed and Ceallach supposed that had something to do with it.

Bryan continued. "You know Adam, of course, but I don't believe you've met Fergus. He is Anna's son and Kathryn's good friend."

Ceallach acknowledged Fergus with a brief nod.

Bruce pulled a young woman forward. "This is Lady Morrigan Macnab."

Ceallach nodded to her. He'd met her before—a warrior in her own right.

Fergus eyed her suspiciously and said, "My pleasure, *Lady* Macnab."

Dressed in her usual men's trews and saffron shirt belted at the waist, she stood straighter and said, "I'm no' a lady but a warrior like yourself."

Fergus stepped back and Bruce chuckled. "That she is, Fergus. None better with a bow and more than competent with a sword. Best beware."

"I shall remember the warning."

"See that you do," she said.

Bruce looked behind him and asked Ceallach, "Whom do you have with you?"

"Your Majesty, I found some Englishwomen in a supply wagon. One is at the hospital looking for her husband. I have just come from burying Lady Radbourne's husband, and now I am ready to turn her over to you."

Immediately Lady Kathryn walked over to her English counterpart and offered condolences. Morrigan and Ceallach stayed behind. Didn't Kathryn know that but for the grace of God her own loved ones would be the ones dead and vanquished? How could she offer solace to the enemy?

But Bruce also walked over to the Englishwoman. "Lady Radbourne?"

She nodded.

"Let me help you from this horse. You may make yourself comfortable here by the fire. I will see to your needs when I've finished with the business at hand."

"I am fine here on the horse, thank you."

"As you wish." With a curt nod of his head, Scotland's king accompanied Lady Kathryn back to the men and Morrigan. "Now, let us get on with this solemn ceremony."

Ceallach had no choice but to await the king and so joined the circle of people.

Bruce addressed them. "These men proved their bravery upon the field of battle under the worst conditions. Fergus has earned my lifelong friendship and gratitude for saving the life of my natural son, Sir Bryan Mackintosh and his wife, Lady Kathryn." Bruce gave Fergus a splendid sword, no doubt from the cache of English weapons. Fergus kissed the blade and handed it back to the king before he knelt in front of him. Bruce then tapped him first on one shoulder, then the other before pronouncing him a knight.

Bruce moved to stand in front of Adam. "Sir Adam. I had the privilege of knighting you when our fight with England began that cold day outside of Greyfriars Church."

"Aye, my king. More than eight years ago."

"We've suffered much since then. Yesterday you helped Sir Fergus save Bryan and Kathryn from the wrath of an English enemy. I cannot possibly reward you with anything that compares to the worth of these two, whom I love."

Adam shook his head. "There is no need to thank me. Bryan is as dear to me as any brother by blood."

Ceallach looked to his own foster brother, Robert the Bruce, and knew that Adam spoke true. Ceallach would lay down his life for the man who was both a brother and his king.

Bruce beckoned to his page and the young boy brought a parchment to the king who took it then faced Adam again. He offered the paper to Adam and he took it. "Adam, I wish to reward you with the newly created Earldom of Moy."

Adam looked stunned. "You are too generous, Your Majesty."

"Nonsense. You've been a staunch ally in the north and have earned a reward. But I suppose now you'll be asking for leave to race home to Moy and tell Gwenyth she is a countess."

Adam grinned. "Aye." He looked up at the sky. "There's still a fair amount of daylight left—I could leave today."

Everyone laughed.

Bruce laughed with them, and then in a more serious tone the king said, "You are anxious to see Gwenyth and your wee ones."

"Aye. They are never far from my thoughts. Our oldest turns five in a few weeks. It will be good to be home for the celebration." He turned to Bryan. "Why don't you and Kathryn come to Moy while Homelea is being rebuilt?"

All this talk of home, of family made Ceallach melancholy.

Where did he belong? His thoughts shifted back to the English-woman, and he turned toward her. She'd acquiesced and dismounted and now sat by the campfire. He stopped in front of her and she stood up from the log she'd been sitting on.

He still had no idea what he was supposed to do with her. "In a few minutes I will be able to bring your plight back to the king's attention, my lady."

"I am not going anywhere, Sir Ceallach." She looked so forlorn. He knew only too well how it felt to be a prisoner, to have others control your fate. But there was nothing he could do about her situation. Radbourne had been a fool to bring her. Brash, stubborn English . . .

He cleared his throat nervously. "Very well." He walked back to the group surrounding Bruce hoping he might soon talk with the king.

"Aye, I *am* worried for your safety," Bryan was saying to Bruce. "Who knows how Edward of England will react to this defeat of his army?" He turned to Adam. "I can't go with you to Moy, but perhaps you would take Kathryn with you?"

Bryan's wife looked very unhappy with that suggestion. "Do you think I will leave here without you?"

Bruce said, "Perhaps you should take a few weeks and accompany Kathryn to Moy, Bryan. I don't believe Edward will be able to convince his nobles to invade Scotland any time soon."

Bryan considered this. "You're probably right. It may take him years to rally them to battle again. I would like to see everyone at Moy and introduce Kathryn to my childhood home." The more he thought about it the more appealing the idea must have been for he said, "Aye, Adam. We'll go with you."

Bruce gave his blessing to the trip and promised that when Bryan returned, he would have the funds to rebuild Homelea. "Now, I have one more bequest to make before I attend to Ceallach and his prisoner. Morrigan, step forward please."

Ceallach was glad to hear that Morrigan was to be the last person singled out. He wanted no reward nor any notoriety for his part in yesterday's victory. All he wanted was to be relieved of the woman who waited for Bruce's attention.

Bruce said, "Morrigan, your family has paid dearly for fighting for Scotland. Your father and brother are dead, and you've been dispossessed from your lands. How long has it been since you saw your mother and siblings?"

"Seven years, my laird."

"Too long. It is past time for you to reunite your family and find yourself a husband."

"I've not given marriage much thought, my laird."

"Aye, you have been serving your country. But now that we have peace once more, you should begin to think on it. I turned your Uncle Angus out of Innishewan on my way to Bannockburn. The estate is yours."

Well done. Morrigan had saved the king's life and survived the dangerous existence of a spy. She deserved to have such a reward for her efforts.

Morrigan appeared stunned at the generosity. "You have defeated the English, my laird. I need no more reward than that."

"Take it. Innishewan is not the prize you remember. I received a report that your uncle gutted it before he left. You won't be able to occupy the castle without considerable repair. Find yourself a husband to help you restore the estate."

"Thank you, my laird. You are too generous. But I have no need of a husband to help me. I am perfectly capable—"

"Of course you are," Bruce said smoothly. "But you will need men to help put it to rights. Perhaps Fergus here could assist you." He turned to the man. "What plans do you have now that you are knighted?"

Fergus said, "I haven't had time to give it much thought. I'm trained as a steward—perhaps I can serve Lady Morrigan in that capacity as she rebuilds."

Fergus looked at Bryan who shrugged and said, "You are certainly welcome back at Homelea, Fergus, when Kathryn and I return there. But perhaps you'd prefer to seek your fortune elsewhere."

"I'd welcome a steward's help at Innishewan," Morrigan said. "I'm not sure you'd earn a fortune, Fergus, but you'll at least have enough to support a wife and family."

Kathryn grinned at Fergus. "All you need now is a wife."

Fergus blushed and said, "Now that I've a way to provide for one, I shall look in earnest."

Hearty laughter followed his exclamation.

"An excellent idea," the king put in. "Fergus, go with Lady Morrigan and be of service to her."

Ceallach saw the dismayed look on Fergus's face and the satisfied look on Bruce's. If he didn't know better, Ceallach would swear the king had stooped to matchmaking.

As the others drifted away, Bruce nodded to Ceallach and said, "I have given it some thought and I've decided that you will be in charge of this female prisoner. As an earl's wife, she would fetch an excellent ransom. But instead, I will hold her hostage to ensure the safety of my own family. Until an exchange of prisoners can be negotiated, Lady Radbourne needs a protector."

Ceallach glanced quickly at the woman, still seated by the fire. "I am not a good choice for this work, sire. I know nothing of women and their needs."

"Who better than a former monk to guard a female prisoner? I trust that the lady will be completely safe in your care. You will accompany her to Dunstruan, a small holding less than a day from here."

Searching for a way to dissuade Bruce, he said, "Why don't you keep her here at Stirling?"

"Stirling will suffer the same fate as other fortresses that have been held against me. With its command of the land, I cannot afford to take a chance on Edward regaining control of Stirling. It will be destroyed."

"I see. A wise course of action, my laird. Much wiser than putting me in charge of this prisoner." Ceallach glanced over at the woman. "If you insist on this, sire, I will obey. But you need to find a woman to accompany Lady Radbourne. She needs . . . she is grieving her loss, Robert. She needs a woman to talk to."

"All right." Bruce thought for a moment. "Dunstruan is less than an hour's ride from Innishewan. Morrigan and her family can live with you until her estate is livable. That should solve several problems at once."

Relieved that he would have help dealing with Lady Radbourne, and more importantly that she would have some sort of female companionship, Ceallach said, "Thank you."

"You will leave as soon as we've dealt with those supply wagons and you've been paid your wages." Bruce paused. "Dunstruan's laird died about six months ago, Ceallach. Dunstruan is to be yours."

"Mine?" Ceallach had spent his adult life not owning so much as the clothes on his back. Responsible for a castle and its lands? For the people there?

"You are a natural leader, Ceallach, and the people of Dunstruan are in need of someone to care for and protect them. That I know you can do."

Ceallach fought back panic. Robert didn't know, couldn't know, what had happened to the one person Ceallach had wanted to save. . . . Even his success at driving Edward of England from the field of battle couldn't erase the horror. His hands shook, and he pressed them against his thighs to hide the tremors. "You are too generous, brother. I cannot accept such a gift."

"Of course you can. You have served me well, especially in the battle yesterday. Take your reward and find some peace from whatever demons followed you to Scotland."

Demons. Ghosts. Memories.

If he refused this gift, Robert would insist on knowing why, and Ceallach could not talk about his past, about Peter. For now he would do Robert's bidding. When the time was right, he would return the holding to the king. "Thank you, Robert. I don't mean to seem ungrateful for your gift. It's just that I . . . am humbled by your faith in me."

Robert observed him closely. "One day I want to hear it all, Ceallach. I want to know what happened in France."

"I was arrested with the others. We were tortured. I escaped. There's nothing else to tell."

Robert shook his head, his expression one of disbelief. "One day," he repeated.

THE DAYS IMMEDIATELY FOLLOWING THE VICTORY at Bannockburn were some of the most joyous and peaceful Robert and his people had known in years. Robert anticipated the return of his wife and daughter from their English prison. Other families also awaited a reunion with their loved ones as soon as arrangements could be made.

Bruce celebrated by dispensing the immense bounty that had been found in the carts the English left behind. A huge sum of currency, gold and silver, and household items of every description made it clear that the English had expected to occupy Scottish castles after their victory. There were money chests for payment of the troops, siege weapons, all sorts of personal weapons and armor, silk tapestries, tents, linen and silk apparel, wine, corn, hay, herds of cattle, flocks of sheep, swine, and war-horses and their saddlery.

Surely every family in Scotland would benefit from the distribution of these goods.

Robert himself spent many hours giving out gifts to his army that first week after their victory. Bryan stayed close to the king, assuring himself of his father's safety before he agreed to leave for Moy with Adam and Kathryn.

Late afternoon sun reflected off an empty golden chalice Bruce had pushed into Bryan's hands. They walked to the king's tent. "Come inside for a moment, Bryan," Bruce said.

Grateful for the promise of something cool to drink, Bryan followed the king into the shelter. They sat down and a page brought refreshments. Relaxed and at ease with his father, Bryan said, "Scotland is yours now, sire."

"Aye, it is. But if she is to prosper, we'll need peace. And if we are to have the dignity of being a sovereign people, Edward of England must recognize me as the rightful king of Scotland."

As long as Edward refused recognition, other monarchs might well follow his lead and Scotland would not be able to deal with other countries as an equal. This would directly impact Scotland's ability to conduct trade and so better the lives of her people.

Bruce sipped his drink before he went on. "Obviously our victory will not sit well with Edward of England."

"No, I'm sure it won't. But that is not your only worry, is it? So long as the pope refuses to allow you back into the Church, you cannot be Scotland's spiritual leader."

"Aye, for myself I would not care. My relationship with my Lord is between him and me. But for a people to be ruled by a man the Church has cast out, well, it will cause no end of problems."

Bryan pondered this for a few moments. "Perhaps in time the pope will rescind his edict against you. I shall pray for that to happen."

"Thank you, Bryan. Your prayers are welcome. And while you are on your knees, ask that Edward might come to his senses as well."

Bryan smiled. "I will. But if Edward doesn't respond, will you continue to wage war until he is forced to come to terms?"

Bruce stood and paced the small enclosure. "I would prefer reconciliation with the English as well as with the Scottish nobles who fought against us."

"You will accept them back into your good graces?"

The king stopped in front of him. "Aye, so long as they swear homage to me and me alone. I'll not abide this loyalty to two kings any longer. People must choose."

Bryan nodded, thinking back to his own wife's divided loyalties. "Aye, that would solve many of our problems."

Robert sat down and picked up his chalice, swirling the liquid as he said, "I have decided to return the Great Seal and the Royal Shield to England. Perhaps such a goodwill gesture will bring Edward around."

"Perhaps, if he is not too humiliated by his defeat."

"Aye, I've had to flee plenty of battles with my tail between my legs. 'Tis not a good feeling, and I doubt Edward liked it much."

"When will you send an envoy with terms for peace?"

Bruce gestured with his cup. "As soon as I can. I am anxious to rid myself of the English prisoners and release my women from captivity."

"I understand, my laird. I would like to go to London with the envoy."

Bruce set the chalice down hard on the table. "Absolutely not. I will not put another loved one at Edward's disposal. You will remain in Scotland. In fact, deep in the highlands at Moy sounds like an excellent idea. Stay there as long as you like."

Three of Bruce's younger brothers had lost their lives at Edward of England's hands. The queen and Bruce's daughter by his first wife as well as his two sisters remained in England, awaiting release.

Bryan nodded. "I have no desire to add to your burden. I will do as you wish. But if Edward refuses your offer of peace?"

Wearily Bruce said, "Then we shall continue to fight." He paused. "I once told you it might be awhile before you could retire to Homelea in peace."

"Aye, but unless we convince Edward to stay south of our border with his army, my wife and family won't be safe."

Bruce smiled. "Then fight we shall, sir knight."

"The very words you used at my own knighting ceremony."

"We have endured much since then."

"Let us hope that the queen is soon restored to you and that peace comes to Scotland with her."

"Aye, let us hope." Bruce stood. "Now, get yourself and your wife to Moy. And don't hurry back."

FOUR

Meals will be eaten in silence.

—from the Rule of the Templar Knights

O*f all the many rules that governed my life as a Templar, this simple rule of silence at mealtime was the hardest for me. Perhaps because we had so little time or opportunity to share our thoughts with our fellows. And maybe that was the very reason for the rule—to keep us from forming attachments. If such was the purpose, this rule had no effect on my friendship with Peter the Weaver. I have mentioned that I was apprenticed to him. We shared a common outlook on life and a similar devotion to God. Of course, the same could have been said about many of our brothers. But Peter and I bonded as mentor and student, and we fought together in Spain. The quiet years in France strengthened our friendship. I felt the same kinship for him as I had—as I still do—for Robert the Bruce. But when Peter needed me most, I failed him.*

That is all I can write just now. Those last days before my escape are too painful to relate. Perhaps another time.

THE TIME HAD COME to take the Englishwoman to Dunstruan. Fergus and Morrigan Macnab left the day before on the two-day ride to Inverlochy to retrieve her family. They would meet up with Ceallach at Dunstruan. Until then, Ceallach would have to deal with Lady Radbourne on his own somehow.

Ceallach stared at the woman walking toward him. Complete responsibility for her sent pure terror racing through him. Abruptly he turned back in the direction he'd come from and walked straight into the king.

"Whoa, friend," Bruce said. He laid his hands on Ceallach's shoulders and steadied him. Steadied his body, but nothing could calm the turmoil of his thoughts. "Where are you going?" Bruce asked.

"To see to the horses."

Bruce looked at him carefully. "The horses are fine, last I saw of them."

"The wagon, then." He made as if to walk on, but Bruce stopped him with his hand.

Quietly Bruce ordered, "You will come with me and prepare to take Lady Radbourne to Dunstruan."

In frustration, Ceallach snapped, "You ask too much of me, Robert."

"I expect too much? I don't see why one woman should be such a bother to you."

Any man who'd led a normal life would know . . . whatever it was he should know. But Ceallach's life had not been normal and he didn't know how to talk to her, how to deal with her obvious sadness. "I know nothing of her needs."

"Food, shelter, safety. That is all you need provide, Ceallach. And she can be given work to do—staying busy will help keep her mind off her difficulties."

Ceallach took a deep breath and let it out. "Fine." He turned back toward the woman and strode up to her. "Come with me."

He glanced back at his brother, furious, for reasons he didn't understand. Bruce shook his head and walked away, leaving Ceallach to deal with her on his own.

Ceallach turned to his charge. Lady Radbourne looked tired and despondent. Ceallach felt a wave of sympathy for her. "The wagons are ready to leave as soon as you secure your belongings." He pointed to her two baskets. "May I carry those for you?"

"No, I can manage," she said.

Ceallach didn't like the idea of her fearing him. If only she knew how afraid he was of her, she would laugh despite her grief. More likely she hated him and what he stood for. He liked that thought even less.

When they drew up before the wagon Lady Radbourne said, "This will not do."

Ceallach just looked at her and she repeated, "This wagon will not do, sir."

"Why not?"

"It lacks shelter from the elements."

"It's less than a day to Dunstruan."

Lady Radbourne became so pale Ceallach stepped forward to catch her—surely she was about to faint.

"Did you say Dunstruan? We are going to Dunstruan?" she whispered.

"Aye." He moved to steady her but she shoved his hand away.

"I'm fine," she said. She drew a steadying breath. "As you can see, sir, the heat will not be good for me. And what if the weather should change? No, this will not do at all."

"Did you think we'd cart you up there on a divan?"

Now her face turned dark. "I thought I'd be accorded the amenities of civilization, but I see that was asking too much."

"Shelter from the elements," he muttered.

ORELIA STARED AT THE HUGE, DARK-HAIRED WARRIOR. He was taking her to Dunstruan, to the place she and John had expected to occupy. How fitting. How perfectly wretched. God certainly had a strange sense of justice. As strange as this man, Ceallach. A man of few words, and even those were terse and decidedly unfriendly. Which was fine—Orelia didn't need a friend. She needed her husband.

She compared her memory of John's physique with the Scot's. Even John, who'd been a fine man, did not approach the perfection of the warrior standing before her. She willed her gaze to remain on his face, but his face was even more riveting than his body.

Not a young face. No, this was a man of some years. A man in his prime, one who obviously trained rigorously for fighting. Deep creases on his forehead spoke to worries and cares and perhaps a burden not shared. Lines around his eyes told her that he'd spent a good deal of time out of doors in a sunnier climate than Scotland's.

That's when she noticed the reddened skin on the side of his neck—a scar unlike anything she'd ever seen. It came up out of his shirt just above the right shoulder and swirled forward into his beard. What would cause such a mark?

She averted her head, not wanting to be caught staring, willing her mind to think of something else. She should fear him, but something in his manner—his lack of ease around her—allayed her fright, and she felt no need to escape from him. But she wished she was going anywhere than Dunstruan, a place whose very name conjured the dreams and hopes she and John had shared. She fingered his cross, which hung from its chain around her neck. *Don't lose faith, Orelia. No matter what happens, you will not be alone.*

She must not dwell on what might have been. *Focus on what you can change, Orelia.* This cart would be bad enough to ride in without the added misery of the elements beating down on her. But the forbidding look on the warrior's face did not bode well. She stiffened her back. She had faced worse opposition than him in her time!

"I will wait in the shade of that tree, sir, until you've made the necessary repairs." She didn't wait for him to respond and walked away. The man would never have thought of her comfort—she would have to speak up if her needs were to be met.

Why was he chosen to be her jailer? His insistence on such crude accommodations only added to her misery. There had been little privacy to mourn her dead husband. This wagon was the final insult, and she just couldn't take any more.

Given a choice, she would sit right here in the dust and die. Then she would be reunited with John. Without him there was nothing to live for. She'd been assured that she would be returned to England when Bruce's wife was freed. But she had no idea how long that would be. In the meantime, she had no say over her life, her accommodations, or anything else. The riches she was to have enjoyed with John had no doubt been given to the victorious Scots. She would return home to England a widow, a childless widow despite her pleas with God to give them a babe.

Her brother-in-law would feign grief over John's death and then would most likely put her on some remote holding to molder away until she died, alone and bereft.

Yes, better to simply lie down and die right here.

Instead she would have to climb into the wagon and ride to the estate that was to have been given to John.

HE HATED TO ADMIT IT but the woman's demand for shelter was not all that unreasonable and would be easy enough to accommodate. But what would Ceallach do if she came up with another request that he didn't know how to respond to?

He found a piece of oilskin and took it back to the wagon. With broken pieces of pikes he managed to create a makeshift cover.

Then he and the men who accompanied him placed provisions in a second wagon that carried additional supplies as well as the household goods Robert had sent along for the castle and its new owner.

As the oxen moved off and started up the trail to Dunstruan, Ceallach pondered the fact that his knowledge of women would be greatly expanded before this responsibility was over.

The trip to Dunstruan should have taken less than a day but by late afternoon they were still an hour away. The track they followed was barely accessible by cart, and the beasts labored to pull the carts, especially the horses. Horses were Ceallach's first love, but unlike the team of oxen, they struggled with the cart in their charge. He was glad to have a team of both—the oxen could be eaten if necessary.

He didn't want to ask Lady Radbourne to drive and, not wanting to add his weight to the wagon, Ceallach walked beside the lead oxen's head to guide them. Two other men dealt with the second wagon and its team of horses.

Silently, he worried about Lady Radbourne. She had eaten very little when they stopped at noon, and what she did eat hadn't stayed down long. The morning's sun had disappeared, and clouds covered the sky. Soon the threatened rain began—a light rain but one that gave no indication of quitting. Lady Radbourne scurried to sit farther under the oilcloth and out of the worst of the wetness. Ceallach pulled his plaid over his head.

But the rain made the cart track slippery where it was rocky and sticky where the dirt turned to mud. The beasts trudged forward, however, and finally, an hour after the rains had begun, the wagons turned onto the path that led to Dunstruan.

Ceallach glanced back to the wagon and the woman huddled there, feeling guilty over her discomfort. He hoped Bruce negotiated her release quickly.

THE OILCLOTH THAT COVERED THE WAGON leaked and Orelia was hard pressed to stay dry. She watched as the Scot pulled his plaid over his head to ward off the wetness. She had once questioned a merchant of such cloth as to its properties and uses and learned that the weave was so tight it was nearly waterproof.

She'd wanted to try to weave it herself—the challenge of counting out the threads to create the variegated checks of the Scots cloth appealed to her. But she hadn't been able to do so without risking John's wrath. Perhaps she'd get an opportunity during her captivity.

The wagon jolted over a rock and sent her scrambling for a hold to keep from tipping out. As the tension eased from her arms, she looked up again. The outline of a modest castle emerged from the wooded hillside. *How long will I be a prisoner in the home I should be sharing with John?* But what awaited her when she returned to England? In which place would she suffer more?

In a few minutes, the cart drew up to the gate and Ceallach halted the beasts. He spoke to one of the guards before turning to her. "Wait here, my lady." With no more explanation than that, he went into the bailey and left her sitting in the rain at the mercy of the elements.

Orelia didn't know how long she must remain in the man's company, but at some point, she would certainly have to take him to task for his lack of simple courtesy.

NO ONE HAD BEEN ON THE WALLS as a lookout and the gates were wide open. Ceallach had no idea if word had been sent ahead so that the people of Dunstruan were expecting him. Lacking that assurance, he'd chosen to leave the wagons outside the gates until he could be sure of his welcome.

A small group of common folk approached him as he walked toward the keep. No one was carrying pitchforks or weapons so he assumed he was safe for the moment.

One man, taller than the rest, emerged as the others hung back. He stopped and tugged his forelock in obeisance. "Sir Ceallach?"

Ceallach relaxed. "Aye."

"Welcome to Dunstruan, sir. I am Devyn the Steward. We have been expecting you."

"You received word?"

"Aye. A messenger from the king came two days ago." He turned slightly to include the others. "We've made everything ready for you."

Heads bobbed in the crowd, and smiles broke out as they realized who he was. A woman stepped forward, the castle keys hanging from the girdle at her waist. Devyn grasped her hand. "This is my wife, Suisan. She has been acting as chatelaine." Suisan reached for the keys.

Ceallach held up his hand. "Keep them, madam." He didn't want to explain that he wasn't planning to stay. "I will rely upon you to continue your duties, if that suits you?"

She smiled. "Aye, my laird. I should be very pleased to oversee your home."

Your home. Robert had been right—Dunstruan seemed to be in good hands. All that was needed was a laird to protect them. They looked at him with such hope and longing that he wanted to turn away and run. Who was he fooling, pretending to be a protector? But he sensed their innate goodness and he could not be impolite. He was here, and for the time being he would pretend that he could be their laird.

But the tightness in his chest told him he would pay a price for this farce. *If they knew me, they wouldn't trust their lives to me.* He shook off the thought and went to the gate to tell the men to bring the wagons in. The beasts, sensing the end of the journey, moved quickly into the bailey.

Ceallach told the guards to see to the animals. Devyn and Suisan and their folk began to unload the supplies. They were efficient and courteous, and he relaxed further. This might turn out to be a pleasant interlude after all. He turned to help Lady Radbourne from the cart.

"Welcome to your temporary home, my lady," he said as he reached for her hand.

But the lady stared at Dunstruan, her expression so filled with pain Ceallach actually took a step backward.

"Lady Radbourne, are you all right?"

A tear trickled from her eye and she swiped it away. "I didn't think this would be so hard," she whispered. "To be here of all places . . ."

FIVE

Brothers may not rise from the table
unless they have a nosebleed.

—from the Rule of the Templar Knights

L*ady Orelia has the most incredibly delicate hands. They
seemed lost in mine as I helped her from the wagon, just as lost
as she seemed on arriving at Dunstruan.*

*She is a beautiful woman, despite her sorrow, and her pres-
ence in my life is a constant reminder of my vows as a Templar,
as a warrior monk. For fifteen years I struggled, as would any
mortal man, to keep those vows. Poverty wasn't difficult—I am
a man of simple needs. Obedience was easy—a military man
learns discipline and the life and death reasons for it. But
chastity. Perhaps St. Paul was mistaken in his belief that man is
better off living chaste. Of course, he did also say better to marry
than to burn. But my vow was to live chaste, and I burned.*

*To ease myself, I often drank more than a prudent amount
of wine and ale. Big as I am, I can down more than most men
and still keep my wits about me. But on more than one occa-
sion, I'm ashamed to say, I drank enough to loosen my wits, my
tongue, and nearly my braes. And each time I drank I got closer
to breaking my vow. It was only a matter of time and wine
until I did so.*

It pains me when I break my word, yet I don't understand why. Why do I cling to those promises, that sense of morality, when God has deserted me? He does not deserve such homage.

ORELIA SAT IN THE BAILEY OF THE CASTLE that had been meant to be her home—hers and John's. Now it would be her prison instead. Her heart felt as numb as the leg that had fallen asleep beneath her. She stood and her numbed leg folded. The warrior stepped forward and grabbed her, steadied her, and helped her down. She leaned on his strength, not because she wanted to be anywhere near him, but to steady herself until feeling returned to her feet.

John. The grief stabbed again. She and her husband had journeyed north in trepidation and hope. Hope that when the Scots were finally defeated they could begin a life where John would not be called to serve in war again. But that hope had been smothered somewhere in the marshy bogs of Bannockburn.

Lady Heathrow had spoken of her anxious desire to return home to her children. Again grief stabbed Orelia. She didn't even have that solace to return to. No child with John's laughing blue eyes or untamable mane of dark brown hair.

Stop. She must stop this at once or her grief would consume her here on the spot, right in front of these uncivilized Scots. She was Lady Radbourne, and she would not give them the satisfaction.

But she was no longer the countess of Radbourne. John's brother Richard would waste no time claiming the title for his own wife. New anxiety rocked Orelia. Would Richard provide for her? He and his pathetic wife would probably gloat. Orelia might be better off here than at home. There was little comfort in the thought.

The needles and pins gradually left her foot and though she still felt unsteady, she withdrew her hand from Ceallach's arm.

"Can you walk now?" he asked.

"Yes, of course." She would not thank him for his concern. She would not give any satisfaction to these people. He led her into the castle, and the interior, though clean, lacked the ornate furnishings of Radbourne Hall.

Orelia's leg gave way and she nearly tripped. Ceallach righted her, and she accepted his help mutely where once she'd have made light of her clumsiness. But her heart would never be light again. Feeling as lifeless as the wooden seat she was led to, she pulled her emotions close. She would not allow these heathens to see her pain.

They had killed John and they could rot. *God forgive me. Forgive me for turning my pain into hatred. Help me forgive my enemies.*

She shivered. How long would she have to stay in such unwelcome surroundings?

ALTHOUGH THE KEEP WAS CLEAN, the inhabitants seemed to thrive in pandemonium, nothing like the orderly life Ceallach had known for so many years in the monastery, and then in Bruce's army. Maybe it was just the constant hum of conversation that caught his attention. In Ceallach's experience, tasks were completed with little or no talking. Here, it seemed that every one was talking at once.

"Where did all these women come from? I only brought one with me and just look . . . just listen."

Devyn the Steward laughed. "My wife has a fair number of female relatives who live and work here."

Ceallach shook his head. "Are they always this noisy?"

"No. Sometimes it's worse."

Ceallach held back a groan of dismay. How would he ever find peace and quiet amongst this cacophony of high-pitched voices? And Morrigan had yet to arrive with her mother and sister. That would mean three more women to listen to. He could only hope that Morrigan, a fellow warrior, would know when to be quiet.

Devyn, seemingly oblivious to the noise, said, "Your men may bed down in the stable. They will take their meals in the hall, of course. Our gates were open when you arrived because we are in need of a repair to the portcullis chain. Perhaps you would take a look at the chain and see if you can repair it somehow?"

"I can do that."

"Good. Then with your permission, I will show you your quarters first."

THE NEXT MORNING Devyn showed Ceallach the weaving hut. A giant loom, similar to the one Peter had loved to work on, stood at one end of the room. Smaller looms for making belts and shawls sat at the other.

"The loom needs repair," Devyn apologized.

"I can fix it." Ceallach said, lost in memories of days spent in just such a hut, working with his friend. *Peter, I failed you.* Ceallach pushed away the images and the emotions.

"My laird?"

Ceallach took a deep breath to clear his head and then walked closer to the loom. One of the side beams was split and would have to be replaced. "Who is your weaver?"

"He died last winter of the same ailment that killed our laird. Suisan can make the smaller things, but she's not skilled at designing material for plaids."

The sight of the great loom rekindled conflicting emotions. Ceallach had always loved working the loom. But he'd not touched one since Peter's death, had not wanted to. He ran his hand along the smooth roller where finished cloth would wind. The loom and the memories drew him.

Maybe it was time to try his hand again. He took a deep breath and released it. "I have some experience. Perhaps . . . perhaps I will weave after I've fixed the beam."

"Excellent, my laird. I'll let Suisan know."

They left the hut, and as they walked toward the front of the keep a group on horseback entered the bailey. Friend or foe? Ceallach couldn't recognize faces from this distance, but the fact that there were women in the party eased his anxiety somewhat.

Ceallach knew he would have to find a smith to mend the portcullis if he wanted to truly secure the castle. Or do it himself. In the long years spent waiting to go on a crusade, Ceallach had not only learned to weave, but also to shoe horses. He might be able to fashion whatever was needed to mend the gate. But the thought of working with hot implements and fire—he didn't think he could do it. Not now—maybe never.

By now he was close enough to recognize Fergus and Morrigan as his visitors. Ceallach strode across the bailey to greet them. In no time he was surrounded by chaos. Suisan and the other women of the castle came out to greet the guests. Devyn and his men were there as well. Only the Englishwoman was absent. Ceallach assumed she was resting, as she'd spent a good deal of time in her chamber since her arrival.

Years of quiet living as a monk and another seven years as a soldier with Bruce had not prepared Ceallach for interaction with crowds. At least not with friendly crowds. In camp, the men had left him to himself, if he so pleased. Certainly his experience at dealing with women, especially more than one at a time, was limited. He withdrew to the edge of the throng and just observed.

He watched as Fergus dismounted and went to help Morrigan from her horse. She refused to take his hand and nimbly swung her leg over the horse's back and dropped to the ground. Ceallach look she gave the poor man did not bode well for

.....ued employment as her steward. Fergus wisely went

.....iorrigan's mother and younger sister dismount.

ɔuisan shooed the servants off to their chores and invited the guests to come into the keep. As Fergus and the others walked toward the steps of the keep, Ceallach stepped forward. "Welcome to Dunstruan."

Fergus said, "We thank ye for the hospitality."

Ceallach exchanged greetings as the women walked into the keep but drew Fergus aside before he entered. "Have you any news from Bruce?"

Fergus shook his head. "Not much has changed. Negotiations for the prisoner exchange have come to a halt."

Ceallach nodded. "We can talk more over food. Come inside."

They sat down at a trestle with Morrigan's family, and she and Fergus made introductions. Devyn the Steward helped his wife with the added work of having guests by setting up an additional trestle. Suisan gave him a hearty kiss for his efforts and Devyn grinned with pleasure.

The natural affection between the two fascinated Ceallach. He couldn't remember his parents ever treating each other with such ease, and theirs was really the only marriage he had first-hand knowledge of. Fergus caught him staring.

"Aye," Fergus said with a nod. "It would be nice to have someone who cared that much about ye, wouldn't it?"

Ceallach wasn't sure he shared the sentiment but he remembered Lady Kathryn's comment at Fergus's knighting ceremony. "Have you started looking for a wife, then?"

"Oh, I'm done looking. I've found her. She just needs persuading."

How had the man found a wife in the few days since they'd left Stirling? His eyes searched the room. "Morrigan?" he asked, dumbfounded.

"Aye."

Ceallach shook his head. "I wish you luck with that one."

Fergus said, "I'll be needin' it."

ORELIA WALKED INTO THE MAIN HALL for the midday meal. There were a number of strangers in the hall today. Perhaps passing travelers had been invited to partake of Dunstruan's hospitality.

As she walked toward an empty table Orelia froze, unable to move forward. She stared at the back of the man seated with Ceallach. John was here. The sight of his dark, unruly hair and broad shoulders made her heart race and she started forward with joy. But then the man laughed a strange-sounding laugh and she realized the absurdity of her reaction.

John was dead. Whoever this man was, his laughter confirmed what her heart didn't want to believe. It wasn't John. Still she stared at the man's back.

As she drew closer he turned away from the warrior and she had her first glimpse of his face. Laughing blue eyes completed the cruel deception. But the similarity ended there. This man had a pointed chin and a scar over one eye. She'd seen him the day Bruce had knighted him. Fergus, if she recalled correctly.

Ceallach stood and the man followed suit. "Lady Radbourne, may I introduce Fergus Cookson."

Fergus bowed but Orelia couldn't move to offer her hand or find her voice to speak. Despite the scar, this man looked remarkably like John. Or was it only wishful thinking? When she was able to speak, she said the first thing that came to her mind. "Are you English?"

He seemed taken aback and she said, "Forgive me. You look very much like . . . an acquaintance in England." She turned to find a seat but Fergus pushed back the bench and moved closer.

He took her hand. "I have upset ye. This acquaintance—ye are fond of him?"

As tears welled, Orelia silently chastised herself for leaving her room. She'd stayed there on purpose, unwilling to break down in front of these people, determined to hide her pain. She feared if she answered the man's question she would burst into tears.

Ceallach unwittingly rescued her when he answered for her. "Her husband was killed at Stirling."

"I am sorry for yer loss, my lady. "

Orelia pulled herself together. She didn't want their kindness, and she didn't want to feel any warmth towards these people who'd changed her life forever. "Thank you," she managed to say before moving off to find a place to sit by herself.

As she ate, Orelia stole glances at Ceallach and his companion. When she saw that the men's attention was diverted, she stared at the one called Fergus.

It had been imagination, wishful thinking. The man looked nothing like John.

SIX

Silver or gold decoration of the saddle, bridle,
or stirrup is forbidden.

—from the Rule of the Templar Knights

A number of events conspired to destroy the Templar
Knights. Word has it that sometime in the year 1305, a knight
by the name of Esquin of Floyran was expelled from the
Templar Order for an infraction of the rules. I did not know
the man nor do I have any knowledge of his crime nor of his
guilt or innocence. But Esquin felt he'd been unfairly treated,
and his subsequent actions were to have a devastating effect
on my life and the life of my brothers.

Esquin alleged that the Order itself was guilty of gross
impropriety, and rumors soon spread throughout France.
When King Philip of France heard the allegations, he brought
them to the attention of the Pope, who promised to institute an
inquiry. He asked Philip to be patient, not to take action until
such time as the pope could look into the matter further.

But Philip's royal treasury owed vast sums of money to the
Templar Order, and these rumors of wrongdoing gave him
just what he'd been looking for—a way to discredit the Order
and thus be excused from his debt. He sent secret directions to
his henchmen throughout France, ordering the detention of all

members of the Temple on the grounds that we had committed crimes too terrible to speak of.

And while we rotted in Philip's jails, he confiscated our properties and wealth, relieving himself of his debt.

MORRIGAN'S FAMILY joined Fergus and Ceallach at their trestle. Fergus blessed the meal and the conversation grew as the meat, cheese, and ale were consumed. Ceallach watered his ale, knowing from experience that doing so would water down his need to drink more than he should.

Ceallach had to ask Morrigan to repeat her question, since he couldn't hear it above the buzz of conversation surrounding them.

She leaned closer. "Have you rounded up your sheep?"

"No, but I've been out to the pasturage to see them." In fact, he'd spent a blessedly peaceful afternoon walking the land that comprised the holding of Dunstruan. He took a bite of bread.

"All of them?"

He nodded, chewed, and swallowed. Why couldn't she let a man eat in peace? "I believe so."

"And are they in good condition?"

"Fair."

"What about the wool?"

"It will do."

He saw more than heard her breath of exasperation and wondered what he'd said to annoy her. The wool was in as good a condition as one could expect having been left until this late date to be gathered.

Morrigan spoke again. "Will there be enough to bother spinning?"

"Aye."

Fergus leaned over to Ceallach and spoke quietly. "She doesn't mean to be annoying. It's just her way." Louder he said to Ceallach, "Can ye be more specific?"

Ceallach frowned, setting down his bread. "The sheep have rubbed it off from here to the far reaches of the estate. It will need to be handled carefully—it's been compressed by the rain."

"You are a man of few words, Ceallach," Morrigan remarked.

"Silence has its rewards," Ceallach replied calmly. He looked across the way where Lady Radbourne sat with Devyn and Suisan. The lady picked at her food, and her sadness tugged at him. As he watched her, she stood and quickly left the hall. *More tears to shed.*

He suspected the lady would not return to the hall, and he allowed himself to be drawn into a lively discussion about the merits of plucking wool by hand versus cutting with shears.

"What do ye say, Ceallach?" Fergus asked.

"These highland sheep shed their wool. 'Tis easy enough to *roo* it from them with your fingers or gather it where they rub it off. No need to use shears."

The conversation ebbed and flowed around Ceallach as he remembered such meals from his childhood. He'd not sat at a table of women, at any table with such conversation, for more than half his life. He wasn't sure if he liked it.

Morrigan turned to her mother and said, "So, how does Grania like married life?"

Eveleen answered, "Your sister and her husband seem quite happy with one another. I have no doubt I'll be a grandmother by Easter."

Ceallach looked at the woman. Though Morrigan was maybe twenty-five, Eveleen Macnab couldn't be more than a few years older than he was, and she would soon be a grandmother. Sometimes the sacrifices of his chosen profession came home with a vengeance.

Morrigan's younger sister, Cassidy, pouted. "I don't see why I can't marry. Evan has asked more than once, Mother, and you refuse."

"Actually," Morrigan said, "I'm the one who said no. Evan will thank me when you've had time to grow up before he weds you."

Cassidy retorted, "Just don't make me wait until I'm an old maid like you, Morrigan."

Ceallach expected Morrigan's quick temper but she surprised him by calmly saying, "That will be enough, Cassidy. If you can't speak to me respectfully, then let's not hear more from you at all."

Cassidy seemed aware that she was treading marshy territory and wisely changed the subject.

Ceallach caught the eye of ten-year-old Keifer Macnab. The boy rolled his eyes. He finished his meal and asked to be excused, evidently as overwhelmed by the chatter as Ceallach. Eveleen gave permission, and the lad shot from his seat like he'd sat on a tack.

Ceallach wished he could join him. Instead he asked Morrigan, "Have you been to Innishewan yet?"

"No. I thought Fergus and I would ride over tomorrow and see what it will take to make it habitable."

Eveleen said, "I look forward to seeing Morrigan engaged in such a womanly pursuit as managing a castle." She turned to her daughter. "Perhaps then you'll stop wearing trews."

"I doubt it. They suit me."

"You'll never find a husband dressed like that, Morrigan."

The young woman's face blushed pink and to Ceallach's surprise, she stole a look at Fergus. Fergus continued to eat his meal and said nothing. But as Fergus looked down at his plate, Ceallach saw him struggle not to grin.

"I could see the need for wearing trews when you were a warrior, Morrigan. But now that we are to have peace with England, you are free to seek a mate and set up a household."

From the stormy look on Morrigan's face, Ceallach guessed that mother and daughter had had this conversation more than once.

"I have other responsibilities, Mother. I have no time nor any need for a husband."

"Perhaps in a few months, then," her mother conceded.

"You are still young, Mother. Perhaps you, too, should seek a husband and help to lighten my responsibility for our family."

Eveleen sputtered and nearly choked. Fergus, sitting next to her, patted her back until the woman's breath came easily. "You are disrespectful, Morrigan. I have no need of a husband at my age."

"But if you would marry, your husband would take responsibility for my siblings, and I would have more time to search for a husband of my own."

Eveleen stared at her daughter, and Ceallach suspected this was an ongoing argument between the two headstrong women. He would not want to bet against either of them in this contest of wills.

To his surprise, Morrigan softened her tone. "Mother, when I find a man who understands what it means to be a warrior, who can allow me to be who I am and not expect me to change for him, then and only then will I marry."

Morrigan did not look at Fergus as she spoke, but Ceallach wondered if the words were meant as a warning to the man. Fergus leaned toward her. "I wish you success in finding this man, Lady Morrigan," he said.

Morrigan looked up at him and swiftly searched his eyes. A second later, she was busily chatting with her sister again.

Ceallach admired Fergus for choosing to court the fiery woman. Few men would be comfortable with her strength, both physical and mental. She did not strike him as some demure and retiring lady. She was more like the ancient queen Boudicca, a fighter and a protector of the weak.

Ceallach himself would not choose such a one. He craved peace most of all. Life with Morrigan would be anything but peaceful.

The conversation moved on to other things. Ceallach paid little attention until Eveleen mentioned that Edward of England had placed a bounty on the heads of the men who had posed as Templar Knights at Bannockburn.

Looking at Ceallach with a directness that told him she knew of his involvement, Morrigan said, "Impostors or not, no one here will even consider turning them in."

Ceallach asked, "Why is that?"

"For one, they led a force that turned the tide of the battle."

Maintaining a calm he didn't truly feel, Ceallach said, "If that is so, then I can understand why Edward wants revenge. He blames them for his loss."

"Well, he must blame someone and he isn't one to examine his own stupidity!"

Her vehemence seemed overly done even for one who fought at Bannockburn. "You don't have a very high opinion of England's king," Ceallach said.

In a hushed voice she replied, "I watched helplessly while he butchered women and children at Midvale. I would like nothing better than to give him a taste of such savagery."

Eveleen said, "Why did you never tell me this?"

Again Morrigan looked at Ceallach as if to reassure him that his part in the battle would remain a secret. "I didn't want you to know more than you should if Uncle Angus questioned you. Some things, the fewer people who know about them the better."

Morrigan's mother looked at her daughter as if seeing her for the first time. "I am proud of you for standing by your principles, Daughter."

"Thank you." Obviously uncomfortable, Morrigan changed the subject, addressing the group again. "Bruce has been lenient, nay generous, with many who opposed him but changed their minds to support him."

Fergus joined in. "Everyone but Clan Comyn. He has been quite harsh in destroying their lands and homes."

"He had the opportunity to destroy Edward's army at Stirling Castle but took mercy on them instead. Bruce has ever been far more magnanimous than Edward or his father," Ceallach said.

"Aye," Morrigan said. "Edward seems ruled by hatred for the Scottish race even more so than by a desire to rule a country where there is no great wealth to be found. Half the country is wild highlands ruled by wilder men." She gestured about her, a bemused, teasing light in her eyes.

Fergus grinned. "Here on the southern edge of the highlands we're close enough to have some of the niceties of civilization. But far enough away to live life as we see fit."

Yet Ceallach feared that Dunstruan wasn't nearly far enough away from England for him to remain here. Once he finished serving Bruce as guardian for Lady Radbourne, he would seek a home farther north, perhaps on a remote northern island. Far away from a defeated king seeking revenge on hidden Templar Knights . . .

When the meal was over, Morrigan asked Ceallach to stay behind. "Walk with me," she said.

He didn't know Morrigan all that well and wondered what she could want with him. She'd made it clear a few minutes ago that she knew, or at least suspected, that he'd been one of the Templars at Bannockburn. Her request to walk with her had sounded more like an order, and he did as she asked out of curiosity.

They walked out of the main hall and into the bailey before Morrigan stopped and turned to face him. "I'm worried about my brother, Keifer. I haven't seen him much since my father died, and I fear he has spent his life solely in the company of women. Keifer needs a man to teach him how to be a warrior."

Ceallach hadn't anticipated this topic of conversation and was momentarily caught off guard. "He is of an age to be fostered," Ceallach said, not sure where this discussion was headed.

"Until I can arrange fosterage, I wonder if you would begin his training?"

Yet another person to be responsible for? What had Ceallach said or done that made people expect so much from him? How could he discourage her? "Can't it wait until he's permanently settled?"

"I suppose it could but I want to put some distance between the boy and our mother. I love Mother dearly, despite our sparring at the table. But Keifer needs to be weaned from her influence if he is to become laird of our clan."

"He's to be laird? I thought you were leading the clan."

"I am. But contrary to my hedging with my mother, I would welcome the right man as my husband. My husband and I can lead the clan until Keifer comes of age. But by then he must be ready to claim his inheritance."

Her plan had merit. "You are wise as well as feisty, Morrigan."

She smiled. "I will take that as a compliment."

He hesitated. "You hardly know me. Why choose me?"

"I know who and what you are."

Her words could be taken as a threat but Ceallach didn't think she meant them as one. He ran his fingers through his hair and decided to test her. "Then you certainly don't want such a man training a young, impressionable boy."

Morrigan crossed her arms. "I don't believe a word of the charges brought against your Order. The king trusts you. That's all I need to know."

He could almost feel some of the weight lift from his shoulders at her declaration of trust. How could he say no to her request? And it would only be for a short time. "All right. I will accept Keifer as my fosterling until you make a more permanent arrangement."

"Thank you." She clapped him on the upper back in the way of comrades and he stiffened, anticipating pain. But the wounds had healed a long time ago. The physical wounds, that is.

"What is it, Ceallach?"

He laughed it off. "Nothing." How long would he keep his emotions locked up tight? How long could he hide his deep need for just such everyday things as human touch? He met her gaze and his pain must have shown. In her wisdom as a fellow warrior she recognized that she mustn't press further.

"We have both seen sights that left scars," she said. She watched him for a moment. "I've found that it helps to talk about it."

"So I've been told." He said no more.

After a moment, she said, "I can only imagine what you suffered. I will pray that one day you'll find the healing your heart needs, Ceallach. Perhaps the love of the right lady will restore you."

He nodded, sensing they both knew Morrigan wasn't that woman. "I don't believe I'm capable of such love anymore, Morrigan."

"I don't believe that, but then who am I to judge?" She smiled ruefully. "Nearly twenty-five years old and as my sister so sweetly put it, an old maid." When he would have protested she held up her hand. "It's all right. Cassidy may be closer to the truth than I'd like to admit." She paused. "Do you need some time alone?"

Morrigan was much too observant. He did feel a bit overwhelmed. "Aye, I do."

"I'll tell the others you have gone to check the sheep."

"Thank you, Morrigan." It felt good to be understood. To be known to some extent, by someone other than Robert. Fergus would be blessed if Morrigan welcomed his suit for her hand.

Ceallach had never considered that he might find a woman who would accept the damaged man that he'd become. But Morrigan's perceptive words made him wish, for the first time, that such a thing might be possible.

TWO DAYS LATER CHAOS REIGNED AGAIN as Fergus and Morrigan's family gathered in the bailey. They'd decided they would all ride to Innishewan to inspect the estate and return before dark. Ceallach wondered if the entire castle would be thrown into such upheaval every time they departed and returned.

Everyone else seemed to be taking it all in stride, so maybe women were just natural harbingers of chaos. With a shout that overcame the noise Lady Eveleen came barreling through the others.

"Where is my son?" she demanded. Fergus shrugged and no one else answered. She turned to Ceallach.

"He is tending to some chores for me."

"Well, he needs to come and mount his horse so we can be off to Innishewan. Where is he?" she repeated.

Ceallach searched for Morrigan amidst the crowd but didn't see her. "I have promised to teach the boy to wield a sword. 'Tis time he had such lessons."

Lady Eveleen paused, looking uncomfortable. Only the most overprotective of mothers would forbid her son to learn to wield weapons. "An excellent idea. But I'm afraid he won't have time today. Perhaps when we return."

"Why not allow him to begin today, Lady Macnab? He's of an age to be fostered, and it's past time to start his training. I am willing to take on the task until he can be placed with a foster family." Keifer was certainly of an age, but was his mother ready to let him go?

Morrigan had quietly made her way to stand by Ceallach.

With a sharp look at her daughter, Lady Eveleen said, "I suppose you've spoken with Morrigan already?"

"Aye."

"Then it will do me no good to discuss it further. I'm glad you thought of it."

He suspected she knew very well that it had been Morrigan's idea. "I'm glad you approve, my lady."

"Yes," she said with less certainty. "I should like to bid him farewell."

"His training has already begun. He's learning the first thing a knight must know."

Anxiously she asked, "And what might that be?"

Ceallach grinned. "The proper way to clean a horse stall."

He saw her shoulders relax and she smiled before she walked away to find her youngest child. It had been difficult for Ceallach's own mother to let him go so that he might learn the ways of men and warriors. It was no different with Lady Macnab.

Morrigan said, "Well done. She would have fought me—thank you for setting her at ease."

"Not at all, Morrigan. It will be . . . good for me to have the boy about."

"You are more than generous, Ceallach," she said, eyes shining. "My brother will learn much from you indeed."

"We'll see about that. I suspect the boy will teach me a thing or two too."

Eveleen returned in a few minutes and seemed resigned to Keifer's staying at Dunstruan. "I've told Keifer I'll expect a full accounting of his behavior when I return," she said to Ceallach.

"A good idea, madam."

She mounted her horse and soon the bailey emptied. Wondering what had possessed him, Ceallach went in search of his pupil.

MORRIGAN HAD INVITED ORELIA to go along to Innishewan but Orelia declined. She didn't feel up to spending time with Morrigan and her mother just yet. Instead she wandered down to Dunstruan's kitchen. The cook was only too happy to have help with the bread making.

Being around other people meant she must hold her emotions in check, think of something other than her grief. The repetitive, mindless work of kneading the dough gave Orelia time to think. Time to pray. And prayer helped to ease her heart. She felt her grief lift bit by bit, day by day. Perhaps she should continue to stay busy instead of hiding away in her room.

To Orelia's surprise Ceallach walked into the kitchen with Morrigan's young brother close behind. The knight spoke with the cook, and she gave the boy a slice from one of the cooled loaves along with a piece of cheese. While the boy ate, Ceallach came over and stood next to Orelia.

"Keifer and I are going to round up the sheep. Would you mind helping?"

She kneaded the dough a final time, shaped the loaf for baking, then set it with the others to rise. She wiped her hands on her apron. "You want my help?" Orelia couldn't disguise her surprise.

"Aye. Everyone else is busy with other chores." He stared at her flour-covered hands. "Never mind. It was a bad idea." He turned to leave.

"Wait. That was the last loaf." The thought of leaving the confines of the castle and taking a walk appealed to her. She took her shawl from a peg on the wall. "I would love a walk and a change of scenery." Even if it meant spending time with the gruff Scot.

"Good. Follow me."

And with no more than that he walked back out of the kitchen, grabbing the boy by the collar as he went. Orelia hastily took off her apron and hurried after them.

She and Keifer fell in behind the knight, not sure if he even knew they were there. Outside the walls of the castle for the first time since they'd arrived, Orelia was astounded by the beauty of the place. She'd been far too miserable and the day's weather too ugly to notice the countryside when she'd arrived.

The castle was situated, like most fortresses, on an outcropping of rock. They walked north toward a forest of ancient oaks.

Young Keifer remained quiet and Orelia wondered if something bothered him. But as they rounded a curve in the path, the lad exclaimed, "Look at that!" And he took off at a run.

"Don't scatter the sheep!" Ceallach yelled.

Keifer's gait slowed but he was still well ahead of them.

Orelia looked to where Keifer had pointed. To their right, the land fell off gently and in the distance, down a gentle slope, sunlight reflected from a deep blue lake. Surrounded on all sides by forest broken occasionally by grassland, the rich summer green and the azure water made a breath-stealing sight. Orelia slowed to take it in then stopped altogether next to Ceallach, staring.

"Have you ever seen anything so beautiful?" she whispered, as if speaking aloud might make the sight disappear.

"Look there," Ceallach said, pointing to the left shore. A flock of sheep moved out of the trees and onto the meadow. A faint trail, brown against the verdant green, wound its way to the water's edge and the sheep followed it, single file.

As the animals reached the water they spread out and drank, the lambs frolicking in the shallow wetness. How Orelia wished she had some parchment to sketch the wondrous view! She continued to stare, forgetting that they'd come out here to round up the sheep.

Ceallach said, "It's glorious, isn't it?"

His voice had lost its gruffness—he seemed as genuinely moved by the pastoral sight as was she. "Yes, that it is." She looked at the blue water. "When I see such beauty I see God's hand at work and

I want to capture it somehow, preserve it so I can see it anytime I wish."

He paused and shifted. "Are you an artist, then?"

"I can sketch. But what I would truly love is to create a tapestry of it."

"Then we'd best round up the sheep so you have yarn to do so." Abruptly he turned and walked away. "Keifer! Come along!" he shouted.

Orelia hurried after him, wondering at his changeable moods. But she forgot the warrior and his moodiness when they came to a small hut. A man worked in a garden behind the round building. From the shade at the side of the hut a good-sized collie dog got to its feet and came over to greet Orelia.

The dog's tail wagged lazily and Orelia offered her hand to him. He sniffed and his tail wagged harder so Orelia scratched his head. When he sat down beside her she knew she'd made a friend.

Ceallach said, "You have a way with animals."

"I was raised on a country estate as was my husband." Indeed the collie reminded her of one of John's favorite dogs on their own estate and for a moment she fought the tears that came with the memory. But crying wouldn't change anything, and it certainly didn't make her feel better. The lovely view of the lake had soothed her heart and reminded her of John's assurance of God's presence. She drew comfort from the knowledge that she didn't have to face her problems alone. She would concentrate on that rather than her sorrow.

A short, dark-haired peasant came out of the hut and greeted them shyly.

"Lady Radbourne, this is Joseph. He and his dog are going to help us with the sheep."

They walked back toward the overlook of the lake but now took a path that led to the lower land where they'd seen the flock. The collie stayed close at the peasant's heels, ears alert, nose testing the air. When they drew closer to the sheep the dog's agitation was palpable. Clearly he wanted to race ahead to join Keifer and get to work.

A word from his owner calmed the dog. They rounded a bend in the path and there were the sheep. They'd moved into the shade of the woods after getting their fill of water. Keifer stood on the edge of the lake, tossing pebbles into the water. "Keifer, come here," Ceallach called.

Orelia quickly counted about seventy-five animals. She spotted the rams with their horns right away. The lambs were all several months old and in good health. They eyed the dog with suspicion, but when he sat on the edge of the herd and merely watched them they soon went back to their feeding.

Great clumps of wool hung from most of the sheep and clung to the branches of heather. "Why did no one shear the wool this spring?" she asked.

The peasant said, "A few of us took enough for our own needs, but didn't see the need to gather the rest."

Ceallach nodded. "It's not too late to remedy the lack. We'll set some of the local children to work collecting it from the woods. We'll roo the rest of it once the sheep are penned."

Using her shawl as a makeshift bag, Orelia gathered wool as they herded the sheep back toward the castle, wondering what it meant to roo a sheep. She would ask Ceallach when she had a chance. Tufts of wool hung from anything the animals rubbed against—trees, bushes, and even stones. The challenge lay in finding it when the darker brown and black fleece blended in with the surroundings. The white wool, though less common, was easier to find. It looked like balls of snow against the green of summer.

Perhaps she should resent being asked to work, but she just

couldn't. The weather and exercise and healing touch of the sun had lifted some of the grief that had followed her here. And like kneading the bread, the task gave her time to think, to remember John and how she had loved him, how she had tried to be a good wife.

At moments like this, she even contemplated not returning to England. After all, that had been their plan, to stay here in Scotland at this very castle. What did she have to return to besides Alice's nastiness and Richard as earl? Yes, she had friends in England but no one who would really care whether or not she returned, if Orelia were honest with herself. And Radbourne Hall would be full of painful reminders of all she'd lost.

But she wasn't the lady of this estate, nor a welcome guest. She was a prisoner, soon to be sent away whether she wanted to be or not. Sent back to Radbourne Hall.

Bringing her thoughts back to the present she saw that they were very near to the castle. With the help of the well-trained dog, Ceallach and Keifer herded the sheep toward the pens awaiting them inside the bailey. Orelia removed the wool from her shawl and placed it in a basket before helping to move the animals into their temporary quarters.

THE ENGLISHWOMAN STOOD NEARBY and listened as Ceallach explained to Keifer what they were going to do. "Sheep are docile if not too bright. They are also stubborn," Ceallach warned Keifer. "We are going to have to catch each of them so I can decide which to keep for slaughter. You may mark those with dye." He handed the boy a bucket and a brush, wondering just how much of the paint would end up on Keifer.

Lady Radbourne said, "What shall I do to help?"

Ceallach had enjoyed showing her the lake—her reaction to the beauty of the place had drawn him to her even as he rejected her mention of God. He didn't understand her, and in his confusion he spoke with more than his usual gruffness. "You can *roo* the excess wool."

She looked puzzled rather than put off. "Roo? Could you explain that, please?"

He scowled, though a part of him wanted to smile, wanted to ease her grief and see her enjoy herself. "I keep forgetting you're a proper Englishwoman. Pluck it off them, like this." He seized a nearby sheep with one hand and laced the fingers of the other hand into the fleece. Gently tugging upward, he loosened a clump of wool. "With your small hands, you'd do better just to comb your fingers through before trying to pluck it free. Here, try it."

She came close to the ewe, which having had quite enough already, began to buck and struggle. But he easily held it in place and Lady Radbourne plucked the wool just as he'd shown her. She placed the wool into the willow basket at her feet.

"These highland sheep molt every spring. Push the wool apart— there where you haven't pulled any away yet." She did as he said and he continued. "See where the wool broke off about an inch from the body?"

"Yes. That's strange."

"Well, it looks strange to you, aye. But 'tis the way of these sheep. The wool keeps growing and the break grows out with it."

The woman said, "And the poor beasts rid themselves of the loose wool by rubbing it off. That's why there was so much of it hanging on the rocks and shrubs."

"Aye, and now we are removing what remains and the sheep will no doubt be glad to be rid of it. Take as much as you can from the back and sides where the wool is in the best condition," he said. "But leave a sufficient pelt to keep them warm this winter. Keifer, mark this one when the lady is done."

"You sure know a lot about sheep," the boy remarked with what sounded like respect.

"My . . . family raised them at one time." Not quite the truth, but close. He and Peter had tended the monastery's flock, and Ceallach smiled, remembering for the first time in years a pleasant time with the older man as they prepared wool for weaving. Working with Keifer reminded him of the teacher-pupil relationship Ceallach and Peter had shared.

Lady Radbourne said to the boy, "We have sheep at Radbourne Hall but the men shear them. We've never *rooed* them." She continued to pluck the wool. "I love the feel of the wool—the oil softens my hands. Is this one finished?"

"Aye, Lady Radbourne. You've done a fine job."

"My given name is Orelia. If we're going to sweat over these sheep, I think it only right that we dispense with formality, Ceallach."

"All right." *Orelia.* A beautiful name for a beautiful woman. He held the animal while Keifer swiped a brush of red dye on its back and then he let the animal go. It raced back to its companions, bleating.

"Listen to him, warning his friends of the terrible fate they must face," Orelia said.

Keifer's eyes grew wide. "They know what the dye means?"

Ceallach laughed and looked at Lady Radbourne. At Orelia. She laughed with them, and he hoped that perhaps her heart had lightened just a bit. As he turned toward the next sheep, he realized that his own heart had lightened for a moment as well.

SEVEN

Brothers must have permission to go out into the city
or when on campaign, to leave camp.

—from the Rule of the Templar Knights

After spending such a pleasant afternoon with Orelia and
Keifer, I find it difficult to write this evening. But I am more
and more convinced that something good may come from
telling my story, difficult as it may be to do so. I would like
to forget it all, but the nightmares won't let me.

On Friday, October 13, 1307, every Templar—15,000
knights, sergeants, chaplains, servants, and laborers throughout the territories governed by Philip of France—were
rounded up in a single day. Only two dozen escaped arrest. We
were accused of heresy, of adhering to doctrine not accepted by
the church. They said we worshiped the devil. It wasn't true,
but that didn't matter.

How do you prove devil worship, especially when it isn't
true? Torture. Torture so severe that a man would confess to
anything his accusers suggested so long as the agony would end.
Methods favored by Philip's minions were the rack, which
stretched a man's limbs until the joints dislocated. Or rubbing
fat on the soles of the feet and holding a flame to them. Some
men were burned so badly that the bones fell out of their feet.

Aye, Philip and his inquisitors said we worshiped the devil, and that we had carnal relations with our brothers. But our real crime was that we hadn't adhered to the vow of poverty. Our biggest sin in the eyes of the King of France was that he was in debt to the Templar treasury and he didn't want to pay it back.

Had he simply confiscated our lands and wealth and forced us to disband, there might have been an outcry. But who would defend us against the accusation of heresy and worse? No one. My body still bears the scars of physical torture, and my heart bears the scars of betrayal. For when pressed to the limits of endurance, with my back repeatedly beaten with flaming pitch, I denied my Lord just like St. Peter. Not only denied him, but admitted to atrocious sins I never committed, anything to make the pain go away.

If not for my sergeant, who by some miracle was in the same cell with me, I would certainly have died. Somehow, Jean Paul got word to friends on the outside, and we escaped from prison. But our escape came too late for Peter.

MORRIGAN STOOD IN THE GREAT HALL and groaned at the amount of work it would take to make Innishewan marginally livable. Uncle Angus had been quite thorough in his destruction of the keep. But the families of the men she'd been fighting alongside, as well as her own family, needed food and shelter. And protection. From the previous owners—her former clansmen—now dispossessed of their lands and homes.

Fergus stood next to her as she assessed what needed to be done. "'Tis not so bad."

"No, as it is, it would make a perfect pig sty. But humans need to eat off those filthy tables."

"They are pretty foul."

"The kitchen is in shambles . . ." She stopped, took a deep breath. "We will start rebuilding here and in the kitchen. The bedchambers and storage areas will have to wait. I'll go into the village and hire some stonemasons."

"What shall I do?"

"Set some men to cleaning the fireplaces and shoveling up these reeds from the floor of the main hall. Until the roof and the walls are repaired there isn't much else that can be done."

He nodded. "I'll make a list of supplies on hand and determine what we need to purchase."

"Good. Thank you for thinking of it."

He laid his arm across her shoulder as if they were comrades in arms. "Ye'll manage, Morrigan. Don't worry. Take one thing at a time. Ceallach has said we can stay at Dunstruan as long as we need to."

He removed his arm from her shoulders, and she relaxed. "Aye, and I'm grateful to him. But I am so looking forward to having a permanent home. I'm sure Mother must feel the same way."

"Where were ye living before the battle?"

She leaned against the cool stone wall behind her. "Near Loch Dee. My men and I came to Stirling at Bruce's call for warriors for the great battle. Mother and the others have been living with relatives in a small cottage near Inverlochy."

"Bruce mentioned that Innishewan was the Macnab stronghold under yer uncle. Where is he now?"

She pursed her lips. "A good question. I don't have the answer."

"Then may I suggest that we need to see to the outer wall and the gate right away. Neither will hold in their present condition if we come under attack. No sense fixing up the keep until we can protect it."

She looked at him with newfound respect. "Perhaps you would oversee that work?"

"Aye. 'Twould be my pleasure." With that he strode off, evidently eager to prove to her that he was a capable steward. He was proving to be useful after all. She wanted to ask him about his eye, how he'd gotten the wound and whether it affected his sight. Perhaps when they had an opportunity to practice in the lists she could ask then.

She pushed away from the wall and looked about her again. So much needed to be done. But Fergus was right—one thing at a time. She'd told Bruce the truth—she had little interest in a husband—no interest and no time. Although now and then she thought it might be nice to be able to share the burden with someone you could trust.

As she'd just done with Fergus . . .

THE FOLLOWING WEEK, after Ceallach saw Morrigan and Fergus off to Innishewan once again, Lady Radbourne asked Ceallach if he would show her the weaver's hut. The small round building sat snuggled up against the south wall of the keep. As they walked toward it, he thought she looked a bit pale. "Are you feeling well this morning, my lady?"

"Yes. I'm fine, Ceallach."

"I haven't used a loom in, well, quite a few years. But I suspect it will come back to me." He just hoped that working with the loom would bring back good memories, not bad.

"A warrior who wove cloth for amusement?"

He would have to be careful how much he revealed. Although he didn't want to lie, she *was* English, would be returning to England soon. And her king had put a ransom on Ceallach's head.

"I was a weaver before . . . this war broke out between our countries."

"I see."

They walked around the corner of the keep and he said, "You said you enjoy creating tapestries—do you weave them or embroider?

"I embroider. I do know how to weave cloth, although I've never tried the checkered cloth you Scots seem to favor."

Ceallach surveyed the inside of the stone hut. The roof was thatched, made so that in good weather such as today, sections could be removed to let in more light. A large fireplace would provide heat when needed. The pegs on the wall set at equal distances and staggered up and down were for winding warp threads. A variety of shuttles insured that he and Orelia would each find one with the balance to their liking.

Peter had favored a particular shuttle to the point where he'd once jested that if he were ever sent on crusade, he would take the thing with him to be sure no one would steal it in his absence.

Ceallach smiled at the memory. It dawned on him that this was the second time that he'd thought of Peter without pain. Or guilt. He'd been afraid that seeing the weaving hut would bring the demons out in force. But apparently he'd been wrong.

"The last weaver must have died," Orelia said.

Her voice brought him back to the present. "What makes you think so?"

"Everything we need is here. A living craftsman would never have parted with his tools willingly."

Again he thought of Peter and his preference for certain tools. "Devyn said the man died last winter along with the laird." What had happened to Peter's loom and tools? Who used them now? Sadly Ceallach wished he had been able to gather at least his favorite shuttle and take it with him. But it hadn't been possible.

Next he examined the largest of the looms, noting that the crossbeam still needed to be repaired. The smaller looms were all in working order. Several of them held works in progress, probably Suisan's.

But if they were going to weave the *brecan* cloth with its variegated stripes and checks, they would need to make their own patterns or find the old weaver's setts. Those he would have guarded carefully and hidden, so no one could duplicate his particular pattern.

"What are you looking for?" Orelia asked as he moved things aside and searched under skeins of yarn.

He didn't answer, but pulled a small package wrapped in a beautifully tanned rabbit's pelt from its hiding place. He unwrapped the hide and carefully held up the sticks decorated in various colors of yarn. "This!"

"Oh, my. That will save us a great deal of effort, won't it?" Her eyes shone, and he knew she was anxious to examine them closely.

He laid the sticks on the worktable aside the big loom. Each stick had been sanded smooth and flat and was wrapped with the precise number of strings of each color needed to create a particular pattern. Ceallach and Orelia could use the pattern to string the loom with warp threads in the correct number, color, and order. Then they would weave the exact same pattern of colors with the weft to create a distinctive cloth for the clothing at Dunstruan.

As she examined the patterns, she asked, "Who taught you to weave?"

Her question caught Ceallach off guard. "Why do you ask?

She looked hurt and he realized he'd been far more gruff than her simple query warranted. Should he apologize? Why did he care if her feelings were hurt? She was nothing to him. Just a duty to take care of—keep her safe and return her to Bruce. But she was also grieving, and he found himself unwilling to add to her misery.

So he softened his voice. "A master weaver named Peter. An Englishman, actually."

"You were fond of him."

"Aye, he was ever patient with me and my big hands. He was older—a few years younger than my father." Ceallach hadn't wanted to learn to weave, but the preceptor had assigned him to the craft and one simply didn't argue or disobey the head of the Order.

"Where is Peter now?"

Another perfectly innocent question, but Ceallach couldn't answer. To say the words aloud seemed almost like admitting to a crime. He should have saved Peter . . . Ceallach hid the trembling of his hands by taking hold of one of the loom's upright posts.

With quiet concern she said, "He is dead, isn't he?"

Ceallach nodded.

"I am well acquainted with grief, Ceallach." She wrapped her fingers around her dead husband's cross. "But we will see our loved ones again in eternity."

Ceallach cleared his throat.

She stared at him. "You do believe that, don't you?"

"I no longer believe in much of anything, Lady Radbourne." He expected a lecture on God and his love.

But all she said was, "How sad for you."

Moving to the shelves that held dyed yarn, she changed the subject, to his relief. "Let's see how much of each color we have—perhaps we can string the warp yet today."

She no longer looked pale—indeed her face glowed with an artist's fervor as she sorted through the yarns.

"I have to replace that beam before we can begin." Again he sounded more gruff than he intended.

But if it bothered her she didn't allow it to show. "Yes, of course. You go right ahead. Which of these patterns shall we try first?" She held one up. "I rather like this one, don't you? I think there is enough yarn here to make a good-sized piece of cloth."

Replacing the beam would take the rest of today and maybe even tomorrow if he had trouble finding the right sized tree limb. As he listened to her excited chatter Ceallach was struck by the realization that women in general, and Orelia in particular, were not the evil temptresses his superiors in the Order had tried to paint.

Did all women have such enthusiasm for tasks of hearth and home? The women of Dunstruan seemed to take pride in creating warmth and shelter—not just the necessities but things of beauty and comfort.

No, there was nothing evil about Orelia at all. She was lovely to look at, yes, but that was hardly a sin. If there was temptation it was not a result of her behavior but of his desire to know more about her, to understand the way she thought. To see the world from a different perspective. Her perspective.

And this desire to know her better, to get to know her and allow her to know him confused and dismayed him.

Her chatter stopped and when Ceallach looked at her, she had a strange expression on her face.

"You aren't listening," she said.

He shook his head. "No. I was . . . thinking how good it is to see you happy. These last three weeks have been difficult for you." Now she looked stunned and her smile faded, as if she remembered that she shouldn't be happy. Hadn't he behaved just the same ever since he'd fled France? Would she live a miserable existence for too many years as he had done himself?

A compulsion to protect her from such a life surprised and scared him all at once.

She turned away from him and began to replace the skeins of yarn. "I should go back to see if I can help in the kitchen."

"Lady Radbourne . . . Orelia. I have said something that made you unhappy. Forgive me."

She placed the last of the yarn on the shelf and turned to him. "There is nothing to forgive, Ceallach. For a few, wonderful minutes you allowed me to forget my grief and I thank you for it."

"I'm glad you had those few minutes, my lady." Sensing that he'd said enough and fearful that she would cry if he said more, he changed the subject. "I'll go look for a suitable log for the beam. You can search through the rest of the tools here and see if there is anything lacking."

She smiled at him. How long had Ceallach lived without the blessing of a woman's smile? Such a simple thing, one that others took for granted. But he could not, for his very soul had languished, although he'd not realized until this moment the depth of that deprivation.

But even he could tell that her smile lacked true joy, was shadowed by grief. This woman had loved her husband. What must it be like to be loved like that? To be the light of another person's life? Such passion had the power to cause deep joy as well as deep pain. Ceallach wondered how she stood it.

They had much in common, this widow with a heart broken by love for her man and a warrior with a heart broken by the God he had once served. But she still called upon that very God for healing, while Ceallach no longer believed he existed. She would become whole again in time, but Ceallach never could.

THE GREAT HALL OF ÐUNSTRUAN, though it lacked fresh whitewash, was pleasing to the eye. The ceiling was domed, and three arches of stone held up the slate roof. The window openings and fireplace reflected the arch in design, lending a harmonious appearance. Effort had been made in the building to use reddish stone in the arches in contrast to the light stone of the walls.

But despite her pleasant surroundings, Orelia picked at her midday meal. It seemed that little she ate agreed with her lately. Most surely it was her grief that made food so unpalatable. Finally she settled for a cup of warm broth and a piece of bread.

Morrigan's mother sat down next to Orelia.

"You didn't go with Morrigan and Fergus today, Lady Macnab?"

"You may call me Eveleen, child. And no. There really is no reason for me accompany to them. It will take the stonemasons and roofers until spring to make the place even marginally livable."

"Oh. That's too bad." It saddened her to picture Radbourne Hall destroyed to such a point. But it soon became clear that her food wasn't going to stay down again. She excused herself and hurriedly left the table.

When her stomach settled again, she went to her chamber and lay down on her pallet. Soon there was a quiet knock at the chamber door. Though she really didn't want company, she told her visitor to come in.

Eveleen walked to where Orelia laid and encouraged her to sit up. "I've brought you some tea, Lady Radbourne. 'Twill calm your stomach."

Orelia took the cup and stared into it. When she looked up she asked, "How did you know my stomach bothered me?"

"You've left the table too many times for me not to suspect. I've birthed five children—four who still live. I know the signs."

Orelia looked at her in confusion. "Signs of what?"

"Are you not with child?"

"With child?" Orelia jolted in agitation, nearly spilling the tea. "No, I assure you I can't possibly . . . in the seven years of my marriage I've never once . . . . no. 'Tis cruel of you to even suggest such a thing!"

"I meant no cruelty, my lady. But this aversion to food—you have no other reason to suspect you might carry a child?"

Orelia shook her head.

"Well, whatever ails you, this tea will calm your stomach."

Orelia sipped the tea. "You are widowed also?"

"Aye. Eight years now."

"Do you still miss him?"

"I do. Not as badly or as often as I once did. But a part of my life is missing since he's been gone."

"At least you have the comfort of your children."

"They are a comfort." She smiled. "Most of the time."

They sat in silence for a few minutes and the tiniest spark of hope lit within Orelia. "John had a fever as a child, and the healer said he would not be able to father children."

Eveleen nodded. "I've heard it said some fevers can make it difficult." Eveleen laid her hand on Orelia's arm and leaned close. "But not impossible."

With all her difficulty in conceiving, it certainly hadn't been the fault of her monthly inconvenience—she was quite regular. With a bit more hope she took another sip of tea and counted the weeks. She smiled when she realized she'd missed her courses twice. In all the stress of the trip to Bannockburn and then John's death, she hadn't paid attention.

Eveleen stopped talking. "Is it possible, then?"

She nodded. "I don't remember having my courses since well before the battle. That is another of the indications, isn't it?"

"Yes, it is. A very good sign." Eveleen reached for her and Orelia allowed the woman to give her a hug. "You are carrying a miracle," Eveleen whispered.

For the first time since she'd learned of John's death, Orelia had a reason to go on living without him.

Eveleen rose to leave. "I will pray for the safe delivery of a healthy son to honor your husband's memory."

"Thank you. I would like to keep this news to myself for a while." Then a disturbing thought came to her. "Will I be able to travel to England when I'm released?"

"I don't see why not, as long as you aren't too close to your time."

"Then would you also pray that I shall soon be released?"

"Of course. You should rest now, Lady Radbourne, and let the tea settle you."

"Please, call me Orelia."

"Good day, Orelia."

Orelia settled back against the pillows and laid her hand on her stomach where John's child waited to be born. She feared news of her pregnancy would dismay John's brother, Richard, who no doubt had already assumed the title of earl. But if she was pregnant—dear Father in heaven, if she had been so blessed—she would return to Radbourne Hall and claim her child's birthright.

THE NEXT DAY DAWNED COLD AND WET. The light mist threatened to become a downpour before the day was through. The dampness seeped into Ceallach's bones as he searched through the woodpile. Fallen limbs and branches had been gathered from the forest to be split into firewood. Perhaps something here would suffice to replace the cracked beam on the loom. If not, then he would have to go out and search the woods himself.

The gloomy weather, unseasonably chilly, matched his mood. What little sleep he'd managed had been interrupted by memories so real they bolted him awake, sweating and disoriented. He couldn't shake them even now, wide awake. Peter's face on that last day haunted him.

Ceallach tugged on a limb that looked like a suitable candidate but it appeared to be caught on something. He gave a good yank and heard Keifer yell, "Ouch!" The boy was supposedly helping but he scampered over the woodpile with a wide grin. Ceallach normally found it hard to resist the lad but today his presence vexed him.

"Get off the pile before you get hurt, Keifer," he said with as much patience as he could muster.

Keifer obeyed and Ceallach went on about his search. He pulled

a stout limb from the pile and set it on end. It appeared to be the
proper length and breadth. He took a piece of string from his
sporran, one that he'd cut to the length needed for the repair, and
measured the log. It would do.

He looked up to see Keifer brandishing a straight stick like a sword
against invisible foes. Amused in spite of his bad mood, Ceallach
decided to put the boy's energy to a more purposeful pursuit. "Keifer,
why don't you put down your sword and groom the horses for me."

"Yes, sir!" Sticking the make-believe sword into his belt, the boy
was off like an arrow.

Ceallach shook his head in amusement and leaned the log against
the bailey wall. He enjoyed the lad's company and would miss him
when he left. Not that he could do anything about it; the boy would
be better off with a proper family, a knight without a past . . . Ceallach
picked up an adze and began to chip the bark from the wood. With
proper care to keep the touch of the tool light and consistent, he
would not have to smooth the wood much before tapping it into place
on the loom.

For a good while, the concentration needed for his task kept his
mind occupied and the night's visions faded. When the bark had all
been removed, he measured the wood twice with the string before
cutting off the ends. Then Ceallach hoisted the log to his shoulder
and carried it to the weaver's hut.

He set the wood down inside the hut and went outside to replace
the section in the roof to ward off the soft rain that had begun to fall.
He came back into the darkened room, propping the door open for
light, and walked to the loom. Gently he ran his hand over the even
surface of the wood as his mind took him back to the day of his arrest.

No, he would not allow himself to feel self-pity. He spun away
from the loom and found a piece of sandstone to smooth the rough
spots on the new beam. When he was ready to take the old beam off

and replace it, he would need help. Until then, he was perfectly happy, if a bit chilled, sitting here by himself and working.

A shadow dimmed his light and he looked up to see Orelia Radbourne standing in the doorway. "Good morning, my lady. What brings you here so early?"

"Good morning to you, Ceallach." She walked to the log and touched it. "You found a piece of wood to replace the beam. Good." She meandered to the worktable and rummaged through the tools scattered there. "How can you see to work in this light?" she asked.

"It's enough." But truthfully, as the rain increased the light was growing worse and with the door open, the rain was coming in.

As if she read his mind, she closed the door. Then she stood before the unlighted fireplace and rubbed her arms. "I'm going to the kitchen for a torch to light the fire." Without waiting for him to agree she walked back out the door.

She had something on her mind, if he was any judge of behavior. Perhaps she would confide in him when she returned. In truth, he was glad she'd offered to light the fire. He'd become quite chilled earlier and would welcome the warmth, so long as he didn't have to handle the flame.

Orelia returned and lit the oil lamps that hung from the walls before thrusting the torch into the wood in the fireplace. It caught quickly and soon blazed brightly. Ceallach moved his stool a few feet away.

Now she fluttered from the workbench to the shelves that held the yarn and then to each of the small looms. Each time she stopped she handled a tool, the yarn, or the work on the loom.

Her fidgety actions unnerved him. "Orelia, cease. What is bothering you this morning?"

ORELIA PICKED UP A SHUTTLE, testing it in her palm as though choosing a shuttle was the most important thing on her mind. But of course, it wasn't. She stood with her back to him, hoping to hide her agitation. "I . . . need to know when I'll be going home to England."

Ceallach stopped sanding the wood. "I expect to hear something any day."

Resisting the urge to slam the shuttle down on the table she said, "What can be taking so long? It's been nearly a month." She must get home before travel became difficult and endangered her and her child. Nothing could be allowed to happen to John's son. It was a boy, she just knew it. Yet it mattered little, only that the child was healthy . . .

But she didn't want to tell Ceallach, didn't want to share her secret with anyone other than Eveleen. At least not until it became apparent, and by then she hoped to be safely home at Radbourne Hall. "I'll just have to pray harder, I guess."

"Aye, if you think that will help." He began to sand the log again, and the rasp of the stone against the wood and the patter of rain on the roof were the only sounds that filled the hut.

"You don't believe in praying?"

"I do not." He shoved the stone hard against the wood as if to emphasize his words.

"Ah, that's right. You said you don't believe in anything. How can you live that way, without daily discourse with the Lord?" she asked him gently.

Pausing from his work, he looked up at her. "Why would I talk to someone who isn't there?"

She gasped. "Ceallach, you mustn't say such a thing. It isn't true!"

He turned back to his work, striking the wood harder than she thought necessary. "It is true for me. He has never been there for me."

How sad he should feel that way. "Never?"

He stilled his hands and reached up to brush the scar on his neck. "When I needed him most he deserted me."

The coldness of his voice nearly made her shiver in response.

"You expected him to follow you into battle?" She paused. "And you believe he did not."

He ignored her. Indeed he seemed oblivious to her presence—staring at something or someone only he could see. His hand stilled on the wood. "I dedicated my life to fighting for his cause, to protecting his people, to living an exemplary life of deprivation and humility. For my efforts he left me to face the devil himself."

She didn't know what to say. John's faith had been so deeply ingrained that she'd never before had a discussion anything like this. She was ill-prepared to challenge Ceallach's misguided beliefs, and so she latched on to the last thing he said. "What happened?"

As if coming out of a trance, Ceallach shook his head and looked at her. "I don't speak of it." He stood and went to the door. "I'm going to find Devyn to help me replace the beam."

He closed the door behind him leaving Orelia alone with her secret and the knowledge that Ceallach had secrets of his own.

EIGHT

Disobedience is worse than defeat.

—from the Rule of the Templar Knights

Orelia suggested that I pray. But all I can hear when I close my eyes are the cries of the innocent, myself among them. Am I strong enough to write it down? I remember only too clearly . . .

Screams—unholy, inhuman sounds. Who would be next? What new torture had our accusers invented since yesterday?

"It doesn't matter what they say or think, Ceallach. You and I—and God in heaven—know the truth. Call on his name and he will strengthen you."

"I'll go next," I said. "They will not take you again. I will not allow it." Peter was older and not in good health. He would never survive a second round.

When the jailer came I stood, offering myself to him, like Christ to Pilate. I held tight to my faith and refused to name others, refused to lie. They beat me with their fists, then flogged me. But they could not break me. For a while.

Not unto us, O Lord. The Templar war cry gave me courage.

How many hours? My God, my God, why hast Thou forsaken me? My tormentors said they would not quit until I

107

confessed. So they flogged me again, this time with a flaming, pitch-covered torch. The fire seared my laid-open flesh and singed my hair and beard, and still I refused. The pain . . . Father in heaven, the pain! Only the threat to torture Peter again forced me to yield. I would have died before submitting, might well die anyway. But I couldn't let Peter suffer again.

Then they promised that if I would yield, they would spare Peter from a second course of torture. So I confessed to heresy, to unnatural acts with Peter, and to grievous crimes against the God I loved. And after I'd betrayed us both with lies, they tossed me back in my cell and dragged Peter off.

I lost consciousness, which was probably a blessing, for if I'd heard his screams a second time I would have surely lost my mind. When I awoke it was to find my friend and mentor lying next to me. I held his hand as he breathed his last.

You were wrong, Peter. God deserted us both.

CLEANING AND REPAIRING INNISHEWAN was a peaceful enterprise compared to dealing with yet another of her sister Cassidy's complaints. And today Morrigan had an added burden—the Englishwoman had come along with them to Innishewan.

"What is wrong now?" Morrigan asked her sister with more patience than she felt.

"I wanted to help the stonemasons, but Fergus made me come ask you for a chore."

Morrigan could guess why. Cassidy's flirting distracted the men from their work. "Why don't you see what's in those trunks in the storage room?"

"It's too dusty in there."

Cassidy pouted and Morrigan's patience snapped. "Then clean the storage room!"

Morrigan's mother and Orelia stood nearby. Morrigan didn't know why Orelia had come along today nor did she know what to make of the woman. Though they were about the same age, they had little else in common.

"Cassidy," Eveleen said. "Either do as you sister suggested or help the kitchen maids scrub out the fireplace. Take your pick but stop arguing."

Cassidy stomped off in the direction of the storage room.

"You have been very patient with her, Morrigan, and I thank you. Where would you like Orelia and me to work today?"

It seemed strange that her mother and the Englishwoman had formed a friendship. But obviously they had. "Could you see if you can find a table that doesn't need repair? Then clean it so we have a place to eat."

Her mother smiled. "Of course."

"Good. And maybe you can persuade Cassidy to stop distracting the men and keeping them from their work."

Eveleen touched her arm. "Do stop fretting, Morrigan. We will all work together so that we can move in as soon as possible."

Morrigan took her mother's hand and squeezed it. "Thank you. Now, off to work with you!"

"Where are you off to?" Eveleen tossed back to her.

She gave her head a jaunty nod. "To fight with Fergus." Morrigan laughed out loud at Lady Radbourne's shocked expression. The pampered lady would no doubt faint to see Morrigan spar with her men.

"Morrigan, you shouldn't alarm Orelia like that," Eveleen chided. She turned to the Englishwoman. "Why don't you go along with Morrigan and see what she's teasing us about?"

"Don't you need help with the tables?" Orelia asked.

Apparently Orelia was as aware as Morrigan that they could not possibly become friends. "No. If I do, I'll get Cassidy to help. Go on."

Orelia asked, "Do you mind, Morrigan?"

She shrugged. "I don't mind." What could it hurt to have the woman tag along?

Despite all the work on the castle, Morrigan and her men had to keep their fighting skills honed. She scheduled training every day for several hours in the afternoon, whether they were here or at Dunstruan. When it was raining, like today, they practiced in the large, open area at one end of the stable.

Fergus was already there, observing several of the men as they fought with swords. He looked surprised to see the Englishwoman but said a quick hello and turned his attention back to the fighting. Orelia found a seat but Morrigan didn't join her. Instead she walked on about fifty paces and leaned against one of the poles that held up the roof and watched. When one pair had finished their bout, Fergus and his partner took their place.

Fergus had become so good with the short sword that except for the scar across his eye, Morrigan might not question his ability to see with it. And yet, if she watched him closely she could discern his techniques to overcome the disadvantage.

When he was done he came to stand beside her.

"Well done," she said.

"Aye, so long as I can keep them where I can see them, I do fine."

Here was a chance to ask him what she'd long wanted to know. "Can you not see at all with the damaged eye?"

"I see light and dark and movement, but shapes are fuzzy." He covered his good eye and looked at her. "You are either a horse or a tree." He grinned, and it amazed her that he was so easy about it.

Encouraged by his straightforwardness, she asked, "How did it happen?"

His grin vanished. "Someone tried to harm Lady Kathryn. When

I objected, he slashed me with a whip." He told her the rest of the story and how he had killed the man at Bannockburn.

She looked at him with new respect. He accepted his lot in life, yet he worked hard to better himself. She sensed that his loyalty, once won, would never waiver. He was a capable steward and a fair fighter.

Maybe King Robert had been right to send him here, after all.

Fergus motioned toward Orelia. "What is she doing here?"

Morrigan jerked her head around. She had practically forgotten the woman was there. "She and Mother seem to have developed a friendship of sorts."

"I suppose she must be lonely, so far from home and all. I wonder how much longer until she's allowed to go home?"

Morrigan hadn't really given the woman much thought until today. She remembered when her father died and how hard Eveleen had grieved. Morrigan was glad her mother had befriended Orelia. The two of them had the bond of widowhood—that must be what drew them together.

She looked back in Orelia's direction and saw that the woman had gotten up and was walking toward them. Now what?

Fergus, ever the gentleman, said, "What can we do for you, my lady?"

Orelia looked from one to another, seeming reluctant to answer.

"Well?" Morrigan asked. The woman probably wanted to leave—fighting was too hard on her delicate sensibilities.

Orelia lifted the hem of her dress to reveal a sheathed fighting knife that she removed and held in her palm. "I wonder if one of you would spar with me?"

Morrigan stared.

Fergus recovered first. "*You* wish to spar? With one of us?"

The Englishwoman gazed at them as if they'd lost their wits.

"Yes, if you wouldn't mind. I haven't practiced since . . . since my husband died."

"You know how to use that?" Morrigan asked.

Now Orelia grinned, evidently enjoying their astonishment. "Yes, I do."

Fergus laughed. "Does Ceallach know you have a weapon?"

Still smiling Orelia said, "I think he's forgotten about it. I did threaten him with it when we first met."

Morrigan whistled. "Well, how do you like that? Fergus, you are better at such techniques; you spar and I'll watch."

Then Lady Orelia shocked Morrigan further by pulling the back of her skirt through her legs and tucking the hem into her belt. Not very ladylike but essential in order to fight without getting tangled in her skirt. Eagerly Morrigan anticipated what was to come.

It quickly became apparent that Orelia's late husband had taught her more than just basic fighting stances and thrusts. Orelia and Fergus circled and thrust and though the lady could not overcome him, neither was Fergus able to dislodge the knife from her hand. Perhaps there was more to the woman than Morrigan credited.

When the combatants called a halt, Morrigan jumped up from her seat. "Bravo! I'm impressed, Orelia."

"I, too, my lady," Fergus echoed.

Orelia took a bow and the tension between them vanished.

Morrigan had few close female friends, had never had the opportunity to form such friendships. As she studied the Englishwoman she considered that maybe she should look beneath the surface to see what else she and Orelia Radbourne had in common.

THE NEXT DAY AFTER DEVYN and Ceallach finished repairing a stall in Dunstruan's barn, they headed to the lists for training. Keifer, as usual, tagged along. Devyn wasn't much of a swordsman, but he was game for a round of practice.

At first Ceallach worked slowly, warming up his muscles and giving instruction to both Devyn and Keifer. They stood on either side of him and imitated his moves.

"Like this, Ceallach?" Keifer asked.

"Aye, use your wrist a bit more."

"How's this?"

"Very good." As Ceallach swung his sword in widening circles, his breathing came harder and he had to warn Keifer several times to move aside. But the boy stayed too close, intent on watching, and Ceallach was forced to shorten his stride and move closer to Devyn. Finally he barked at Keifer to move off and work alone while he and Devyn sparred.

With the boy a safe distance away, he found his rhythm again. His last conversation with Orelia came back to him.

You don't believe in praying?

I do not.

In anger and frustration he increased the intensity of his attack, pushing his practice partner back until Devyn cried out. Only then did Ceallach realize he'd backed the man to the curtain wall, completely unaware of where they were and what he was doing. Once again the demons had been let loose.

Ceallach lowered his sword. "Forgive me, friend."

Devyn looked at him with a fearful expression. "You fight like the very devil himself."

Keifer rushed over. "What happened?"

Ceallach closed his eyes and raised his face toward the sky. "I'm . . . all right," was all he could manage to say. Yes, the devil himself dwelt inside Ceallach, always searching, waiting for Ceallach to weaken, to let him out. Ceallach shuddered and lowered his head. If Ceallach were a stronger man, he would be able to control this monster that threatened to dominate his every move.

He couldn't take a chance on harming the lad or anyone else. He'd sworn off whiskey after that night of the battle, but now he questioned the wisdom of it. Where would he find the strength to deal with his fears; how would he fight the demon? It fed on turmoil, on emotions, and whiskey deadened his sensitivity.

Wiping the sweat from his forehead he said, "That's enough for today."

Devyn eyed him warily. "Are you sure you're all right?"

"Of course. Keifer, clean the weapons and mind you don't cut yourself." Then he stalked off, aware of the puzzled look on their faces. Aye, well, Ceallach was puzzled too.

He went to the well and brought up a bucket of water thinking to wash his face and hands, then thought better of it. One of the joys of life outside the cloister was the freedom to bathe at will. He went to his chamber and, finding a drying cloth and a precious bit of soap, he headed to the river.

But as he approached the bathing pool he could hear the murmur of female voices. Was it wash day? Or were they bathing? Either way, he couldn't join them. Why couldn't they live by a schedule so a man might know what to expect?

Vexed at the loss of opportunity, he started back to the castle. No, he would find another spot. He'd be considerate and bathe downstream, but bathe he would. He followed the well-worn path along the banks and soon the voices faded.

He would have to speak to Devyn and Suisan about establishing a schedule. How could he function without structure, predictability? Aye, a lack of predictability was exactly what frustrated him in dealing with people, especially women.

He found a pool, not as deep as that by the castle, but sufficiently large that he could float for a bit. He stripped off his clothes and entered the stream, drifting peacefully on the water. Then he washed himself, ducked under the water one last time and waded ashore. After drying off, he wrapped his plaid around his waist for modesty and sat in the shade of a giant willow. The warmth of the day and the babbling water lulled him into a state of drowsiness.

As he drifted between wakefulness and sleep, he became aware of the pounding of his heart as he imagined . . . the entry in his journal last night had been the hardest he'd written yet. He needn't fear hell or Satan—he'd met both in a prison in France. Where his God had deserted him and his mentor and friend.

Birds chirping in the trees overhead brought Ceallach back to the present—to a lovely summer day and a life that no longer seemed to hold any meaning.

MORRIGAN FLOATED IN A DEEP POOL in the creek near Dunstruan. Orelia and Eveleen had joined her on this lovely summer day. They had disrobed down to their shifts and Morrigan had grinned as she watched Orelia unstrap the knife from her calf. Now they lazed on the water, circling their arms to stay afloat.

Eveleen said, "I'm so glad you decided not to go to Innishewan today, Morrigan."

"There isn't much more you or I can do until the roof is fixed. Fergus can oversee the workers as well as I can." And though it was true, she couldn't help but wish she were spending the day with him and not with her mother and Orelia.

Morrigan had enjoyed the other day at Inneshewan. It had given her a chance to know Orelia better. Morrigan watched now as Eveleen and Orelia swam close together, whispering to one another.

The two swam toward her, grinning, and Orelia said, "Eveleen and I agree, Morrigan. Fergus definitely likes you."

Morrigan playfully splashed water at Orelia. "Don't be ridiculous."

Eveleen paddled over to them. "Orelia might be right, Daughter. I've caught him staring at you when he thinks no one is looking."

"What if he does? It doesn't mean anything." Did he really watch her? She'd thought so but was afraid it was only wishful thinking.

Orelia and Eveleen exchanged looks "Well, then you better not get caught looking back or he'll think it does mean something," Eveleen said.

"I don't look at him. I practically ignore him."

Orelia smiled. "I noticed that you ignore him. Except when you are practicing in the lists. Or arguing with him about the repairs to Innishewan. Or inquiring about that mysterious eye patch of his."

"Or asking for his advice," her mother added.

Morrigan stood up, water sluicing off her. They made it sound like she was pining for the man. It wasn't true! "He is my steward. Of course I talk to him." When no one offered disagreement, she returned to the water and the three of them paddled about.

Orelia swam close to Morrigan. "Would it be so awful if he did like you?"

Morrigan treaded water. This familiarity with another woman felt odd to her. Yet she longed for a confidante, someone who would understand these new feelings and her confusion over them. Someone her own age. "Well, I guess it would be all right. He's . . . rather handsome, don't you think?"

Orelia's arms stopped and she sank into the water, sputtering as she took in a mouth full of water. Morrigan reached for her but Orelia moved to where she could stand in chest deep water, her expression troubled. "When I first saw him at Dunstruan, I thought he was John. My husband."

"That must have been awful," Eveleen said.

Morrigan said nothing. She was just beginning to grasp the depth of emotion one could feel for a man and could not imagine what Orelia had suffered.

Orelia moved to shallow water, and Morrigan and Eveleen followed. They each found a rock to sit on, feet dangling in the water. Orelia seemed to need to share, to talk of her feelings. "I only thought it was John for a moment, but yes, it was hard. Wishful thinking. They don't look that much alike."

"'Twas understandable. You loved your husband, and denial is part of grief. But you have much to look forward to," Eveleen said.

Morrigan looked at Eveleen and then at Orelia. "What can a widow look forward to? Will you remarry, Orelia? Mother never has." Morrigan watched as a look passed between her mother and Orelia. "What?" she demanded.

"I've kept this to myself—only your mother knows—but with each passing day the joy . . . I am expecting a child, Morrigan."

"Oh. A baby." Looking down, Morrigan traced her finger along the rock she was sitting on, absently rubbing back and forth. Her face softened as she imagined what it must be like to have a child by the man you loved.

"Yes, God has blessed me in my sorrow. John will live on in this child," Orelia said reverently.

Morrigan's hand stilled and she looked up. "I'm happy for you."

"Thank you."

Eveleen said, "One day, God will bless you with a husband and children, Morrigan."

They would expect her to deny such a thing, but Morrigan

couldn't. Such thoughts had been on her mind much of late. "Aye, I believe he will."

Eveleen raised her eyebrows. "So, Orelia and I are right—you haven't been ignoring Fergus."

Morrigan smiled. "No, I haven't." She traced the rock again. What would they think if she voiced her concern? Would they understand, not make fun of her? She took a deep breath. "Do you think he'd notice if I wore a dress now and then?"

Orelia laughed, but not in derision. "Notice? Oh, yes, he'd notice, don't you agree Eveleen?"

"I do indeed."

Morrigan took another fortifying breath and nodded. "All right. Who will sew it?"

"I will." Orelia and Eveleen answered together. The three of them laughed, sharing a moment of camaraderie and joy. Orelia and Eveleen rejoiced because they'd known the pleasure of loving and creating a child from their love. And Morrigan rejoiced because a certain man was indeed watching her as she suspected.

THE WARM AFTERNOON SUN felt wonderful and while the others continued to swim, Orelia climbed out and got dressed. She wandered downstream, searching the creek bank for wildflowers to make a bouquet. She added her latest find to the ones in her hand and raised her head.

Orelia knew she shouldn't stare, 'twas impolite. Ceallach stood with his back to her, still as a deer that knew it was being stalked. His back was bare—he'd removed his shirt—and he was apparently adjusting the folds of his plaid. His damp, disheveled hair told her that he'd already taken a swim, so she was in no danger of embarrassment from having him disrobe further.

Yet from what little she knew of Ceallach, she was sure he

wouldn't like to have her see him thus. She began to turn away to give him privacy when her gaze lowered from his head to his shoulders and she saw the scars. Deep and red even after what must be years of healing.

She nearly reached for him, barely restraining a gasp, the instinct to comfort overwhelming. Yet the scars were well beyond need of such emotion. What ever could have caused such marks?

The welts and stripes rippled and bunched with the movement of his muscles. Deep striations, ridges of flesh, shiny reddened skin that looked fragile. Now she could see the full extent of wounds that were barely hinted at by the redness on his neck. Here lay clear evidence of the reason for his secretiveness about his past.

Slowly he turned and saw her standing there. She knew when he realized what she was looking at. A moment's hesitation, a hitch of his shoulders. Without a word he pulled on his shirt and drew the laces at the neck closed. Only then did he speak to her.

Quietly, his voice hoarse with emotion, "Go away, Orelia."

Why did his words sting so? Because behind them she heard the anguish of a sheep without a shepherd. A man who'd lost his faith. It wasn't just her that he hid from; it was their Lord. From the looks of his back, he'd suffered unbearable pain. "Who did that to you?"

He shook his head, and droplets of water splashed his shirt.

She walked forward, stopping an arm's length away. He stood with his head bowed and again he shook his head. "Leave it, Orelia. Forget what you saw. The wounds healed a long time ago and I am not in need."

But she couldn't let it go, couldn't leave without knowing who had done this to him and if this had driven him from his faith. "You were whipped, weren't you? Why?"

He raised his head and looked at her. Angrily he said, "I was punished for crimes I didn't commit."

Puzzled, she quizzed him further. "I don't understand. Why?"

With finality he said, "It doesn't matter. It's done."

"And this is why you believe God has deserted you?"

He looked toward Dunstruan. "May I walk you back to the keep?"

Orelia wanted to press him to talk about what happened, not only so she could understand but to try and help him heal the wounds she could not see. But now was not the time.

They did not speak on the walk back to the castle.

LATE THAT NIGHT a violent gust of wind agitated the coals in the fireplace into swirls of light that quickly ebbed into darkness. The gusts also crept through the drafty main hall of Dunstruan Castle. Over the years the once heavy tapestries that lined the walls had become threadbare and moth-eaten, allowing a breeze to waft through Ceallach's hair.

Ceallach sat in the glow from the dying fire, waiting for morning. He couldn't sleep. The gale had risen, causing the shutters to bang against the walls. His sword lay on the bench next to him. The noise of the wind, the smell of smoke that seeped into the room from the fireplace, the faltering light, all contrived to bring back the nightmare that had plagued him since he'd left France. Tonight, before the crashing shutter had brought him upright in his bed, the nightmare had been unusually vivid.

Probably as a result of his conversation with Orelia this afternoon. A noise from behind startled him and he jumped to his feet, sword at the ready.

"Ceallach," a soft feminine voice said. Orelia came into the light. "Did the wind awaken you, too?"

Her hair hung in a thick braid over one shoulder. He couldn't speak, feared to speak, unsure if he was in his right mind. Sometimes the demons lingered, teasing and goading him. He continued to hold his sword on the chance that the woman wasn't real but a tormentor from the darkness of his past.

He shook his head. The vision remained. "Orelia?"

She looked at him as if his wits might be addled, adding weight to the possibility that she was indeed, real. "Yes," she assured him. Wisely she remained where she was.

He lowered the sword but did not lay it down. Not yet. "Why are you not abed?"

She gestured with her hand, pointing back up the stairs. "I heard a noise."

"The shutters banging."

"Oh. How silly of me." She stared at him. "Are you all right?"

He took a deep breath and laid the weapon back on the bench. "Aye."

"May I come by the fire?"

"What? Ah, yes."

"Will you put some peat on it? We may as well be warm if we are going to be awake." She smiled.

The rare smile surprised him. But then she certainly had reason to be sad. Something in him wanted to be the cause of her smile, and to give her reason to grace him so again.

Yet he could not relax—any more than he could get close enough to the fire to add peat as she'd asked. He sat down again, pretending he hadn't heard her.

She shook her head and placed a brick of peat on the fire, stirring the embers until it caught before turning her face to him.

"Why did you accompany your husband to Stirling?" he asked.

Guiltily, he acknowledged her pain and the cause of it; he wanted to share the darkness tonight, not be alone in the shadows. Orelia had shadows of her own to face. Why could she smile? Why could he not?

She continued to crouch before the fire, poking at it now and then.

"King Edward was convinced that Bruce could not beat him in a pitched battle. John was to receive . . . Scottish lands upon the victory. I came with him so that we might occupy the castle immediately." Her shoulders stooped a bit more. "This castle," she whispered.

Her obvious distress overwhelmed him. "I'm sorry, Orelia. I didn't mean to make you cry." What should he do? How could he comfort her? He knelt beside her and laid his hand on her shoulder, his fingers brushing the thick braid of golden hair. She reached up, still staring into the fire, and placed her small hand on top of his fingers. His heart raced. But he dared not remove his hand and take away whatever comfort she felt from it.

Then her words struck him full force. "This castle? Edward planned to give *Dunstruan* to your husband?"

He felt her take a deep breath, then she twisted to face him and their hands parted from their resting place. The room seemed colder somehow.

She wiped a tear from her eye. "Yes, Dunstruan."

"Father, have mercy," he said under his breath. How could she stay here, knowing if her husband had lived this would have been their home?

She looked at him strangely. "I thought you didn't pray, Ceallach."

He dismissed it with a wave of his hand. "A force of habit, nothing more."

Her expressive face and eyes were full of questions, but to his relief, she let it be. "It's all right, being at Dunstruan. I have made peace with God over John's death and my sojourn here. I believe God has a purpose, a blessing that will come of my hardship. In fact, I am sure of it."

"I am amazed at your ability to see good in such a tragic situation." She amazed him and disturbed him—disturbed that buried piece of him that used to know how to love and be loved. Something near his heart warmed like the flame she had coaxed from the fireplace.

"It's easy to feel blessed when life is going well, Ceallach. Not so easy when it feels like God has deserted you. I confess, in those first days after John's death that's exactly how I felt."

"And now?" Did he really want to hear what she had to say? Would her words brand him as weak?

"Now? Now I see God's hand in my decision to accompany John. We had no hope of having children—having a son—so we came here to expand John's holdings. John wanted his younger brother to take on more responsibility for the inheritance that would eventually be his."

She stood up and smiled again and he thought it strange. "My husband was told he couldn't father children. A childhood fever, you understand."

"A fever." He nodded although he wasn't altogether sure what a fever had to do with begetting children. Still, he certainly wasn't going to ask for an explanation of such a subject from her.

"John was wrong not to believe that God would hear our prayers for a child."

Ceallach stood also, uncomfortable with looking up at her as she paced. "Wrong?"

Turning to face him, she fingered the cross she'd taken from her husband's body. "John's last words to me were a reminder that no matter what happens, I am not alone." Tears ran down her cheeks but instead of wiping at them she placed her hands on her stomach. "My faith has sustained me and I have been blessed. In this John could not have been more right."

Ceallach couldn't quite grasp her meaning. "What are you saying, Orelia?

Beaming with obvious happiness she said, "I am carrying John's child, Ceallach. A miracle and a sign of God's gracious love."

Ceallach could only stare at her. Her prayers had certainly been answered and he was happy for her. But she was carrying another man's child. The tiny flame near his heart sputtered and nearly went out.

ORELIA YAWNED and pulled her nightdress close to ward off the chill. The fire had burned down again. How long had she been talking with Ceallach? And why did he stare at her so? "Now you will understand why I am anxious to return to England."

He seemed to come out of a trance. "Of course. You must claim the child's inheritance."

She glanced at the window opening. "It will soon be light. Perhaps I will return to my bed and rest a bit more."

"Yes, of course." His voice sounded strange.

She looked at him. "But you will not."

"Nay, I'm done for the night. Go on. I'll keep watch."

What a strange thing for him to say. 'Twas only the wind causing trouble tonight. But she did find it reassuring to know that he would keep them safe. "Thank you for keeping me company, Ceallach. For letting me talk about John. It eases the pain to remember him. And to think ahead to the joy of having his child to raise."

She started for the stairs when he called to her. "Orelia?"

She turned back to him.

Looking decidedly uncomfortable he asked, "Would you add some more peat to the fire?"

"If I don't, you will sit here in the cold, won't you?"

He didn't answer, and she wondered about his aversion to tending the fire. She walked back and after building up the flames she looked at the scar on his neck.

One of the kitchen servants at Radbourne had been burned in a cooking accident and her skin had looked much like this. How had Ceallach received this mark? He'd looked stricken when she'd first seen him tonight, as if he'd seen a spirit. What secrets did he hide? Remembering his look of terror, did she really want to know? "Some day I would like to hear your story, Ceallach."

"My story?"

"Why you fear the fire. How you came to have those scars on your back."

She saw his shoulders rise and fall with a deep breath. But he didn't look as despairing as he had earlier. Orelia was drawn to the big man. His size and quiet dignity gave shelter without realizing, without awareness. Like a shade tree giving shade simply by existing.

"Goodnight, Orelia."

She would not get an explanation tonight. But one day soon, she would insist. "Goodnight, Ceallach."

She climbed the stairs to her chamber pondering the fact that she had made a number of friends here among her enemies. Eveleen, Morrigan, and perhaps Ceallach, too. How could she explain the comfort she drew from his presence? He asked for nothing in return, was unaware of his affect on her. So she gave him the only gift she could, a smile she hoped conveyed her appreciation. Gentle reminders that God still loved him, no matter what had happened to make Ceallach think otherwise.

The wind had died down, and she crept quietly to her room. Before climbing under the covers, she knelt and said a prayer for Ceallach, that he might find peace from whatever plagued him from the past. And with her hand on her stomach, she prayed for the safety of the future she carried.

NINE

Each brother knight is allowed three horses; at the
discretion of the Order his squire may have one also.

—from the Rule of the Templar Knights

Morrigan *once said that the love of a woman might heal
me. For a time I hoped that woman might be Orelia, that
perhaps she would stay at Dunstruan. But it cannot be. She
carries a reminder of the life she left in England.*

*Even were it not for the babe, Orelia wouldn't want a
man as scarred and weak as I am. The scars on my body are
not the worst of it. Those I can hide from sight. 'Tis the scars
on my heart that I fear will never heal.*

Especially if Orelia leaves Dunstruan.

ANOTHER WEEK WENT BY, nearly six weeks since the battle, and
still there was no word from Bruce that the prisoner exchange had
been arranged. Knowing that Orelia was anxious to go home and
why it was important for her to do so, Ceallach sent Fergus to
Stirling to find the cause of the delay.

While they waited for Fergus to return, Ceallach and Orelia and
even Morrigan prepared the wool for spinning. First the wool was
sorted according to fiber length. Long-fibered fleece made the best

yarn for the hard cloth with its tight weave that could keep out all but the worst weather.

While Orelia and the other women pulled handfuls of the sorted wool through a coarse metal comb, Ceallach prepared the large loom with warp threads. There was sufficient yarn from last year to weave a good amount of cloth. The weaving hut filled with the women's chatter and Ceallach discovered with some surprise that he enjoyed their company.

When Fergus hadn't returned within three days time, Ceallach worried that Edward of England had returned or some other calamity had befallen Scotland's king. Ceallach would have to go to Stirling himself. But late the afternoon of the fourth day Fergus rode into the bailey.

Everyone gathered around to hear what he had to say. The poor man barely had time to dismount from his horse before the questions started.

Ceallach waded into the group. "What delayed you, Fergus?"

"Nothing serious, but it will take some telling. May I have a drink for my parched throat before I begin the tale?"

"Of course," Ceallach said, relieved that at least war hadn't broken out again.

They sat at a table in the main hall. Morrigan brought bread and drink and then sat beside Fergus as he explained his delay. "When I arrived at Stirling, they were beginning to tear down the castle. I learned that Bruce had moved his headquarters to Dunfermline Abbey and so I had to ride there."

Ceallach nodded in agreement with Bruce's choice. "The abbey has accommodations fit for a king."

Fergus set down his mug. "And a queen. Bruce is anticipating the arrival of his wife—he asked you to come to Dunfermline."

"What of the Englishwoman? Is she to go with me?"

"Aye. Bruce expects to exchange the prisoners any day."

Ceallach, Orelia, Morrigan and Fergus left Dunstruan the next day and set out for Dunfermline Abbey, a dozen or so miles east of Bannockburn. The abbey had ample accommodations for royalty and guests, having been used as an occasional royal residence since the days of Malcolm Canmore, three centuries past.

The trip was uneventful and when they arrived at the abbey, Ceallach escorted Orelia to her chamber. Knowing she would be anxious for news, he said, "I will return as soon as I can. You should probably rest."

"I'll try."

He left her, not at all sure how he felt about leaving her for good. One thing he did know—he would miss her company.

Fergus and Morrigan had gone off to see about purchasing some horses, and Ceallach went to find Bruce.

"Ceallach, welcome. It's good to see you again. How are things at Dunstruan?"

"Your Majesty." Ceallach bowed. "Dunstruan is doing well. I brought the Englishwoman with me. Fergus said you'd arranged for her release?"

Bruce's face clouded. "So I thought. I have only just received a letter from Edward of England." Bruce held a piece of parchment aloft and shook it in the air. "Not only is the wretch ungrateful that I returned his shield and seal, he refuses to agree to terms for peace. And he has reneged on the agreement to exchange the prisoners."

Robert stopped and stood very still, obviously on the verge of completely loosing his temper and taking his frustration out on his guest.

Into the quiet Ceallach softly said, "I am sorry to hear that, my laird. Especially about the queen."

Bruce pinched his forehead with the fingers of his left hand and bowed his head, eyes closed. "Eight years. He's held my wife prisoner for eight years, Ceallach."

Ceallach wondered what it must be like, to miss a woman so. It was just as well that he would never know, for the blessing of love could easily turn to a curse. Bruce lifted his head and pounded his fist into the palm of his other hand. "I'm done with patience, Ceallach. If this is how Edward reacts to my gesture of conciliation, then he and his people shall taste my anger."

"You will invade England?"

"Aye. I've sent for Douglas and Bryan. We are going to harass the northern English towns—Edward's subjects will pay for his arrogance. They will know the displeasure of the king of Scotland."

Ceallach said nothing as he considered the wisdom of taking part in these forays into English territory. "How far south will you go, my laird?"

"Not far enough, in truth. If we want to hit Edward where it would do the most damage to him, we would need to go as far south as London. The northern provinces don't have the population or political clout of London and its surrounding shires."

"But you can't get to him there without risk of capture, so you think that if we strike hard enough and often enough in the north we can still get Edward's attention?"

"Aye. The northlands are poorly defended—we'll be able to plunder at will as long as we stay away from the garrison at Carlisle."

Ceallach nodded. It could work. Aside from the goods and beasts they would capture, they might put enough political pressure on Edward to force him to let Bruce's women go.

"You needn't worry about capture, Ceallach. We'll ride fast, strike quickly and be gone before the English army can ride north to respond."

Ceallach thought of the work that needed to be done at

Dunstruan. But Devyn and the others were more than capable of handling it while Ceallach was gone. "I'll send Fergus and the women back to Dunstruan. I wouldn't mind tugging at Edward's nose, so long as he is far away."

"You still have a price on your head, Ceallach. I would understand if you didn't want to do this."

Ceallach grinned. "So when do we leave?"

Bruce clapped him on the back and laughed. "As soon as Bryan gets here."

Bryan Mackintosh arrived two days later and Bruce immediately called a meeting with his lieutenants. Ceallach, Bryan, and Douglas stood in the king's solar.

"We will leave in two days' time. Ceallach will see to the horses—make sure they are in good health. Douglas, I need you to oversee provisioning, and Bryan will see to the weapons."

Bryan said, "Are you planning to go with us, Your Majesty?"

"Of course. Why wouldn't I?"

"Much as I hate to deprive you of the fun of sleeping on the ground and eating cold oat cakes, it might be best if you stayed here," Bryan said.

Bruce was scowling in a way that clearly said he wouldn't entertain an argument on the subject. But Bryan forged ahead anyway, and Ceallach suppressed a chuckle. Robert's son took after him in many ways, and just now the younger man's tenacity probably wasn't appreciated.

"Explain yourself, stripling."

Undeterred by the king's obvious displeasure, Bryan explained. "Our purpose is to gain Edward's attention and focus it on the plight of his Scottish prisoners. If you are not party to these raids, then when Edward complains to you of them, you can promise to punish the culprits."

Bruce stared at him a moment. "I can claim the raids weren't sanctioned, in other words."

"Aye, and promise there will be no more raids if he releases your queen."

Ceallach saw the wisdom in this. "If Edward still refuses to negotiate Elizabeth's release, we can continue raiding. You could even lead the next raid to make your point."

"Your suggestion is a good one, Bryan. Since I don't know anything about this planned raid, you may leave whenever you are ready. And be careful."

That last sounded more like a concerned father than a king, and Ceallach thought again of the price Bruce and his family had paid for his crown.

Three days later Ceallach, Bryan, Douglas, and a group of about sixty men set off for England, entering the country at Norham castle, just south of the border. As they skirted around the imposing keep, Bryan said, "Kathryn was held prisoner there earlier this year."

"I'd heard something to that affect. How did you get her out?"

"We were lucky—her kidnapper moved her and I was able to ambush them and free her."

They camped that night north of Newburn, and Bryan called all the men together. "I want to be sure that the objectives of our raiding are clear to all of you. We will burn crops, destroy settlements, and steal livestock. Whatever we can't carry off to Scotland is to be destroyed."

Ceallach asked, "What if we are offered a ransom to leave a place in peace?"

Bryan grinned. "We will gladly accept cash donations to the King of Scotland's treasury."

The men laughed and Bryan continued. "There will be no looting or robbery once a ransom is paid. The English won't pay if they can't trust us to keep the truce they pay for. Is that understood?"

Heads nodded in agreement.

"We will stay clear of castles—they will have trained men at arms who could make life difficult for us. Instead we'll visit manors, villages, and monasteries."

The next day they rode south to Newburn and stayed there three days, unhindered by English soldiers. From there Bryan led them to Newcastle where he offered to leave the town alone for a ransom payment. When the town leaders refused, Bryan ordered the men to burn buildings and crops and intimidate the town just as William Wallace had done in 1297.

Ceallach enjoyed being on campaign, especially as it became increasingly clear that the English could not put up any sort of defense. And even more because there was no loss of life. He and the rest of the Scottish marauders continued south to Durham where the residents wisely paid Bryan not to destroy their crops and buildings.

Following the old Roman road, they swept through the valleys and carried off cattle. Ceallach had a few anxious moments as they neared Carlisle's garrison of trained troops, but the Scots were able to relieve the garrison of sixteen fine horses before heading north and burning the towns of Brough, Appleby, and Kirkoswald. Returning home they trampled crops along the way with the stolen cattle and horses.

Upon their return to Scotland, Robert congratulated them on a job well done. Ceallach helped distribute the livestock and other goods he and the others brought back.

Anxious for the return of his wife, Bruce sent an envoy to Edward, demanding terms. Ceallach and all of Scotland were well aware that the longer Robert and Elizabeth were separated, the longer it would be until they produced a male heir. Now that she was a mature woman, her childbearing days were dwindling and the monarchy lay in peril.

WHILE THE KING AWAITED WORD from England, Ceallach headed back to Dunstruan. He'd been gone more than three weeks and Ceallach's impatience grew as his horse trotted around the last bend in the rough track leading to the castle. Dunstruan came into view and Ceallach halted the horse. There was nothing extraordinary about the fortress. It looked much the same as many others—curtain walls surrounding a stone keep.

Yet his heart stirred at the sight. When had this pile of stones come to feel like a home? Dangerous thoughts for a man who wanted to leave when his time as Orelia's warden was finished. Ceallach had not been given a definite date for Orelia's return to England, but both their departures from Dunstruan could not be far off. The thought did not cheer him.

He rode into the bailey and the usual chaos of greeting and homecoming prevailed. He smiled and searched the crowd for Orelia. Since the day she'd seen his scars—and the night she'd calmed him after his nightmare—she was often on Ceallach's mind. He needed to know she was well.

He would have to tell her that he didn't know when she'd be released from Dunstruan. He finally saw Orelia standing off to one side, not really a part of the castle folk—a guest, not a resident. She appeared to be in good health, to his relief.

From across the crowd Orelia questioned him with a lift of her brows. He shook his head—he would have to give her the details later. For now his silent message told her that her visit had been extended. Orelia disappeared inside, no doubt wanting time to absorb her disappointment.

While he took refreshment, Morrigan and Fergus sat down with him. "Devyn says the corn is ready to harvest so there is no need to delay," Fergus said.

Morrigan grinned. "In fact, we've been making preparations

while you were gone. The harvest will begin in the morning. Keifer can barely stand it, he's so excited."

Harvest. Ceallach could remember watching his father's workers bringing in the corn and everyone enjoying the games and festivities afterward. The idea of such a celebration at Dunstruan appealed greatly. "Lucky for us that Devyn saw to the planting this spring or we'd have no reason to celebrate. Tomorrow we harvest!"

When he'd finished talking with Morrigan and Fergus, Ceallach went in search of Orelia. He found her in the chapel, a small, plain room that Ceallach had not visited in his time at Dunstruan. A tiny window high on the wall and two candles provided light. There were no benches—just the stone floor and a kneeling pad along the rail. Orelia knelt there in front of the altar.

His foot scraped the floor as he turned to leave, and she looked up as if startled.

"Ceallach?"

He hesitated. "I did not mean to disturb your prayers."

She smiled, and he would swear that the room brightened. He must stop thinking such foolish thoughts, especially about a woman just two months widowed who carried proof of her husband's love. An Englishwoman who must leave to claim her child's inheritance.

"You didn't frighten me. I was praying for you, and you appeared as if conjured from my petition. Come. Kneel with me for a while."

He drew a deep breath. "Praying for lost causes, are you?"

She glanced down to where her fingers clasped the necklace she always wore. When she looked back at Ceallach she said, "Perhaps. But you are only lost because you refuse to listen to the shepherd's call. I seem to remember your telling Keifer that sheep are stubborn."

He rubbed the scar on his neck. "I believe I also mentioned they are docile and not too bright."

Her expression was that of an exasperated mother to a wayward child. But she smiled and stood. "You have news for me?"

"Our raids went well, but there is still no definite date for the exchange of prisoners."

"I thought as much. Yet another matter to pray about." A tear welled from her eye and fell slowly down her cheek. She brushed it away.

He put his arm about her shoulder in a brotherly hug. "I'm sorry. I know you're anxious to go home."

After a moment, she moved away. "Stay with me here a while, Ceallach."

He swallowed, uncomfortable knowing that she would be praying for him but he couldn't pray for her. Yet he could not refuse her request for company. "All right."

They knelt in front of the altar and Orelia bowed her head. Ceallach glanced her way and saw her lips moving. And like the gentle nudge of a shepherd's staff, her faith prodded at him. He bowed his head before a distant God and offered a halting, awkward prayer for Orelia and her child. It wasn't much; but it was something.

EARLY THE FOLLOWING MORNING, Ceallach finished his contribution to the harvest celebration. Sitting on a bench against the stable wall, he wrapped the final twist of twine around a ball of wool.

Keifer sat down next to him, his bright red hair glinting in the sun. "What are you making?"

He watched intently as Ceallach picked up a needle and thread and began to stitch together a cover of soft leather stretched tight around the twine.

Ceallach smiled at the boy. "What do you think it is?"

"A ball."

Ceallach nearly laughed out loud at the lad's reverent utterance. "Aye, it's a ball. We will use it for a game later today."

Keifer's eyes were bright with anticipation. "Will I be allowed to play?"

This was the third such ball Ceallach had made since he arrived home yesterday, but the boy didn't know that. Ceallach made the last stitch and tied off the thread, then handed the finished toy to Keifer. "The answer is yes. But you may play with this one now."

Pure joy lit the child's face as he took the sphere into his hands and juggled it up and down, catching it in either hand. "Thank you, my laird." Then Keifer threw his arms around Ceallach's neck in a brief but breath-strangling hug. Though Ceallach had to swallow hard at the boy's display of affection, Keifer simply backed up and tossed the ball to Ceallach. With a grin, he threw it back.

After a few minutes of play, Ceallach asked, "Have you completed your chores?" He threw the ball.

Keifer caught it. "Aye, my laird. You said we couldn't leave until they were done."

"Then go and find young James to play catch with you until we're ready to depart."

Keifer raced off in search of Devyn and Suisan's son. Ceallach shook his head. Keifer was an active lad, always in motion. Ceallach had been challenged more than once to find things to keep the boy occupied, both physically and mentally. Although he enjoyed Keifer's company, he would be happy when Morrigan found a permanent foster family for the lad. Ceallach was growing entirely too fond of these people and this place.

Thoughts of Morrigan made Ceallach wonder if Devyn and Susian and the others were ready for the trip to the cornfields. Dunstruan's cook had been feverishly preparing food for them to take along for a harvest picnic. Ceallach walked across the bailey and saw that the picnic supplies were already loaded into one of the wagons along with the sickles that would be used to cut the stalks.

The corn had been planted on the hills to the west, and though it meant taking a rugged uphill path, most people would walk there rather than ride in the bumpy wagons that would be used to haul the harvested corn back to the castle.

Ceallach spoke with the captain of Dunstruan's meager guard. The portcullis had yet to be fixed so they relied on the stout wooden gate for defense. Ceallach wanted to ensure Lady Eveleen and Suisan's safety, since they would remain at Dunstruan to see to the games and food for this evening.

Soon they were ready to depart—Fergus, Morrigan, and Orelia waited for him to give the signal. But the boys were nowhere to be seen.

While Suisan went to find the ever-wayward twosome, Ceallach went over to Orelia. "Are you sure you want to walk, Orelia?" he asked quietly.

"Yes. It won't hurt me, you know." She smiled to soften her words. "The exercise will be good for me, and I really don't want to be bounced until my teeth jar."

He nodded at her sensible explanation. "All right. But if you get tired, say so." He grinned. "No one will think anything of it if a delicate English flower has to ride," he teased.

She swatted his sleeve and Ceallach felt . . . like a cherished friend, like someone who mattered. He must rein in such senseless thoughts. But it made him feel good to see Orelia shake off her grief for a moment and smile. She had much to live for and seemed determined to make the best of her situation, despite the delay in going home. While she remained, he was determined to make it as pleasant as possible for her.

They arrived at the fields without incident, Orelia walking the whole way. Devyn divided the workers and sent them to cut the stalks. The women and children would follow behind the men, gathering and tying the harvested stalks into sheaves. The men held races, seeing who could cut their way to the top of a ridge first. Ceallach won two of the three races he engaged in.

He and Fergus stood side-by-side, wiping sweat from their faces and looking down from the ridgeline after Fergus finally beat him to the top. Below them, the women and children worked in pairs, gathering stalks together and winding twine about them.

A growing number of sheaves stood ready to be hauled to the wagons. Ceallach pointed to where Keifer and James manfully struggled to carry one between them. He lost track of the number of times the sheaf or one or the other of the boys fell until the poor mistreated corn was finally loaded on the cart.

"What a pair of rascals those two are," Fergus said.

"Aye. They need a close watching. It seems Morrigan and Orelia have struck up an unlikely friendship," Ceallach commented, watching the two women work together.

"Aye, so I see. I can't understand what they have in common, to have so much to say to one another." Fergus shrugged.

"Women always seem to have much to talk about." Ceallach shook his head in bewilderment. "I'm hungry—let's load the wagons so we can have our picnic. I'd offer to race you to them, but—"

Like a small boy, Fergus took off running and, unable to resist the challenge, Ceallach raced after him. They reached the bottom of the hill at about the same time and bent over, panting and laughing, beside the two startled women.

Keifer and James raced toward them, jumping on the men's backs. Ceallach and Fergus fell to the ground as if tackled. And Ceallach laughed aloud when he held Keifer at arm's length. Sputtering, the boy flailed about, trying to reach Ceallach. When Keifer leaned hard into Ceallach's hand, he released him, and Keifer came stumbling toward him, then over him, falling down on his other side. Again,

Ceallach laughed. Keifer giggled beside him, lying still for a moment.

The gentle late summer sun shone through a thin layer of clouds, warm but not too hot. All around him, Ceallach could smell the earth where it had been trampled, and the grassy smell of the severed corn stalks. And above him stood the two most beautiful women he'd ever seen. Hands on their hips in mock aggravation, Morrigan and Orelia shook their heads—one blond haired, one black—at the men's antics.

Life was good. At such a moment as this, life was very good. For the first time in many years, Ceallach lifted his face to the sky and smiled. Maybe God had listened to Orelia's prayers for him after all.

Fergus reached up to Morrigan for a hand up and when her hand touched his he pulled her down on top of him. She shrieked and called him a few names Ceallach didn't realize ladies knew. Her skirt flew up and Orelia hastily reached out and pulled it back for modesty.

Skirt? Heavens above!

Orelia caught his eye and grinned, then barely shook her head to warn him off before he commented on Morrigan's unusual attire. Perhaps she understood better than he did how Morrigan had decided to wear women's clothing for a change.

Ceallach stood up, as did Fergus, who hauled the still squawking Morrigan up beside him. Fergus leaned close and whispered to Morrigan and she quieted immediately. The two walked off, leaving Ceallach alone with the widow.

He turned to Orelia. "What did Fergus say to Morrigan to quiet her so quickly?"

Still grinning she said, "I didn't hear it but I suspect he threatened to kiss her."

"Kiss her!"

Orelia looked at him strangely. "Well, yes. It's what people do when they are attracted to each other."

"Well, aye. I mean, I'm sure you're right . . . well, how about that."
He wasn't sure what to make of such a thing.

The other women had been busy spreading out the picnic lunch
underneath a sprawling old oak. Ceallach's hunger and thirst overcame his amazement, and he offered his arm to Orelia. "Shall we join
the others?"

Several fallen branches served as seats for the hungry harvesters.
Ceallach noted that Morrigan and Fergus sat on different branches
but close enough to talk. Ceallach led Orelia to the wagon where
they each found bread and cheese and early apples. They carried the
food to a seat with the others.

They didn't tarry once the meal was over. Everyone pitched in to
load the sheaves so that they could return to the castle for the celebration. As they walked home behind the creaking wagons, a number
of the women began to sing and soon some of the men sang along.

Several of the tunes were familiar from childhood and Ceallach
joined in. The walk to Dunstruan passed quickly, and soon the gates
were opened for them to pass into the bailey. They unloaded the corn
into the storage area of the barn, but one sheaf was kept aside for the
night's festivities.

The corn was no sooner unloaded until Keifer ran over to
Ceallach. "Will you show us the game now, my laird?"

Ceallach ruffled the lad's hair. "Aye. And when you're done
playing, don't forget that you are to decorate that sheaf of corn for
tonight."

"I won't—James is going to help me."

"Good." The activity would keep them both out of trouble.

"What game shall we play?" Morrigan asked.

Ceallach produced the balls he had made as well as a long, narrow
piece of netting he'd had Suisan fashion out of string. *Jeu de paume*—
handball," he said.

"I've heard of it," Orelia said. "The French play it, do they not?"

"Aye. It is very popular with the royal family there." Ceallach pointed to the hitching post to his left. "We need to stretch the net across the court and fasten it to something on either side."

Morrigan took one end and Fergus the other and after quite a bit of laughter and a good deal of trial and error, they stretched it and hung it to Ceallach's satisfaction.

Ceallach clapped his hands and rubbed them together. "All right, we're ready. Who will play first? Orelia?"

She shook her head and Ceallach realized that running to and fro and risk tripping on her skirts was probably not a good idea for one in her condition. Suisan and Devyn gamely agreed to play while Ceallach acted as teacher and arbitrator.

As they lobbed the ball back and forth across the net to each other, Ceallach taught them the intricacies of keeping score. When the adults grew tired, Keifer and James and other children took turns.

Orelia came to stand by Ceallach as he watched the children play. "Your game is a big success." She paused. "Have you been to France?"

As casually as he could he said, "I lived there for fifteen years." He hoped that would satisfy her curiosity.

"Really? I would love to go there some day."

He'd seen Paris in every season, since his monastery had been but a few miles on the outskirts. But he wanted to end this conversation before it touched on things he'd rather not talk about. Before she could ask more questions, he shouted at the boisterous boys. "Take care you don't damage the net, lads." He moved away from Orelia, relieved to end the topic of conversation though bereft of her company.

He nearly ran into Morrigan who was stomping toward the front gate. Even in a dress she walked with a purposeful stride. Her expression was both angry and frightened. Ceallach followed her, instinctively grabbing up his sword, as did Fergus and Devyn.

No one questioned Morrigan—Ceallach had left the gates open so the locals could join them, and he and Fergus assumed there was a threat. When the three of them rounded the corner into the main area of the bailey, Morrigan stopped and Ceallach halted behind her. Fergus went to her side, weapon at the ready.

Strangers sat astride their horses in the bailey of Dunstruan.

TEN

All actions undertaken on campaign shall be done
in accordance with strict military order.

—from the Rule of the Templar Knights

Days and nights had no beginning or end as I lay moaning in agony in the belly of a ship bound for Scotland. My sergeant, Jean Paul, as fine a Frenchman as ever lived, escaped the inquisition and torture by feigning a feeble mind. Nothing could have been farther from the truth. Jean Paul's brilliance at scrounging and haggling had amused me on our trips to the Parisian marketplace near our Order's house. But now his skill saved my life.

Three days after Peter died, Jean Paul negotiated our escape from prison. Ever resourceful, Jean Paul found us passage aboard one of several Templar-owned ships that had escaped King Philip's greed. Scotland's king was the only monarch in Europe who offered us safe haven. In return for sanctuary, we sold the ship and its contents to provide Bruce with money and weapons for his fight against England. For these past seven years I have lived as a wanted man, bitter and alone except for Robert. But now my life is bittersweet—there is a light in the darkness—another man's woman.

CEALLACH STARED AT THE UNFAMILIAR mounted men who had ridden through Dunstruan's unguarded gates.

"Hello, Uncle Angus," Morrigan said as the leader and two of his men dismounted.

Not strangers to Morrigan, then. Ceallach lowered his sword when he saw Morrigan signal behind her back not to draw their weapons. He saw Fergus sheath his sword and Ceallach followed suit.

"Hello, Niece."

This must be the uncle who'd once been laird of Innishewan. Ceallach quickly counted—Angus Macnab had two dozen men with him. Ceallach's half dozen soldiers and Morrigan's score of fighters stood among the crofters and farmers gathered for the harvest celebration. The numbers were in their favor.

Still fear tightened Ceallach's stomach. Not for himself but for the women and children.

Orelia. Fighting panic, Ceallach searched the crowd for her blond hair. With relief he saw that she had quietly moved with the other women close to the door of the keep. If fighting broke out, Ceallach hoped she would follow the women inside and bar the door.

"Whose keep is this?" Macnab demanded.

Ceallach stepped forward. "'Tis mine, Ceallach of Dunstruan." Though he knew the answer, he asked anyway. "And who are you?"

Angus smiled, but the smile lacked any warmth. "I am Angus Macnab, laird of Clan Macnab."

Asserting his right to lead the clan—a right Bruce had taken from him—didn't sound like the words of a man who'd come on a social call. Morrigan took a step forward and Ceallach saw Fergus reach out a hand to hold her back. But she wasn't seeking confrontation any more than Ceallach was. Ignoring the reference to his leadership of the clan, she said, "Will you join us for our harvest celebration? We are just about to set out the evening meal."

Though Ceallach would as soon send the man on his way, highland hospitality demanded such an offer. Morrigan had made the correct gesture, but was it prudent?

"I thank ye for the hospitality, lass. But I'll just take what I've come for and be gone."

Eveleen had been making her way to the front of the crowd and now she stood before Angus. "You can't have what you came for Angus. 'Tis no longer your right to train him."

"And I say it is my right. The boy is my brother's son—who better to foster him?"

Keifer. Where was the boy? Ceallach did not dare seek him out for fear of giving away the child's location. Had Keifer been with Orelia and the other women near the keep's door? Ceallach didn't remember seeing him there.

Ceallach tried to catch Fergus's attention, but the man's gaze didn't leave Angus and the threat he represented. Eveleen stood between opposing clans of armed men. Somehow Ceallach must get Eveleen behind him before a fight erupted. Again Ceallach stepped forward, placing himself between Eveleen and Angus. With his left hand he tugged on her skirt and after a moment's hesitation, she backed away. Hopefully she took herself to safety.

"While I'm sure Lady Eveleen appreciates your offer, Keifer is my fosterling," Ceallach said as he moved closer to Morrigan, who was unarmed and thus also in danger. He didn't have a weapon to give her and couldn't have done so anyway without provoking Angus. But a tug on her skirt, and then a second, accomplished nothing. She did not back away as her mother had done; she stood firmly where she was. Now what? If she had a weapon, he knew she could hold her own and Ceallach wouldn't worry. As it was, he wanted her out of harm's way.

A quick glance at Fergus—who was flexing his hand as if to grasp his sword hilt—confirmed that the situation might turn ugly at any moment.

Angus took a step closer, now no more than a sword's length in front of Ceallach. "Nice of ye to offer to foster him, but the boy is my kin. I'd appreciate it if ye'd turn Keifer over to me." Though he spoke to Ceallach, Angus glared at Morrigan.

Morrigan glared back. "No! Keifer stays here!"

Angus looked away from her. He peered over Ceallach's left shoulder toward the sound of children's voices. Ceallach recognized Keifer and James—in their usual high spirits and unaware of the drama being played out in the front of the bailey. To Ceallach's dismay, the voices grew louder.

Eveleen stood at the corner of the keep, her expression one of panic. As the boys burst around the corner, she reached for Keifer but snagged James instead. Keifer dodged his mother's outstretched hand and in his headlong rush to resist capture, came to a halt less than an arm's length from his uncle. Keifer held a battered corn stalk that had obviously been used as a target for the boy's swords. James backed away and ran off but Keifer stayed where he was, glancing up at Angus and back at Ceallach.

They stood thus for barely a minute. In one swift move Angus unsheathed his sword while his man seized Keifer's tunic. Macnab's man handed the boy to Angus who now held Keifer in one hand and his sword in the other.

Ceallach withdrew his sword but he couldn't engage Angus's blade in such close quarters without endangering Keifer.

Angus held his blade so close to Keifer's neck it drew a trickle of blood. Ceallach suspected Macnab had no real interest in training Keifer—he simply wanted the future laird of Clan Macnab in his control. To do with as he wished. Which meant Morrigan, the current laird, was probably in danger as well. Angus pressed his advantage, retreating toward his horse with the boy as his men guarded his back.

As Morrigan lunged toward her brother, one of Angus's men grabbed her arm.

But Fergus thrust his blade and then his body between the woman and the scoundrel trying to harm her, breaking the man's hold on her. The man's blade must have cut Fergus because he cried out and clutched his arm, his weapon dropping to the ground.

Morrigan picked up his fallen sword and, skirt or no, engaged the outlaw's blade.

The skirmish distracted Angus, and Ceallach saw his opportunity. Locking gazes with the frightened boy, Ceallach gave a quick nod and after a moment's consideration, Keifer poked the cornstalk into his uncle's eye.

Angus howled and his grip loosened long enough for Keifer to wriggle free.

Ceallach yelled, "Run to the keep, Keifer!"

The boy hesitated for a moment before he remembered his training and obeyed his commander. Bellowing in rage, Angus, eye watering profusely, attacked Ceallach. Angus's blade slid off of Ceallach's and he stepped in, separating Macnab from his horse.

Macnab must have realized what Ceallach had done and tried to work his way back toward the beast. But Ceallach continued to press him away from the horse and away from his men, isolating him. Macnab's impaired vision made him no match for Ceallach. With a quick flick of his blade, Ceallach knocked his opponent's sword to the ground.

When his men saw that Angus had been disarmed, they attempted to come to his aid but Ceallach and Morrigan's men drove them off. Seeing there was nothing they could do to free Angus, his men scrambled to mount their horses. To Ceallach's dismay, no one had thought to close the gate, and all but five of the Macnab men managed to get away.

The five were quickly subdued. Ceallach ordered his men to put the prisoners in Dunstruan's dungeon. Satisfied that Macnab no longer posed a threat, Ceallach approached Fergus and Morrigan. Any triumph at capturing Angus disappeared when Ceallach saw Fergus sitting in the dirt.

Morrigan kneeled beside Fergus, holding her bare hand over a bleeding wound on the man's upper arm. "What were you thinking? You could have been killed!" she scolded.

Blood oozed from under her fingers, and Ceallach knew they must get Fergus inside and stop the bleeding. "Fergus?"

Fergus pushed at Morrigan. "Me? *I* could have been killed?"

Ceallach tried again to get their attention. "Morrigan?"

"Never mind that. Can you walk?"

"Aye, just help me up and don't be falling on me this time."

Ceallach hid a smile and offered his hand to help Morrigan to stand but she waved it aside. Still holding fast to Fergus's wounded arm, she stood up, tripping on her skirt and muttering, "What was I thinking, wearing a skirt and trying to fight in it yet?"

She helped Fergus up but he nearly swooned. Morrigan steadied him, and the two stared at each other, barely aware of Ceallach's presence. Fergus said, "But ye look so lovely, lass." And with that he passed out from the loss of blood.

Ceallach caught him before he hit the ground and carried him into the keep where Morrigan hovered over him and Suisan sewed up his wound. Suisan assured them Fergus would recover as long as the wound didn't fester.

Although he was weak from loss of blood, Fergus soon revived. "Stop fussing at me, Morrigan. I'm fine. Help me to my room, if ye must, and then let me be."

Morrigan had a pallet made up for Fergus in front of the fireplace in the main hall. "You'll sleep right here where I can stay by you and see that you don't bleed all over everything again."

Fergus protested but Morrigan stood firm. Seeing that Fergus was in good hands, Ceallach went to find Keifer. The boy and his mother sat at a small table in the kitchen. Eveleen made a place for Ceallach to sit on the bench beside her. "What will become of Angus?" she asked quietly.

Keifer's pale face surprised Ceallach—the encounter must have shaken the boy. Ceallach laid his hand on the lad's shoulder. "I will turn Angus over to the king. 'Tis up to Bruce to decide Macnab's punishment."

Keifer said, "Why'd he try to take me?"

The boy's gentle heart had learned the first painful lesson of combat. "Your uncle wanted to hurt you because you are to be laird of Clan Macnab. Angus forfeited his right to the Macnab lands when he chose not to support Scotland's king."

Keifer studied his fingernails. "Will he try to hurt me again?"

"I don't think so."

Keifer took a deep breath and released it. "I best learn how to fight just in case."

Keifer had just taken his first step toward manhood. "Aye, it's not a game, Keifer. Your quick thinking today saved you and your sister, lad. You were brave and resourceful, and that is something no one can teach you to be."

Ceallach observed Eveleen, and the brightness of her eyes told him she realized the import of today's events as well.

Keifer stood up from his chair. "I'm going to see if Fergus is all right."

Ceallach nodded and the boy left. Ceallach stood to leave as well, but Eveleen took hold of his hand.

"Thank you. Your training saved his life today."

Ceallach appreciated the praise, but was simply relieved that all had turned out well. "He's a good lad—he'll make you proud one day, Lady Eveleen."

"He already has."

The fight and Fergus's injury dispelled the festive air and no one felt like continuing the celebration. Keifer stayed close to Fergus until Eveleen sent the boy off to bed.

Ceallach urged the crofters who'd come for the holiday to remain at Dunstruan for the night. He feared Angus's angry men might lie in wait for the unwary. As the night was warm, most of the people made themselves a bed in the hay of the stable.

Late that night, when the castle had finally quieted, Ceallach found himself restless and not ready to sleep. He decided to check on Fergus. Firelight was the only illumination as he made his way across the main hall. Halfway to the fireplace he heard the murmur of voices and saw two silhouettes sitting on the pallet. Fergus and Morrigan.

Afraid to move and give himself away, Ceallach stood still. He watched as Fergus leaned close and said something that made Morrigan throw back her head and laugh. They sat close to each other, and Morrigan reached up and touched the mark above the man's eye.

Nothing like a mysterious scar to draw the attention of the ladies. Ceallach reached up and touched his neck where the tip of his own disfigurement was visible. He'd never seen the damage to his back but from what he could see of the redness on his neck, he was better off not knowing.

He brought his attention back to the couple in front of him, again thinking he should leave but afraid if he moved they would notice him. Perhaps they would turn their back at some point so he could leave them undisturbed.

Fergus took Morrigan's hand and spoke to her with obvious

sincerity. That Morrigan allowed the man to hold her hand seemed like a good sign to Ceallach. Morrigan answered and as she leaned into Fergus's arms, Ceallach saw his chance to leave unnoticed.

He walked to his chamber wishing he could talk to Orelia in the privacy of a torch-lit room.

A FEW DAYS AFTER THE HARVEST Ceallach sent Angus Macnab and his men to Bruce, accompanied by several of Morrigan's warriors. Ceallach doubted Robert would give Angus a second chance and fully expected Bruce to imprison Macnab for life.

The weather turned cold and wet and as he tramped through the rain to the weaver's hut, Ceallach was glad they'd had such fine weather the week before to bring in the corn. He opened the door to the hut and warmth and light dispelled the gloom of the day. A kettle hung in the fireplace keeping water warm for tea, and a plate of sweet cakes sat on the stone mantelpiece.

Orelia sat at one of the small looms, weaving a belt. "Good morning, Ceallach."

"Good morning, Orelia. Is Keifer here?"

"No, he's not."

"He should be along shortly. I told him to meet me to help us with the warp." Ceallach walked across the room to the large loom. He'd strung the warp threads earlier, painstakingly counting out the threads and colors to produce the desired pattern. It would take the three of them working together to ensure that the warp threads were evenly wrapped about the release spindle. Ceallach was anxious to begin weaving the pattern he and Orelia had decided on.

The door flung open and hit the wall, bouncing off it and banging shut behind Keifer. Ceallach suppressed a grin. The boy may have taken a step toward manhood, but there was still a long road ahead.

Without stopping her work, Orelia calmly said, "Keifer, the door has a handle so it can be closed without such a bang."

Keifer walked over to her side, a mischievous grin on his face. "Aye, my lady. I'll try to remember."

She reached out and playfully slapped the boy's arm. "Ceallach and I need your help to make sure the warp threads are even."

The three of them worked together—Ceallach turning the spindle while Orelia and Keifer untangled and stretched the threads. When all the warp was on the proper spindle, Orelia patiently showed Keifer how to tie the knots at the other end. Ceallach watched—his big hands made such small work difficult, and he enjoyed seeing Orelia and Keifer work together.

If a stranger happened upon them, they might think the three of them a family. Ceallach dismissed the fanciful thought.

As he tied the knots, Keifer asked, "What will the king do to Uncle Angus?"

Evidently the threat of his uncle bothered Keifer, and Ceallach wanted to put his mind at ease. "Angus will no doubt spend a long time in prison."

"I'm going to train as a knight and fight with Robert the Bruce," Keifer informed them.

"Aye, part of your training will be in warrior skills, Keifer. But you must also know how to lead your clan, which is what Adam Macintosh will teach you."

Keifer made a face of displeasure. "Why can't I stay here and learn that?"

"I wish you could—I'll miss your door-opening method."

Keifer grinned. "May I go now? James and I want to practice."

Ceallach gave permission and Keifer didn't disappoint. He flashed them a grin as he deliberately closed the door the same as when he'd come in.

Ceallach set up the weft, aware of Orelia watching him. "I expect to hear from Robert any day about your return to England."

She handed him the shuttle. "Oh. Well, that's good."

Thinking to distract her, he asked the first thing that came to his head. "How did you meet your husband?"

He'd struck up the right conversation because she smiled. "My grandparents had a small cottage near Bolton Abbey, just a few miles north of Radbourne Hall. The waterfall and general wildness of the place reminded my grandmother of the Scottish highlands where she grew up."

He raised his eyebrows. "Your grandmother was Scottish?"

"Yes, from Lochaber."

"Well, that explains it then." He was smiling.

"Explains what?" she asked, following his lead.

"Your fondness for *brecan* cloth."

She took the shuttle from him and took a turn at the weaving. In the glow of the fire and the ease of their hearts, neither one looked forward to her leaving.

ELEVEN

Brothers shall avoid rumor, envy, and slander.

—from the Rule of the Templar Knights

The days until Orelia must leave race by faster than a ship in full sail. The date for the prisoner exchange has been set and this time Robert will not allow anything to come between him and the return of his wife. Robert and Elizabeth have spent most of their marriage apart, and I do not envy them the difficulties that may lie ahead as they rebuild their relationship. My brother vacillates between joyful anticipation and fearful apprehension, and we are all avoiding his temper as much as possible.

As for me, my dread of Orelia's departure remains steadfast. I could almost selfishly wish that she did not carry her dead husband's child, or better yet, that there was no inheritance for the child to claim. Then they could remain in Scotland. With me.

MORRIGAN'S MEN delivered Angus to Dunfermline and returned with news. Bruce himself had led another raid into England. The raid made way for another round of negotiations, this time at Dumfries. Edward's emissary agreed to the prisoner exchange, but talks broke down when Robert insisted on being recognized as Scotland's king. Finally, they agreed that the prisoner exchange would take place the beginning of October, more than three months after the English defeat at Bannockburn.

With a heavy heart, Ceallach made preparations to take Orelia to Dunfermline.

The night before they would ride south to return Orelia to England, Ceallach thirsted for strong drink as he hadn't since coming to Dunstruan. But he would not give in. He would not. The strange part was that the demons weren't chasing him, at least not the demons of old. No, these were new ones, awakened with the touch of a woman's hand.

Orelia. Fair Orelia with her glowing hair and faithful heart. How he would miss her!

Instead of a bottle of whiskey, he sought her company. What he would do for solace when she left, he didn't know. But tonight she was here, and he found her sitting by the fire in the solar.

When he entered, she smiled a smile that seemed touched with the same melancholy he felt. Could that be true? Did she regret leaving?

She was spinning wool in the light from a candle, and her movements were captured in the shadow on the wall behind her. Gracefully her hand fed the wool onto the spool while the other spun the spindle. Her hair hung in a braid over her shoulder. He knew he was staring, but he wanted to remember her just so.

A slowly lengthening string eased from the spindle, and he picked up a spool and began to wind the newly made thread on it.

"Thank you," she said. "The light is growing dim. I hate to set the spindle down. Are you able to build up the fire?"

Her voice did not chide or belittle. He wished he could do this for her, but he hadn't mastered the fear yet. "Perhaps you should retire."

"It is early yet." She stopped the spindle. "Who will fix the fire for you when I'm gone, Ceallach?" she asked gently.

For a brief moment, he let himself think of how cold he would be without her. "No one, I suppose."

She set the spindle aside. "Then it is time for you to tell me what you fear. Maybe then it will no longer have such a hold on you and you will not freeze when I have gone."

The thread ran out. There was no more to wind, and he let his hands fall to his lap. He gazed up at her, at her beautiful, patient face. She laid several logs on the fire and poked at them until the flames crackled cheerfully.

"Perhaps you are right." Maybe this is what it would take to control the demons, especially once she was gone.

They sat facing each other on the benches before the fireplace. Where should he start? He rested his forearms on his thighs, and with his head bent so that he wouldn't have to see her expression, he said, "My true name is Marcus of Kintyre." Then he told her all of it, about his training as a knight and taking the Templar vows. About the years of contemplation and preparation for war. About life in the monastery and about Peter, his teacher and friend.

"We were working at Peter's loom that evening, getting the warp ready for a rug he had designed. The king's soldiers forced their way in and arrested us, dragged us away and threw us in a dungeon. We didn't know what we'd done wrong."

"They arrested all the Templars in France that night, didn't they?"

"Aye. We had grown wealthy, and the king was deeply in debt to us." He paused to gather himself. If he was going to tell the rest . . . how could he say the words? He'd never told anyone, not even Robert.

Orelia's gentle voice said, "You didn't do anything wrong, did you?" It was more a statement than a question.

He raised his head and studied her. "I'm no paragon, Orelia. But I didn't do the things they accused us of. And neither did Peter."

She nodded. "Go on."

He hung his head, unwilling to watch her face when he said, "They accused us of defiling the cross, of . . . of sorcery and devil-worship."

She reached for him but he pulled away. "They said . . ." He took in a deep breath and let it out. "They said we committed unnatural acts with each other, Orelia. I loved Peter like a father. A father!" He jumped to his feet. He paced in agitation. "They tortured him, and he confessed to everything. When it was my turn, Peter urged me to just get on with it—confess to it all. He said that God would know the truth. But my pride wouldn't let me—it took them two days to break me. Then I confessed to everything, everything but . . . I would not besmirch the friendship I had with Peter with such a foul lie. That's when they lit a torch and . . ."

Tears poured down his face and he hated the weakness—hated it! He turned his back to her and, head bent, rested his hands on the stones of the fireplace, closer to flame than he'd been in seven years.

Ceallach looked down into the fire. "My back was already flayed open from the whip, and the torch singed the open skin. Why they didn't kill me, I don't know. Finally they threatened to torture Peter again if I did not concede.

"So I confessed to all of it to save Peter from another round, and they threw me back into the cell. But my confession meant nothing—they dragged Peter out of the cell again. I begged them to take me; I promised to confess to anything if they would spare Peter."

He turned and looked at Orelia, at the tears that glistened on her cheeks. He would finish his tale, and it would end his friendship with the only woman he had ever cared for. No woman would want a man like Ceallach, a man who had failed to protect someone he loved.

"My body gave out and I lost consciousness. When I awoke, Peter had been returned to the cell and lay dying by my side. If I had confessed sooner, had not angered them with my stubbornness, Peter would still be alive. But my pride wouldn't let me."

He dared to look up into her eyes. There was nothing but compassion in them, a tenderness despite knowing his innermost secrets. He had expected to feel humiliation when he finally told someone. But he didn't.

The candle had begun to gutter in a final pool of wax, and the fire had burned low. The spindle and spool lay at rest and strangely, so did his heart.

ORELIA'S WOMANLY INSTINCTS told her Ceallach would not welcome her touch and certainly not her pity. "Your friend might have died no matter what you did or said."

"You don't really believe that, Orelia."

She stood and walked close to him, stood in front of him, but didn't touch. He looked as if he might break if she did. "Yes, I do believe that. You blame yourself for his death and yet, from the sound of it, you could have confessed to killing the pope and they'd have taken Peter away anyway."

"Then why did they allow me to live? I would have gladly given my life for Peter, but they didn't take it. They took him." Ceallach sank to the bench, his head in his hands, and sobbed.

She suspected that Ceallach had never truly grieved for his friend until now. Whether he welcomed her touch or not, Orelia could not deny him the solace of human touch. She sat beside him and laid his head on her shoulder, stroking his back. "It does not sound like they were trying to spare you. Your scars testify to that. It is only your strength and God's grace that saved you."

As his sobs subsided, the full import of his words washed over her. Fear ran through her body, chilling her.

Fear for Ceallach. A Templar Knight and a wanted man.

He clung tightly to her for a moment, then pushed away and dried his eyes on his sleeve. He stood abruptly and strode away from her as if he couldn't bear to be comforted any longer. However, when he faced her, she brought her hand to her mouth to stifle a gasp. In his vulnerable state, his feelings for her were unmasked.

"Ceallach, I can't . . . Surely you know . . ."

He raised his hand as if to stop her words. She could almost see him pull himself together, could definitely see his relief that she didn't actually comment on his feelings. She would not distress him further by mentioning it. Nor would she name her own feelings, for she had come to care for this gentle man who feared the fire's flames. However, there was something more pressing to discuss.

"The Order was disbanded, was it not?" she asked.

He reached up and absently touched the scar on his neck. "Aye, the Order was disbanded by the pope, and the Templars who didn't confess were excommunicated."

"Ah, then you are still within the good graces of the Church."

He shook his head. "Nay. I recanted my confession—I've been branded a heretic."

It was worse than she'd thought. "And now Edward of England has placed a ransom on you."

"Aye."

"Yet you plan to accompany me to the border? You mustn't, Ceallach. 'Tis too great a risk."

His expression was tender as he said, "You are not my enemy, Orelia."

"No, I am not. You will never be my enemy. But I cannot speak for others. Must you ride with us tomorrow?"

"To see you safe? Aye."

"Does no one else know?" she whispered.

"Only my foster brother."

She stared at him. "You trust me with this."

He looked down at the floor and again rubbed his neck. When he gazed at her again, he seemed more settled. "I tell you these things because you are my friend and you need to understand why I am . . . why a warrior would be afraid to light a flame."

If only she were free to care for him, she would hold him close and not let go. She laid a hand on her stomach, reminding herself of Radbourne and the reason she must return there. "You need not be ashamed, Ceallach, not with me. And you needn't fear that I will reveal your secret."

She reached for his hand and he allowed her to take it. "Tomorrow I will leave to secure my child's future. But I will never forget you or our friendship."

He invited her close and she moved into his arms with an ease that surprised them both. The child moved within her as if in greeting its father. But Ceallach wasn't her husband, could never be her husband, and this child would never know its father.

They parted. "I want to say good-bye here, tonight, in private." She wiped a tear from her cheek. His eyes were bright, and she knew he was affected too. But he would not say so, because she was not his and never would be. She belonged at Radbourne, raising John's child. And Ceallach belonged . . . nowhere.

He lifted her chin. "Tell me those are the foolish tears of a breeding woman, and that you will not cry tomorrow."

"That is exactly what they are. I am English, despite my grandmother's Scottish blood; I don't belong here and I must go home."

"If things were different . . ." He shook his head and reached into the folds of his plaid, withdrawing a small piece of parchment, folded and sealed with wax. "Take this, but do not open it unless you have need of me."

"Why would I—"

"You may need my help but would hesitate to ask. What is written here will assure you that I will come."

She took it and tapped it with her finger. "You expect me to grow old and never open this after you arouse my curiosity so?"

"If you don't need me, don't open it. It's that simple. There is nothing there of any consequence unless you are in trouble and wonder if I will help."

The tears started again. "Very well." She tucked the missive under her belt. 'Twas time, but she couldn't let him go without one kiss, one taste of him to remember him by. He gazed at her and she moved back into his arms. He touched his lips to hers, and she yielded. For one, too-brief moment they were of one accord.

She broke away, missing his touch and knowing she would never feel it again. Brushing away her tears, she said, "Good-bye, Ceallach."

He stared at her. Clearly the kiss had affected him, too. Why had she made their parting so much harder for him. For them both?

"Good-bye, Orelia," he whispered. Then he slowly walked away.

ROBERT THE BRUCE HALTED HIS RETINUE on a wooded hillside overlooking the English border. Ceallach glanced at the position of the sun and determined that they were early for their rendezvous with the English. Bruce had been uncharacteristically silent during the ride. The king of Scotland and victor of the battle of Bannockburn had dismounted, and now paced back and forth like an anxious bride-groom.

But the king wasn't the only one whose nerves stretched thin. Ceallach fought his need to look at Orelia, to study her face so that he would not forget. But no one must suspect his feelings for the young widow. There could be no conjecture about the babe's paternity.

When the negotiations had become final and a date for the exchange set, Bryan had gone to Moy to fetch his wife, Kathryn. She would act as the queen's lady in waiting, providing feminine companionship. Bruce didn't know what condition Elizabeth would be in. She had not been subjected to living in an open cage like Bruce's other womenfolk, but had spent most of her imprisonment under house arrest at various manor homes.

But Elizabeth had spent the better part of the past year in Rochester prison, which could not have been kind to a gently bred woman. She might need a woman to confide in.

Elizabeth and Bruce's daughter Marjorie and the other Scottish prisoners had been transported to Berwick by ship. Berwick remained in English hands, which so angered Bruce that he refused to have the exchange there. The exchange would take place near Norham Castle, close to the English border.

Bryan motioned for the others to dismount and give the king room.

Ceallach got down from his horse and walked over to stand by Bryan. "Our king appears nervous," he said softly.

"Aye, he was calmer before the battle."

Ceallach wanted to tame his own nervous stomach and sought distraction in conversation. "They've been separated a long time."

"Eight years, and after only four years of marriage."

Ceallach wondered what kind of woman Elizabeth Bruce might be. How had she withstood prison and separation from her husband? "Did you know the queen?"

"I joined their household as a squire a year after their marriage. It seemed to be a union of great warmth and mutual respect." Bryan paused, seeming lost momentarily in memories. "I remember when she was taken. He nearly resigned the crown."

Further talk halted when the lookout announced the approach of riders. They remounted and rode slowly down the hillside. Ceallach could only imagine the king's emotions as he rode toward his wife and the daughter he hadn't seen in eight years.

Robert had received occasional letters, but eight years was a very long time. People change, most especially someone who has been a prisoner. How would he and Elizabeth ever put their life back together?

Bruce halted, and Ceallach could see him moisten his lips and fiddle with the reins. His features were tense, and Ceallach was amazed to discover that he understood. Here was no king, just a man, a husband who feared what he might discover when he next beheld his wife. Had Elizabeth become bitter in her prison? Could she forgive him for his inability to rescue her?

Ceallach had no trouble imagining the horrors of imprisonment. While Elizabeth would have been spared the depravity Ceallach had known, the loss of freedom gnawed at a person's soul.

As they approached the English riders and their Scottish prisoners, he noted Elizabeth's bright blond hair and the straightness of her posture as she sat upon her horse. Bryan motioned for his men to bring forward the prisoners who would be exchanged for the queen.

Ceallach was afraid to look at Orelia, afraid his feelings were written on his face for everyone to see.

Orelia urged her horse forward then looked at Ceallach for the last time. She smiled bravely. He nodded, desperate not to show his feelings. Not the love, not the fear, not the grief. He managed to smile back.

The two groups faced each other. The men accompanying Elizabeth held back while she allowed her horse to advance. Robert dismounted and everyone followed suit. Then the king walked to his wife's horse. Neither moved but searched each other's faces. Then with a cry Elizabeth dismounted and threw herself into Robert's waiting arms.

Though they were a good twenty feet away from the couple, Ceallach turned around to give them privacy. Seeing his movement, Bryan stationed his horse nose to tail with Ceallach's, providing a screen of sorts.

"I feared how this would go," Bryan admitted.

"So did I. This is a good beginning, don't you think?"

They glanced over the horse's backs at the still embracing couple. Bryan grinned. "Aye, most encouraging." His grin disappeared. "He never stopped loving her, Ceallach. Not all this time and despite . . ."

Ceallach recognized Bryan's struggle, as if he didn't want to tarnish the reputation of this man he so obviously admired.

Softly, he said, "I've heard the rumors, Bryan."

"It's not as if he chased after women." Bryan defended his father. "Rather they were drawn to him, his power and position." He paused. "I cannot judge him. I don't know if I would have done any different in his circumstances."

Seeking to reassure him, Ceallach laid a hand on his arm. "I do not accuse him. Only Elizabeth has that right."

Bryan signaled to Kathryn and she walked forward. Ceallach glanced up to see the royal couple walking toward them. Elizabeth seemed apprehensive, and he saw Robert strengthen his hold on his wife's arm.

Bryan knelt and took his queen's hand to kiss it.

Elizabeth's voice shook as she said, "Rise, Sir Bryan." He did as she said, and, in a most unqueenly fashion, she hugged Bryan tight. Ceallach studied Robert, whose eyes appeared over bright.

When the queen released him, Bryan gently drew Kathryn to his side. "Your Majesty, may I present my wife, Lady Kathryn."

Elizabeth grasped Kathryn's hand and squeezed it. "How kind of you to welcome me. I am pleased to see Bryan well married. We will talk more later."

Bruce introduced Ceallach. "My lady, this is Ceallach, my foster brother." He leaned close and whispered something in her ear. She drew back, her expression quizzical. But she simply extended her hand. "I'm pleased to meet you, Ceallach."

Ceallach bowed over her hand. "And I you, my queen."

The queen turned to Robert. "We are on Scottish soil, are we not?"

"Aye, my love, that we are."

"Then let's not waste another minute." She looked at Robert as if no one else stood near. "Take me home, Husband," she whispered.

TWELVE

No brother may leave the field of battle while the
Order's standard is still flying.

—from the Rule of the Templar Knights

*Orelia was right. Talking about Peter's death and my part in
it has brought me a sense of peace. Unburdening myself to her
healed me even more than writing it down. But in revealing
the torture, I fear I lost her admiration and respect. Still, what
difference does it make? She has gone back to England, to the
life waiting for her there. I remain what I have always been—
a warrior waiting for the next fight to begin.*

ORELIA TURNED IN HER SADDLE, looking for Ceallach. He sat on
his horse, there on the hill, and tears came to her eyes. He'd been a
stalwart friend and she would miss him.

She would never see him again. Her home was at Radbourne,
raising John's child to one day take on his inheritance. Ceallach
certainly could not come to England, not with a price on his head.

She touched her stomach. Surely the child would be a boy. God
had been kind enough to grant her fervent wish and given her John's
child. Was she asking too much that the babe be a boy?

She attempted a smile—determined not to show her sadness—
and waved at the warrior before facing forward for the ride south. A

part of her would always remain in Scotland with the brave knight whose friendship she'd grown to cherish. She wiped away tears, unsure if they were tears of joy or pain. Her condition made every emotion sharper and she didn't trust her heart just now.

The journey was blessedly uneventful and although the men complained about the slow pace and the need to find shelter at night, they were kind enough and watched out for her. Orelia took care to eat well and get as much sleep as possible. Nothing could be allowed to harm Radbourne's heir. Though she was grateful for the gentle palfrey that carried her, by the final day of the journey she was more than ready to get off the horse and stay off.

But she worried about her welcome at Radbourne Hall. Alice had certainly made her dislike of Orelia clear, so clear that Orelia had followed John to Scotland. How would Alice react to the news that Orelia carried John's heir?

Wearily she dismounted at last in the courtyard of Radbourne Hall.

"Welcome home, Orelia," Richard said as he helped her dismount. For one brief moment, looking at the brother who favored John so closely, Orelia nearly threw herself into Richard's arms. But since they had never been particularly warm toward each other, she merely nodded in greeting.

Composing her emotions, she responded with the dignity befitting a widow. She suspected she would need to draw heavily upon decorum and faith in the days to come. "Thank you, Richard. I am glad to be here."

Alice stepped forward and gave her a light peck on the cheek. "Welcome, Orelia. You look tired."

Orelia nodded. "More tired than I've ever been."

"We'll not fatigue you more by insisting on visiting with us right now." Richard held out his hand. "Come, Alice will take you to your room. When you are rested, you may tell us everything you know about . . . John's death. And your imprisonment."

Richard seemed sincerely grief stricken at his brother's death, but Orelia sensed a lack of sincerity in Alice. She gave herself a mental shake. Such foolishness. She was allowing her feelings toward the woman to overshadow all else and cloud her mind.

Gratefully she settled into her room. Alice and Richard now occupied the master chamber and Orelia was glad to be spared from sleeping there with nothing but her memories. Just seeing the house and grounds had been painful enough reminders of her loss.

For two days she stayed in her room, taking meals there, resting and restoring her strength. Not only physically, but also preparing to tell Richard and Alice about John's death and then, the news that would change everyone's future.

THE FIRST THING ORELIA NOTICED when she left her room and came down the stairs into Radbourne's main hall was the smell of beeswax candles. There were few windows in the hall, and candles or torches were necessary even in daylight. But Orelia had always burned tallow candles, leaving the more expensive beeswax for special occasions and guests.

As she made her way to a table to break her fast she noted the new tablecloths of Irish linen. Again, such costly items were not unheard of at Radbourne but were not used every day. Perhaps Alice had ordered them used to celebrate Orelia's return. She would thank the woman for such thoughtfulness.

Richard sat down beside her. "Good morning, Orelia. It is good to see that you are feeling rested enough to come down this day."

"I'm glad to be home."

"As we are to have you. I thought the Scottish pretender would never let you leave. I traveled to London twice to encourage Edward to have you released quickly, to no avail."

She was grateful for such efforts on her behalf. "Thank you, Richard."

Orelia had learned from Ceallach that it had been Edward who stalled the negotiations, but she chose not to point that out to her brother-in-law. Thinking of Ceallach made her feel almost homesick, and she stifled a smile at her fanciful thought. She was home here, at Radbourne.

Discreetly she laid her hand on her gently swelling stomach. So far, her clothing concealed her condition. Without John to protect them, she felt especially protective of his heir. She needed to be fully prepared for battle before she disclosed her news. When they had finished the meal, Richard said, "Come. Alice will meet us in the solar so you can speak of John in private."

Orelia stopped inside the door of what had been John's favorite room. If the changes in the hall had been subtle, those in this room were not. John's desk, a perfectly usable piece, was replaced with an ornately carved, obviously costly one of oiled English oak. There were no longer rushes on the floor but a fine and no doubt outrageously expensive carpet.

Beautiful new tapestries lined the walls, and the glazed window had been replaced with an exquisite stained glass picture of John the Baptist baptizing Christ.

"It's lovely, isn't it?" Alice stepped forward from the shadows and took a seat in one of the chairs.

"Stunning." Orelia nearly objected to its obvious expense until she remembered that she no longer had responsibility for the treasury of Radbourne Hall. But she must object sooner or later before these two spent all of her child's inheritance. Resolved to speak up when the time was right, she sat in the chair Richard held for her. Another extravagance—chairs with backs instead of the perfectly acceptable benches John had furnished the room with.

The final realization that John was truly gone, that her life had changed irrevocably, came when she happened to glance at Richard's hand and saw that he wore the ring that signified he was the Earl of Radbourne. She stared at the ring. "You had a new ring made?"

"But of course. King Edward has named me earl. I *am* John's heir, Orelia. There was no reason to wait for your return."

"Perhaps not." Richard's decision not to join the army had certainly worked in his favor. "But you might have waited to ascertain whether or not I was with child," she said, trying to keep the reproof from her voice.

"Come now, Orelia," Alice said. "Be reasonable. There was no reason to think such a thing. After all, you failed to conceive for seven years. Why would we think that might change?"

Richard and Alice's shallow faith had always been a source of concern for John. With as much wisdom and grace as she could muster, Orelia said, "Perhaps if you believed in a faithful God you would not have been so quick to dismiss the possibility."

Richard stepped into the fray, attempting to soothe any ruffled female feathers. "I'm sorry if your sensibilities are hurt, Orelia. I meant to keep you from having to deal with all manner of legalities. All is settled and you may now get on with your life."

"Unfortunately, Richard, there is one small problem with your plan. I am, indeed, carrying John's child."

Richard and Alice looked at her in shock, and Orelia shivered as if a cold wind had blown through the room.

Richard recovered first. He looked at Alice before saying, "That's not possible."

Orelia sat up straighter in her chair. "Of course it is. Your brother and I were man and wife and acted accordingly."

"Are you certain of your condition? Sometimes when one wishes for something hard enough, the body is convinced it's so," Alice said in a sweet voice that barely hid the daggers in the words.

The two days of rest had given Orelia the strength she needed to deflect Alice's accusation that Orelia was losing her mind. "Yes, quite sure."

"Well, this is good news, isn't it dear?" Alice said with not the least bit of sincerity.

But from the look on the man's face it was anything but good news.

Hoping to lessen the blow and yet determined to set the situation to rights, Orelia said, "King Edward will no doubt make you the child's guardian, Richard, and give you control of the estates until John's child reaches its majority. We will all live here and nothing will change."

But from their distressed faces—and the changes at Radbourne Hall—it was obvious that Richard and Alice had quickly gotten used to their new rank. And to their belief that their child, not John's, would one day inherit the earldom.

ALICE AND RICHARD SAT in the beautifully appointed solar of Radbourne Hall. Orelia's news was only minutes old but Alice was determined that her child would one day be the Earl of Radbourne. Alice had no intention of giving up what she'd gained. "The child is not John's," she asserted.

Richard jumped up and paced the room. "You are accusing Orelia of being unfaithful to my brother. I find it hard to believe of her."

"Why, Richard? You know how desperately she wanted a child." Inspiration struck. "For that matter, so did John. They may well have agreed to an indiscretion so that she could get with child. With John to claim it as his own, no one could or would dispute the child's legitimacy."

"No one should dispute it now."

Determined to manipulate her husband to her will, she tried another tack. "You are very loyal to your sister-in-law, Richard." She tapped two fingers against her cheek. "Perhaps the child is yours."

Richard strode to her and raised his hand to strike her. But he let his hand fall as he said, "That's a ridiculous accusation and you know it. If you count the months, it is plain that the child could very well be John's. You go too far, Alice, with your accusations. My brother was a man of honor, and so am I."

"Yes, and what will you get for it? The opportunity to guard a property that will be given to some other man's child. Not your own kin, but a stranger's seed."

She could see from his expression that her seed of doubt had taken root. She would feed it until he believed her, believed that Radbourne was in danger of being inherited by a child of outside blood.

She softened her voice. "Richard, we may yet have a son. We mustn't take the chance of denying a true Radbourne of the title." He started to protest and she interrupted him. "It is easy to step aside for Orelia's child when we have only a daughter. But, I, too, am expecting, and this time it may be a boy."

It was a lie; she wasn't pregnant. But she must get him to see this her way. She could entice him into her chamber and get with child again. Indeed, she would do so. She must bear him a son or all was lost. She must ensure that a Radbourne—her son—would carry on the name.

He came to her and held her hands. "Are you feeling well this time?"

"Yes, quite well. Are you happy, Richard?"

He gazed at her with obvious concern and yet, a tug of doubt lingered. "Of course. I simply worry that this is too soon after losing the last babe."

THE MARK OF SALVATION

"I will be fine, Richard." She placed her hand over her empty womb. "I will do my best to produce a son this time."

He hung his head and she smiled in victory.

"What shall we do about Orelia, then?" he asked.

She sensed that he now harbored the hope of his own son becoming earl one day. Still, Alice knew of his respect for Orelia. She would tread carefully. "I know that it is difficult for you to believe badly of Orelia. I myself prefer to think that she and John agreed to this deceit. But it is possible that she was mistreated in Scotland and would rather believe the child is John's than face revealing her ordeal."

John stared at her. "I never considered such a thing, but it is possible. Poor Orelia."

Alice wanted to shout in victory. The seeds of doubt were in full bloom now. "When the child is born we will put it about that both died in childbirth. Tragic, but these things do happen."

"You . . . you mean to harm them?"

Clearly Alice's husband wasn't made of stiff cloth. She would have to be the strong one. "No, of course not. We can keep them imprisoned here at Radbourne—no one need ever know of their continued existence." Alice doubted they could actually do this, but insisting on killing the pair at this moment would only make Richard resist her. Best to reveal that part of her plan at a later date.

"All right, I'll agree to this unless the child favors John. If so, we will accept his parentage and I will acknowledge him as heir."

"By all means, Richard." But Alice had no intention of accepting Orelia's child, whether or not he favored John. All Alice need do was produce a son for Richard, and the poor sot would do whatever she asked of him. Their son would be the next earl.

CEALLACH RETURNED TO DUNSTRUAN a few days after seeing Orelia safely to the English border. For several days Ceallach busied himself with overseeing preparations for winter, although in truth the steward and his wife could handle such details perfectly well without him.

When staying busy didn't remove his melancholy, he went one afternoon to the weaver's hut. The *brecan* cloth that he and Orelia had designed awaited finishing. As he sat at the loom, sliding the shuttle back and forth and working the pedals in the proper sequence, Ceallach's thoughts drifted. The light in the hut seemed dim and he stopped weaving to go outside and see if the autumn sun had gone behind a cloud.

It had not. He returned to the loom and his thoughts went back to Orelia and her sunny hair and smile. A wave of longing now shadowed him, and he realized that he missed her. They had shared a comfortable companionship here in this small hut not unlike what he and Peter had once shared.

But of course, his feelings for Orelia ran in a much different direction than what he'd felt for Peter. Aye, his emotional tie to the woman combined with a physical yearning scared him almost as much as the thought of lighting a fire.

He reached to tamp down the row of yarn and nearly cursed. He'd pressed the fourth pedal when he should have pressed the second, and the last half dozen rows of the design were wrong. He would have to tear out the work and start again. Disgusted with his inattention and certainly not at all soothed by it, he dropped his shuttle into the tool tray and stared into the unlit fire.

A scratching sound pulled Ceallach from his reverie and he turned to find Keifer standing in the doorway. "May I come in?"

The boy's quiet entry let Ceallach know that Keifer felt as lost as he looked. "Of course. You don't look too pleased with yourself today."

Keifer stood next to Ceallach and heaved a dramatic sigh. "Morrigan says I must go to Moy in the spring."

"Aye. We talked about this before. Adam Mackintosh will foster you."

"But I want to stay here with you."

Ceallach wanted to hug the boy for saying so. But Keifer stood ready to take another step toward the man he would become and Ceallach resisted the urge to give comfort. "I would like that, too, Keifer. But you must do what your sister thinks best."

Ceallach suspected that much of the boy's reluctance came from a fear of the unknown. "When it's time, I'll go with you and stay at Moy until you are settled."

Keifer's eyes shone. "Really?"

"Aye. Rest your mind." Ceallach found it easy to make such a promise—there was nothing holding him at Dunstruan. Indeed, maybe he'd just keep heading north when he left Moy.

Keifer walked over to the loom and ran his hands across the cloth. "Are you going to finish this?"

Ceallach looked at the wrongly woven section. "Aye. I promised Lady Radbourne."

"I liked her."

Ceallach swallowed. "I liked her too."

Keifer said, "This last part isn't right."

Ceallach began to remove the threads. "I know. Will you help me fix it?"

"Sure." Deftly Keifer pulled the weft threads back through the warp. "Before she left I helped the lady finish the belt she was working on. She told me our hearts are like this cloth."

Intrigued, Ceallach asked, "What did she mean?"

Keifer shrugged a shoulder. "She said if you make the weave tight enough, water can't get through to get you wet. But when it's that tight the light can't get through either. She made it sound like that wasn't good."

Ceallach smiled as he pictured Orelia making such an analogy for the boy. No doubt, knowing Keifer, she had felt sure the boy would share that bit of wisdom for Ceallach's benefit. "Lady Radbourne is a very wise woman."

"And pretty too."

"Aye, and pretty too."

They worked together on the cloth for three days until it was finished. Ceallach and Keifer removed the material from the loom. With Suisan's help they fashioned it into plaids for each of them. A smaller piece became a woman's shawl. This Ceallach tucked away in his saddlebag, taking comfort in the thought of riding to England and giving it to Orelia. Yet fully aware that he could not.

Weeks passed and Ceallach could not find peace anywhere at Dunstruan because the vision of a blond-haired Englishwoman followed him everywhere.

Finally, he told Fergus and Morrigan he had to go to Dunfermline to serve the king. They assured him that Innishewan would not be finished before next fall and they would gladly remain at Dunstruan. After promising Keifer he would return in the spring to take him to Moy, Ceallach rode in the direction of his king.

The decision gave him peace of mind. When he arrived at the abbey, Bruce was glad to see him and found work for him to do. For the first time since the prisoner exchange, Ceallach slept well.

But he dreamed of Dunstruan.

ROBERT THE BRUCE looked at his fragile, unsmiling daughter, the heir to the Scottish crown. As a twelve-year-old child, she had spent the first months of her imprisonment in England hanging in an open cage on the wall of the Tower of London. Rage and hatred for Edward I of England, the current king's father, filled Robert as he envisioned this cruelty to his child.

When even Edward's own subjects had complained of his treatment of a child, Marjory had been taken to a nunnery in Walton and kept in near isolation for the past eight years. She had not been allowed to talk to anyone. As a result she was quite shy and rarely voiced an opinion. Hardly suitable traits for ruling a country as fractious as Scotland. And after all she'd been through, he wished to spare her more heartache—would do anything to see her happy.

He held out his hand and she came to him. "Come, sit down. I have something I must talk to you about."

She did as he asked and even smiled at him. He returned the smile and said, "Marjory, you are heir to the throne of Scotland."

She shrank back into her chair. "I know." She sounded less than enthusiastic, relieving him of the possibility that she coveted the throne.

"I see the thought doesn't give you pleasure."

"Nay, Father. But I will do my duty."

"That is what I want to talk to you about. My brother Edward has fought alongside me to win our country's freedom. He feels that he has earned a stake in who should govern Scotland when I die."

She looked at him sadly. "Are you ill?"

He smiled at her concern. "No, I am not, other than the malady that lays me low now and then. I am well, but you . . . I worry about your health, Marjory. You are not strong, and I would not wish upon you the burdens of ruling. I would rather see you take a husband, someone who could make you happy and give you a normal life. God knows you've had little enough of that."

Marjory's mother, Isabella of Mar, had died shortly after the girl was born. Bruce had married Elizabeth de Burgh when Marjory was eight, and the two had gotten on well enough. Those first four years of their marriage had been fraught with danger and intrigue, and he'd seen little of his daughter. He did not know her well at all. "Tell me, do you fancy any of the young men you've met?"

Her smile was shy. "You will laugh."

"No, I promise. I want only to make you happy, if it is within my power. I won't deny you, child."

"Walter the Steward has been kind to me."

She blushed and Bruce wondered just what form this kindness had taken. He would speak to Walter. But to his daughter he only said, "Walter is several years younger than you but I have never found him wanting. Is . . . has he . . . does he return your regard?"

"Yes."

"Then no doubt Walter will soon be coming to speak to me. That brings me back to the issue at hand."

"I don't want it, Father. Give the crown to Uncle."

"How will Walter feel about that?"

Angrily she said, "It won't change his feelings."

Glad to see that spark of life, Robert said, "If that is true, and Walter asks for you, you shall have my blessing."

"But what of the succession, Father?"

"I will call for a parliament to settle the succession on your Uncle Edward, should Elizabeth and I not have a son."

Marjory's relief showed plainly that Robert had made the right decision.

January 1315

SLEET PELTED THE WINDOW of her chamber on the late January day that Orelia and John's son was born. As she held him for the first time, tears poured down her face. The birth had been later than she'd calculated—it seemed that she might have conceived on that last night with John rather than earlier as she'd thought.

But John's son looked healthy and whole and she praised God for the babe's safe delivery. That was all that mattered.

"What will ye name him?" Mary, her maid asked.

Mary had been her maid since before Orelia's marriage. A more loyal and constant friend could not be found, and Orelia was grateful to have the woman attend her and her son.

"Iain."

"'Tis a strange name, my lady. Where did ye find it?"

"It is Gaelic for John, for truly God has been gracious in giving this child to comfort me."

"Aye, that he has." She reached for the child but Orelia held him away from the woman.

"Ye need to rest, lady. I'll see to the babe."

Orelia was tired, but she feared for her son and didn't know why. "Mary, please grant a new mother a boon. Don't take the child from this room unless I am with you."

Mary looked alarmed. "What is it? What do you fear?"

"I don't know. I . . . oh, I'm probably being foolish. But I don't trust Lady Alice."

Mary nodded. "Nothing foolish about it. I don't trust her none either."

Orelia breathed a sigh of relief. "We will keep that opinion to ourselves, Mary. But we must be vigilant with Iain."

Mary took the child and kissed his precious cheek. "None shall hurt this wee one without harming me first," she said fiercely.

With that assurance, Orelia gratefully slipped into a much needed sleep.

And dreamed of Dunstruan.

Thirteen

Brothers shall wear their hair cut short and are
not permitted to shave.

—from the Rule of the Templar Knights

T*is spring and I returned to Dunstruan as I promised Keifer. I went with him to Moy and stayed several weeks. But I didn't head north as threatened. Dunstruan called to me, and I returned there to help with the lambing. The sheep remind me of that day at the lake with Orelia.*

Everything at Dunstruan seems to remind me of her and of the fact that her child must be several months old by now. I had hoped she would send me word of her safe delivery, but I've heard nothing. Which is as it should be. What would her dead husband's family think if she sent word to a man in Scotland? They would think the worst of her, and much as I long to know that she is well, I want her happiness more.

TRUE TO HIS WORD, Robert the Bruce called for a parliament in April 1315 at St. John's Kirk in Ayr to settle the succession to the Scottish throne. Ceallach and Bryan accompanied the king to the church where they greeted James Douglas; Thomas Randolph; the king's brother, Edward; and Marjory's betrothed husband, Walter the Steward.

Ceallach entered one of the private solars of the kirk where the meeting was to take place. Most of the participants had already arrived. While many stood in the back of the room, Bruce's inner circle took seats at a huge table made from a slab of what must have been a gigantic tree. The tabletop had been polished smooth and reflected the sun that came in through the kirk's stained glass windows.

Bruce waved Ceallach to an open seat next to Bryan Mackintosh. Bruce called the meeting to order. "Gentlemen, in the interest of ensuring the smooth transition of power when I die, our first order of business is to settle the succession of the crown. My daughter, Marjory, is the heir presumptive to Scotland's throne, and I am pleased to announce her betrothal to Walter the Steward."

Shocked silence followed the king's announcement. Ceallach suspected that a number of the men present may have harbored the hope of wedding their own sons to the king's daughter and thus to the crown. Everyone stared at young Walter, a lad of just eighteen, who'd beaten out all of the competition for Marjory and her inheritance.

The glowering looks were impossible to ignore. Bruce stared back before saying, "You might offer congratulations, gentlemen."

A chorus of less than enthusiastic toasts were offered.

Walter stood and addressed the king. "If I may, sire?"

"Of course."

Walter cleared his throat. He appeared understandably nervous to address so many of his elders. "It is true that the king has given me his blessing to marry Marjory. But your unspoken fears that I seek the crown through her are unfounded. I have no aspirations to marry a queen. I want only to serve my liege, King Robert, and to make Marjory happy."

James Douglas said, "Marjory has not had a normal life. None would fault her for wanting some happiness and peace." He looked at Walter, who nodded his agreement and sat down, visibly relieved.

Bruce placed his hand on Walter's shoulder, patted it, then pointed at the assembled nobles. "Our continuing war with England requires a firm hand on the helm of state. I have spoken with Marjory, and she and I agree that she does not have the disposition to rule. Nor does she have the desire."

"What do you propose, then, Your Majesty?" Thomas Randolph asked.

"I have advised Marjory to waive her rights in favor of my brother, Edward. He is experienced in the art of war and leadership. If I should die without a legitimate male heir, the crown would pass first to Edward, then to his sons. Failing this, it would pass to Marjory and Walter's heirs."

Heads nodded.

Douglas asked, "What if the succession falls to a minor child?"

Bruce looked at Bryan, a man who was, in reality, Bruce's oldest child, born out of wedlock while Bruce was still in his teens. "Then I propose Sir Bryan Mackintosh, Earl of Homelea, to act as regent until the child comes of age."

There was a great deal of loud discussion at the table and in the audience as all eyes turned to the man sitting next to Ceallach. Few would deny that Bryan had earned respect as a warrior and a man of wisdom. If he were to advocate his claim to Scotland's crown as Bruce's only male child, many would support him simply because of his excellent reputation.

But the legitimacy of Bruce's crown was already in question by his detractors—would Bryan add fuel to the fires of discontent or strengthen his father's grip on the throne?

Bryan stood and cleared his throat. The crowd hushed in anticipation. "Thank you, Your Majesty. You honor me with your trust in presenting me for such a critical position. But if I were to step so close to the throne, I might very well weaken it. I would not give your enemies any reason to disparage your legitimate heirs and their claim to the crown."

There was a stunned silence before Bryan continued. "May I suggest your nephew, Thomas Randolph, as a more suitable regent. He and I are of the same age and experience, but no one can dispute his right to guide the throne of Scotland."

Bryan sat down amidst hushed conversation throughout the room. Ceallach marveled that Bruce had made such a public bid for power for his illegitimate son. And even more at the young man's wisdom and diplomacy in refusing the position.

No one seemed to want to disagree with their king, no matter what their assessment of the situation. Yet someone must. Quietly, Ceallach spoke. "He's right, Robert. There's not a one of us here who doesn't think highly of Bryan, but Thomas is a better choice."

Ceallach saw Bruce struggle within himself, struggle with his love for his son and his duty as king.

Finally, Bruce nodded. "You are right, of course."

Ceallach could almost hear a collective sigh of relief from the audience. Robert had proven himself to be a valiant warrior and brilliant general during wartime. He had just shown his nobles that he would also rule wisely in times of peace.

Bruce turned to Randolph. "Thomas, will you accept this responsibility?"

"Aye, my laird. I am honored by your trust."

Bruce looked at Bryan, and Ceallach saw pride mixed with regret cross the king's face. Then he took a deep breath, as if putting the issue to rest. Bruce sought out his brother. "Edward, is this act of succession agreeable to you?"

"Aye, brother. It is."

"Good. And with the rest of you?"

The room resounded with votes of affirmation. No one raised an argument against the plan. Robert, looking far more relaxed with that business finished, said, "I will have the succession papers drawn up so all of you can sign them before this parliament adjourns. Now, there is other business we must consider. The English have been levying Ireland to provide supplies and manpower for their fight against us."

"And they've complied?" one of the nobles asked.

"What choice do they have? The people of Ireland are suffering, as we have suffered, from the heavy hand of English power. I have received an appeal from the O'Neills, the royal line of Ulster, requesting my aid and offering the throne of Ireland to my brother, Edward, if we will assist them against the English. Perhaps it is time for the Celtic peoples to unite against their common foe."

Edward Bruce stood up. "If we unite with the Irish we can threaten Edward with our ability to launch a combined army against the west of England. This might well be what it takes to force Edward to recognize my brother and bring peace to Scotland."

Bruce said, "I propose that we send an expeditionary force to Ireland under my brother's command. He will seek out those who support such an Irish-Scottish union."

There was some lively discussion as to the best way to support their Irish brethren, but in the end all agreed to Bruce's plan. Clearly Ceallach's colleagues were determined to have Bruce recognized as their chosen king. They would do whatever it took to bring Edward of England to that admission.

Ceallach volunteered to accompany Edward Bruce to Ireland. Not only could he serve his king, but the activity and distance from Dunstruan might finally bring an end to his preoccupation with Orelia Radbourne.

IAIN WAS A HEALTHY CHILD, praise God. But his downy reddish hair was a legacy from Orelia's grandmother. What a time for it to surface with John not here to defend his heir! Alice, large with child, smirked each time she saw the boy.

When Alice was delivered of a healthy male child in late July, Orelia feared that Alice might voice aloud her accusation that Iain was not John's child.

While Alice was still abed after the baby's birth, Orelia left Iain in Mary's care and went in search of her brother-in-law. She found him in the solar at his desk, the ornate monstrosity that had replaced John's. Orelia was determined to win him to her side once and for all and remove his wife's unspoken threat. Richard was a fair, level-headed man. She simply needed to make her case, appeal to his love for his brother, to his honor.

He beckoned her to come in, and she walked across the new carpet and stood before him. He continued to peruse the parchment he was holding. But she would not be intimidated by his rudeness. She sat down in the chair before the desk. "Richard, have you received word from Edward making you Iain's guardian? I would be relieved to know that I will have your wise assistance in guiding the affairs of the estate."

Deliberately he set the paper aside. "I'm afraid I've had to send a second missive to Edward apprising him of all the facts of the case."

Orelia strove to hide her agitation. She smoothed her skirt and as calmly as she could, she said, "Of what facts do you speak?"

Richard's expression became condescending. "We both know that my brother was unable to have children. We both know that John's hair was dark like my own. Obviously your child is the product of an unfortunate incident which you are understandably reluctant to reveal."

She stared at him. "Incident?"

John shuffled papers on the desk in front of him. "There is no need to distress yourself, Orelia. The child was obviously conceived within days of my brother's death, when you were first held captive. Frankly I'm saddened that you insist otherwise, but I can understand why you would want to believe the child is John's."

Indignant at his implication she jumped up from the chair. "This *is* John's child! How can you think I would lie with another man?"

"I don't think you would willingly do so, Orelia. Of course not. Obviously, you were mistreated during your stay in Scotland and the child is the result. But I'll not have some Scottish by-blow inherit my family's estate and wealth."

She placed her hands on the desk and leaned forward. "The child was conceived just before John died, Richard."

"Perhaps. But he'd not fathered a child before—what are the chances it could've happened in those last days? And then there is the additional issue of the boy's red hair."

With fraying patience and growing apprehension, she said, "My grandmother was Scottish, Richard, and she had red hair. That is where Iain's hair color comes from."

Richard stood up, towering over the desk, over her. "Because of the love I hold for you and my sympathy for your misfortune, I won't turn you or your . . . child out. My brother would not want that."

She straightened and smacked her hand on the top of the desk. "Your brother would want you to recognize his son!"

"If you become hysterical I shall change my mind. We cannot have hysterical women at Radbourne Hall. It isn't good for any of the children." He perused the document he'd been reading. "If you remain calm and quiet, I will allow you to stay. You and . . . Iain will be well cared for and will want for nothing."

Fighting tears of frustration she said, "Nothing except Iain's inheritance."

"Don't be difficult, Orelia. To be clear, if you are not compliant, I will publicly denounce you and set you on the street to earn your living. As it is, to avoid scandal, Alice and I agree that you should live quietly here at Radbourne."

Alice had put Richard up to this, Orelia was sure. But how could Orelia possibly overcome Alice's hold over her husband? He was even more besotted—and deceived—by Alice now that she'd borne Richard a son.

"You needn't bother yourself. I'll take my son to live at Bolton in my grandmother's cottage."

"No, I'm afraid that won't be possible."

"Am I your prisoner?"

"In a manner of speaking, yes. I regret the necessity, but Alice is adamant that your behavior should not reflect poorly upon us."

"If you truly believe this is not John's child, why don't you just send us away?"

"I will honor my brother's love for you."

"You mean it would reflect poorly on you and Alice if we did not stay."

"I will honor my brother's love for you," he repeated.

She gave one parting shot. "You would honor your brother more if you didn't want his title so badly that you would cheat his son of it."

"Enough! You will stay in the cottage beyond the garden. You will not leave Radbourne without permission. Do I make myself clear?"

"I shall petition the king!"

"Don't bother. I have already informed him of the unfortunate treatment you received in Scotland and the resulting child. Edward will not come to your rescue. Resign yourself to a quiet life at Radbourne."

Orelia could think of no other argument that might sway Richard. The injustice of it! She shook with rage. But for now she must do as he demanded. Somehow she would find a way to get the title back for John's son. She would not rest until she had. "May I take Mary with me?"

"Of course. And Orelia? Don't try to leave or I'll lock you in the room in the tower."

Trembling, Orelia went to her room and to the chest that held Ceallach's parchment. Opening the lid, she reached in and fingered the paper. She needed a male champion, someone to vouch for her time in Scotland. Should she send for Ceallach? But would Richard believe him? Surely not, and Orelia could not endanger Ceallach, especially when there was so little hope of changing Richard's, or Alice's, mind.

She would have to bide her time. She thought of the strong resemblance in looks between John and Richard. Would Iain's hair turn color? Or would he grow to look enough like John to make a case for his claim? And if not? What if the boy continued to favor Orelia's side of the family?

If he continued to favor her grandmother, then he would never be the Earl of Radbourne and all would be lost.

THE ROAD LEADING TO DUNFERMLINE ABBEY was lined with wedding guests on an overcast day. Robert the Bruce stood on the steps of the church with Walter the Steward, his daughter's young bridegroom. Remembering his own anxious thoughts at his wedding to Elizabeth de Burgh, Robert sought to calm the man. Yet when he took stock, Walter appeared perfectly at ease.

"Are you nervous?" Bruce asked.

Walter shook his head. "I know that Marjory is God's choice for my wife. Maybe I'll be nervous later, tonight." He blushed.

Bruce refrained from chuckling at the boy's admission. Instead he said sincerely, "If you love her and tell her so, all will go well."

Walter swallowed and his Adam's apple bobbed. "You've been married twice. Were you nervous?"

"Oh, aye. The first time, I had the same fears as you. I especially worried that I wouldn't know how to please her. But you will find your way. Together."

Walter nodded and Bruce continued. "Marjory is much like her mother—fragile and rather meek. But she must have an inner strength to match my own or she would never have survived the deprivations of her imprisonment."

"I have sensed that." Walter looked down at his feet, then raised his head and looked Bruce in the eye. "I admire her greatly, my laird."

"And I am pleased that she has chosen her husband so wisely, Walter."

The rain that had plagued Scotland for most of the past three weeks had taken a rest, although the skies remained gray and threatening. Robert just hoped the weather would hold off until all were safely indoors.

Trumpets sounded and both men took their cue, looking up to see Marjory coming toward them astride a white horse. Robert's heart stopped at the sight of his child in her wedding finery. The people lining the road were throwing rose petals in her path, showering the bride with color.

The perfume of the flowers wafted subtly on the air and Robert glanced to where his wife stood. They exchanged a knowing look, a look filled with the memory of their own vows, of Elizabeth's ride to meet her groom. Robert remembered his joy at knowing that she was his to love. That same feeling was reflected on Walter's face, and Bruce relaxed. Marjory had indeed chosen well.

The horse stopped and Marjory's friends helped her to dismount. They draped the train of her dress behind her and led her to stand before the two men. Marjory gave her hand to her father and he raised it to his lips and kissed it. Then he joined the young couple's hands together, giving over his daughter into the young man's care.

Bruce was glad to see his daughter well wed. It seemed that

Walter indeed cared for her—he wasn't put off by her shyness or lack of beauty. Indeed, he catered to her every wish, and it gladdened Robert's heart to see it.

The two exchanged their vows on the steps in front of the crowd. Then everyone adjourned into the abbey to celebrate the wedding mass.

How could it be that his daughter was twenty years old and a woman grown? Bruce sat beside his wife and held her hand, wondering where the years had fled. The years of hardship and denial had aged Elizabeth, but she remained beautiful. Now in her thirtieth year, she despaired of giving him a child. She insisted that the fault lay with her, that Marjory and Bryan were proof of that.

Perhaps she was right. But Robert had not given up hope; he prayed daily that God would bless them as he had Sarah and Abraham.

NEARLY TWO YEARS after Bannockburn, Edward of England still refused to acknowledge Robert the Bruce as the rightful king of Scotland. Orelia wasn't surprised when she heard that Bruce had taken to raiding northern England again in retaliation. She knew that Radbourne Hall was situated far enough north that Bruce might come there. But the estate lay in a sheltered valley, and Richard assured everyone that the Scots would not find them.

Orelia's enforced stay at Radbourne had been a subdued, daily trial. But when she heard of Bruce's raids she thought of Ceallach and wondered if he might come to England with his king. And if so, might he come to Radbourne? How she longed to leave this place that had become a prison.

Orelia sat at the loom in the weaving hut Richard had built adjacent to her cottage. As she passed the shuttle back and forth her mind seemed to weave its own tapestry of recent events. The spring and summer after Iain's birth had been unusually wet and that year's harvest was poor. Fortunately, the previous harvests had been abundant, and Radbourne had a good supply of grain in storage.

Orelia passed the shuttle through another time and pulled the beater bar down to tighten the weave. The wet weather remained, and she was weaving a tight, woolen cloth to shield them from the rain. But unlike the checkered cloth she'd woven with Ceallach at Dunstruan, this cloth was a dark blue with only a faint red stripe in it. Plain, like Orelia's life.

She shook off her melancholy and resumed passing the shuttle through the open shed of the warp. Last October had marked the one-year anniversary of Orelia's departure from Scotland, and she fought to repress the memory of Ceallach as he watched her leave. If she'd known then how much she would miss him, would she have gone?

She didn't know the answer to that question. Some days she was sure she would have stayed in Scotland—coming back had accomplished nothing except imprisonment. But as long as she remained in England she might be able to restore Iain's inheritance. When he was old enough to defend himself from Richard and Alice's accusations, Orelia would take Iain to London to see the king.

But for now she took pleasure in the milestones of raising her child. A few months ago, Orelia and Mary had celebrated Iain's first birthday in the small stone cottage where they lived in quiet obscurity.

They'd had another wet spring and summer. The weather and the enforced exile combined to make Orelia restless. With each passing day, Orelia prayed that her brother-in-law and his wife would release her. But Alice's behavior since the birth of her own son had been erratic, and Richard did nothing that would upset his wife.

The days passed and Orelia concentrated on taking delight in her child. The child whose red-tinged dark hair and laughing blue eyes so reminded her of John. His paternity became clearer with each passing day. Did Richard not see it?

FOURTEEN

Dormitory lights shall remain burning throughout the night to discourage unnatural behavior.

—from the Rule of the Templar Knights

I *am tired of fighting and I want to go home. How many soldiers have written those words over the ages, I wonder? I've been fighting in Ireland this past year as it seems not all the Irish share Bruce's desire for a united Gaelic army. But with our latest victory here in Kildare, the last of the Irish resistance is overcome. Edward Bruce will soon be crowned High King of Ireland. Now we need not fear that Ireland will fall to England's power; Scotland's western seaboard will be protected.*

I cannot imagine these tidings will bring Robert much joy, under the circumstances. News of his daughter's death reached us just a few hours ago. My prayers are with him and Walter and the babe. No one seems to know if it was a boy or girl.

Aye, I am praying again. I have not decided for sure that anyone is listening, but prayer seems to give me the peace for which I've been searching. Peace that I have found nowhere else. Perhaps that is proof enough that God exists.

CEALLACH WAS NEARLY AS GLAD to be back in Scotland this time as he'd been after his escape from France. The past year in Ireland fighting against his fellow Gaels had made him anxious to return to

Dunstruan and take up the life of a rural sheep farmer. He'd had time enough away from the place that the memories of Orelia shouldn't haunt him. Or so he hoped.

But before he went home he wanted to pay his respects to Bruce. He went to Dunfermline, and soon after arriving he faced his foster brother in the privacy of the king's solar. They sat in comfortable chairs before the fire. A servant brought refreshments and closed the door behind him when he left.

Once they were alone, Ceallach said, "I am truly sorry about Marjory's death, Robert. How did it happen?"

Bruce looked pained. "A fall from a horse. She was not the best of horsewomen." He stopped. "When it became apparent she would not live the surgeon was called. He . . . had to cut the child from her as soon as she died."

Ceallach closed his eyes and thought of young Walter the Steward. What a horrible decision for a husband to have to make. "And the babe?"

"A boy. Healthy except for an injury to his leg, either from the fall or from the surgeon. Walter has been quite distressed, as you may imagine."

The talk of childbearing reminded Ceallach of Orelia, and again he wondered how she had fared in delivering her child. The child would be nearly a year and a half old by now. Ceallach forced his thoughts back to the present.

Robert asked, "What news do you bring from Ireland's new king?"

"Your brother sends you greetings. He still must subdue a few more Irish chieftains but essentially he is in command of the country."

"Good. I hope this gives him the contentment he's searched for. I love my brother, but Scotland truly is too small for the two of us." He set his glass down and tapped his fingertips together several times. "I've decided to raid England again, Ceallach. Would you like to come along?"

This surprised Ceallach. He'd thought the raids were over. "What has Edward done to anger you this time?"

"He still doesn't acknowledge me as the rightful king of Scotland. Says I'm a propped up puppet with no support from my people. I thought I'd show him the reach of my 'propped up' government by harassing his subjects."

Ceallach considered whether or not he would go with Robert or return to Dunstruan. "When do you plan to leave?"

"I can wait until you've had time to see to things at Dunstruan."

"How far south do you expect to raid this time?"

"At least to Ripon, if not further."

Ripon, Ceallach knew, was less than a day north of Radbourne Hall. Perhaps he could inquire after Orelia's welfare. Or even see her. He shook his head to rid it of such a fanciful thought. He would do nothing to jeopardize her life or that of her child. He just needed to know they were well and safe.

"Aye, I'll go with you."

A messenger called Robert away, and Ceallach stood in the solar and stared at a painting hanging on the wall. He smiled, remembering when it had been painted, the year Ceallach joined the Bruce household as a foster son. Robert's stern father had threatened them with a thrashing if they so much as moved during the sitting. The warning had been needed—he had followed Robert into any number of rousing adventures.

Just as he was about to do again.

ORELIA SAT ON A WOODEN BENCH in the small garden behind her cottage at Radbourne, watching Iain play. She took advantage of the listless summer sun this morning to be outdoors for a change. Iain ran about on sturdy legs, chasing after a butterfly that flitted cooperatively amongst the rock-strewn paths.

Iain was the image of his father, and Orelia's heart clenched at what John was missing—at what the child was missing by not knowing his father. Nearly two years after John's death, Orelia could only conjure the image of his face when she looked at their son. Her memories about what he had been like were fading as well, and she'd begun to tell Iain stories to help her remember.

The cottage had proven very agreeable. A path led to the main house, but was quite overgrown with grass, as only the servants who brought food and other supplies used it.

Though hard to imagine, Orelia had not stepped foot in Radbourne Hall for nearly a year, nor had Alice come to the cottage. Richard visited regularly to make sure they were quite comfortable and faring well. His visits were surprisingly pleasant; she sensed that he came to the cottage to escape Alice's sharp tongue as much as he did out of duty.

But otherwise Orelia might as well have lived miles away. The arrangement suited Orelia just fine, although she feared that as Iain grew older, the confines of the cottage would not be sufficient. She must speak to Richard. It was time to resume some semblance of normal life; to visit her old acquaintances, to find new friends. Her grief was at last subsiding, and it was time to think upon the future. Surely Richard did not intend to keep up this charade; Iain was clearly a Radbourne and must take his rightful place some day. In the meantime, Orelia needed to return to her own life as well.

The scrabble of pebbles on the garden path drew her attention and she looked up as Mary walked into the garden. The maid wrung her hands, her expression anxious. "My lady, the earl and countess are walking down the path. They'll be here in a few minutes."

Orelia stood up from the bench. She went to Mary and laid a hand on her arm in reassurance. "Take Iain inside and I'll see what we have in the way of refreshments." Mary glanced down knowingly and Orelia clasped the material of her skirt to hide her trembling hands.

Richard and Alice coming together to visit? Were they here to at last acknowledge Iain as John's heir or did they have darker intentions?

Mary took the toddler by the hand. Iain protested at being separated from the butterfly he was chasing, but Mary deftly distracted him with the promise of a sweet. "Come, let's wash your face and make you look a proper gentleman for your aunt and uncle."

"Thank you, Mary." Orelia followed them into the cottage. She put water over the fire to heat and readied her meager store of tea to offer refreshment. The wet spring weather hindered the growth of herbs as well as crops, and supplies for tea were dwindling.

Soon the sound of footsteps announced her guests, and Orelia carried Iain outside to greet Richard and Alice. Even for such an informal visit, they were dressed as if they were visiting royalty. Clearly their new station in life suited them.

They were followed by their sullen, five-year-old daughter, Anna, and a maid carrying a child that must be young Richard, six months younger than Iain. Except for the reddish tints in Iain's dark hair, the boys could be brothers. Certainly no one would dispute that the two were cousins.

Richard allowed his gaze to go from one boy to the other and silently acknowledged the resemblance with a sigh. With a brief glance of malice toward Iain, Alice came forward and greeted Orelia with a kiss to the cheek and a false smile on her face.

A cold kiss of disaffection, like the one Judas gave the Lord. Orelia suppressed a shiver of dread. Her motherly intuition sensed danger for her son. Was she being foolish? Orelia didn't think so. As soon as possible she would pull Mary aside and warn her not to let Iain out of her sight.

Richard looked at the child in Orelia's arms and his expression showed his lack of ease. What was the purpose of this visit?

Orelia handed Iain to Mary. "Why don't you take the children into the garden?"

"No! Young Richard must stay with me!"

Alice's outburst shocked Orelia. "I'm sure the servants can watch—"

"My son is too delicate to play in the open air." Despite her obvious devotion to the boy, Alice made no move to take him from the maid and hold him.

"Alice," Richard said, his voice placating and patient. "Remember we came to talk to Orelia. We mustn't have little ears about."

Alice threw a cold look toward her husband, and Orelia was again surprised, this time by Alice's obvious animosity. Then she smiled warmly at him, changing her demeanor with frightening speed. "Yes, you are right. Go on, let the boys play together with Anna."

Alice's changeable moods had Orelia questioning the wisdom of letting Iain play with his cousin. But Mary could be trusted to watch over him so Orelia dismissed her misgivings. She cleared her throat. "How nice of you to visit." Orelia forced some warmth into her voice and invited her guests into the cottage.

Orelia served refreshments, then sat facing Richard and Alice before the fireplace in her tiny parlor. Orelia made small talk wondering how long it would take for Alice or Richard to reveal the reason for the visit. No one mentioned the similarity between the boys, but the knowledge seemed to hang in the air around them.

"The wet weather doesn't bode well for the crops again this year," Orelia commented.

Richard cleared his throat. "No, not at all."

Silence.

"I thank you, Richard, for allowing Iain and Mary and me to live in such a lovely place. We quite like it here. Although I do miss having visitors."

Silence.

Alice raised her cup of tea and sipped from it.

Orelia thought she detected a glazed appearance in Alice's eyes and wondered if the woman felt ill. Did Richard not notice how strangely the woman had behaved earlier?

Very deliberately, Alice set her cup down. "We are expecting visitors of our own soon but regretfully, you will not be joining us." She looked at Richard as if daring him to contradict her.

Richard explained. "We are having a celebration of young Richard's first birthday and have invited quite a few friends. From London."

His meaning was quite clear to Orelia, even without Alice's hostility. The guests must not see either her or Iain. If someone should happen to see Iain, they might remark upon his resemblance to his late father. Such a remark could very well be repeated—the idea of John's wife bearing him a child after his death would be an interesting topic of conversation that could eventually make its way to King Edward.

Richard could probably explain away his earlier assumption that the child was the result of "an unfortunate incident," as he'd put it. Few would doubt his word on that. But how would he explain that after seeing the child he continued to insist the child was not his brother's?

The answer would be obvious—they wanted the title. And while Orelia wasn't sure how convinced Richard was, Alice had never hidden her desire to have her own son become the earl.

But Iain would have to live long enough to be identified. Orelia's blood chilled at the thought. She considered confronting Richard and Alice with her suspicion, but feared their reaction.

Alice's facial expression became cool and she looked at Richard.

Some sort of understanding flowed between them. "The boys look nothing alike, Richard. I don't know what all your fussing is about."

Richard looked uncomfortable but remained silent.

Alice went on, "Still, Orelia and her . . . son must remain hidden until our celebration is over and the guests have left. I think they would be more secure in the main house."

Orelia couldn't believe Richard was nodding, agreeing with Alice's absurd statement. She did not want to stay in the main house. Here in her own little cottage she had control of her life and of Iain's. In Radbourne Hall, Alice controlled and manipulated the inhabitants. Who knew what Alice might do in order to remain the Countess of Radbourne?

Panic nearly undid Orelia. She must dissuade them, if only for a short time. "That isn't necessary. I will ensure that your guests don't even know anyone is in this cottage. There is no need for us to stay in the Hall."

With calm assurance, Richard set down his cup. "I'm afraid I must insist."

Orelia's cup rattled as she placed it on the bench beside her. "If Iain isn't John's child, why concern yourself with what your friends think?"

Richard eyed his wife. "Come, Orelia. Surely you can see that the child looks like John, just as I do. But everyone . . ." He seemed to search for the right words and failing, simply looked away to the window, misery on his face.

"Everyone believes that you both died," Alice put in. "We can't have your ghosts scaring our visitors."

"Wh—what?" Orelia fought for breath. "You've told everyone I *died*?"

Alice rose. "We had to tell them something. There were too many inquiries." A catlike smile grew across her face. "The whisper of a horrible illness, spreading like wildfire in Scotland, and how you apparently succumbed to it explained your quick demise and the reason we did not have a public burial. People were actually relieved to have not been exposed."

Alice bent, took a sip of her tea, and stared at her husband but spoke to Orelia. "Your son will never take his father's place at Radbourne. It belongs to young Richard."

Not bothering to hide her trembling, Orelia stood. She was enraged and terrified at the same time. These people would do anything! They could kill her and Iain now at any time and no one would ever ask! How could she have become so cornered? How could she have been so foolish, thinking she could remain here and some day they would do the honorable thing?

"You . . . acknowledge Iain as John's son?"

"What difference does it make? The lie is told and I'm not about to have you return from the dead," Alice said.

Richard made a sound as if he was choking, and Alice gave him a sharp look.

Something wasn't right between these two, and again Orelia felt reluctant to leave the cottage. "So you will lock us away in the tower room?"

Richard looked directly at his wife before returning his gaze to Orelia. "You will remain in that room, yes. But if you give me your word to stay there, I won't lock you in."

Alice said, "Well, I think we should lock the door."

"Alice," Richard warned.

Alice stood abruptly. "Fine. Now that everything is settled to *Richard's* satisfaction, I shall leave." Alice stalked out the door.

Orelia considered trying to escape from Radbourne rather than submit to this new form of imprisonment. Richard and Alice might lock her away permanently. Or worse.

Richard shoved his hands through his hair. "Orelia, I'm sorry.

Please be patient with Alice. She has not been herself since the boy was born. I keep hoping she'll get better."

Richard's confession astonished Orelia, and his distress was not feigned, of that Orelia was certain. She felt as if she had been hit; her head spun. Was this man friend or foe? Was there still hope that he might do the right thing? That this was all Alice's idea? "She doesn't seem quite . . . rational, Richard. Have you talked to the healer?"

Richard stood and paced in the small space before Orelia's fire-place. "Yes. Alice is taking some potion that is supposed to calm her nerves but . . . you saw her. She is either angry or anxious, rarely at ease. And I fear for my son if she doesn't stop coddling and spoiling him."

Should she believe Richard? Or flee Radbourne? Everything in her said she should leave as soon as possible, that Alice meant her and her son harm. But Richard might be willing to protect her. "When your guests have left, will we be allowed to return to the cottage?"

"Yes, of course. I mean to right this wrong I've done to you and my brother's son, Orelia."

"What?" Astounded at his words, Orelia had to remind herself to close her mouth.

"Let me explain. When you first arrived home Alice convinced me that your child wasn't John's. She said at best you and John had agreed to allow someone else to father a child on you; at worst you'd been raped by some Scotsman."

Orelia couldn't find her voice to answer such an outrageous accusation. She stood and faced Richard, checking her desire to slap his face. "How dare you—"

"Calm down, Orelia. I'm trying to apologize for entertaining such thoughts. Although it pains me to admit it, if Iain didn't look so much like John, I might still believe Alice and not you."

"But you do believe me?"

"Yes."

Orelia shook her head in disbelief. "You will truly acknowledge Iain as John's heir? Even though you've told the king and everyone else that I died?"

Richard appeared chagrined. "I will throw myself on Edward's mercy, explain that I feared for my wife's . . ." He paused, put his hand to his forehead and rubbed it. "You've seen Alice. I fear for her mind. That will help explain our lie to some extent, but I am ready to face the consequences of my own actions."

"But why, Richard? What do you gain from this?"

Richard's expression became grim. "Even though I have not behaved as such, I am a man of honor and no one, not even my wife, will force me to continue in such a reprehensible fashion. But please, Orelia, I beg you not to say anything of this to Alice. I fear . . . I'm not sure what she'll do from one day to the next. Let me see to things."

"Would she harm the children?"

He swallowed so hard Orelia could see his Adam's apple bob. "I honestly don't know the answer to that. She has said she'd rather see Richard dead than see him denied the title."

Orelia gasped. "'Tis worse than I thought."

Once again he ran his fingers through his dark, wavy hair. "Much worse than I would have believed possible. I can't go to London to see Edward and leave her here unsupervised, so I've sent for Alice's cousin, George of Wellsey."

With delight she said, "John's squire." She hadn't seen George since he and John left the tent that day of the battle. "How is he? I had heard he suffered a wound at Bannockburn."

He waved his hand. "A minor injury—he's fine."

John had trusted George with his life, so Orelia felt sure she could trust George with Iain's.

"She's always been fond of the man, and he's agreed to watch over

205

things here while I go to London. He'll keep her calm while I see the king and locate an appropriate healer for Alice."

"Why not wait until Alice is better to see the king?"

"I have waited long enough. The lie doesn't get any easier to defend the longer it lives. Best to clear this up and see to Alice's malady afterward. Then you can resume your life, once you are brought back among the living."

He gave her a rueful smile, and again Orelia saw his resemblance to her dead husband. The likeness among the Radbourne men was truly uncanny. Irrefutable. Orelia stood and went to Richard, giving him a hug.

Though he resisted at first, he obviously needed comfort and soon wrapped his arms around her. "Can you move to the tower by tomorrow, Orelia? Placate her on this?"

"Yes, I will do it for you." She pulled away. "Thank you, Richard. For doing the right thing when it means losing so much."

He dropped his arms. "If I had only—"

"Let me finish. The title means little, but your acknowledgment of Iain as John's true son . . . your nephew . . ." She wiped away a tear. "That means all the world to me. Thank you."

"I am only sorry it has taken me so long. Just take care while you're in the house; keep away from my wife." He glanced outside. "I'd best go find her." Richard left the cottage and Orelia stared after him, lost in thought.

Smiling, she rose and carried the cups to the kitchen area of the small hut. Her prayers had been answered! Soon she and Iain would be free to live where they chose—Radbourne Hall or perhaps she would inquire about the availability of her grandmother's cottage near Bolton.

A scream split the quiet morning. A woman's scream.

Mary!

Orelia jumped up and nearly flew out the door in the direction of the pond.

She heard Mary shouting for her as she drew closer to the spot where a wooden pier jutted into the still waters of the fishing pond. Mary came running toward her, a wailing Iain in her arms. Not the worst, praise God.

"Oh, my lady. He fell on the pier and gashed his head." Mary stopped in front of her.

Blood poured from a cut on the child's forehead. Orelia gently pushed his hair back and took a closer look. The injury was not nearly as bad as the amount of blood indicated.

Someone came up behind her, and Orelia turned to see Richard, his expression questioning. Behind him Orelia could see Alice walking away from them and toward the cottage.

"Is he all right?" Richard asked. "Shall I carry him?"

"It's kind of you to offer, Richard, but I think Iain will resist going to anyone but me just now."

"Ah, yes. You're right. Shall I send for a healer?"

Orelia took her sobbing son from Mary and began to walk to the cottage. "No, Mary and I have the skill and supplies to take care of him." She smiled at Richard, grateful for his concern, especially in light of Alice's evident lack of the same.

Richard addressed Mary. "How did this happen?"

Orelia looked at Mary, but the woman would only repeat that Iain had fallen. Mary refused to look at Richard.

"I'm sure it was an accident, Richard." Although if that was true, why hadn't Alice stayed to reassure them? What was she trying to hide? Or was Orelia letting her imagination get away from her now that Richard had confessed to Alice's unbalanced behavior?

Richard watched his wife before saying to Orelia. "I'm going to take Alice home. Please send word if Iain requires anything, anything at all. Otherwise I'll see the three of you tomorrow."

Richard left while they tended to Iain, and Orelia observed Richard and Alice walk up the path to Radbourne. She and Mary took Iain inside and soon his wound was cleaned and bandaged. Mary took him to the bedchamber to change his bloodstained clothing.

Orelia followed them. When his clothing was changed she held him in her lap, something Iain rarely allowed anymore unless he was tired or in need of comfort. She kissed his forehead. In addition to the cut, he was scraped and bruised from his encounter with the wooden piling. But it could have been so much worse.

Mary fussed about them, bringing Iain his favorite toy and a cup of tea for Orelia. As she set the cup beside Orelia, Mary said, "I'm so sorry, my lady. I should have been more vigilant. I should never have let Lady Alice hold his hand."

Immediately alert, Orelia said, "*She* was holding him?"

Mary clasped and unclasped her hands. "'Twas Lady Alice's idea. I protested but she insisted."

Alice had insisted? "Are you sure it was an accident?"

Mary shook her head. "I'm not sure at all."

Suspicious she said, "What do you mean?"

"I can't swear to it, my lady—I was distracted for a moment. But I believe Lady Alice pushed the child. I grabbed him just in time to keep him from going in the water."

"Dear God in heaven."

Silence grew between them as each woman thought of the child being lost in the depths of the murky water.

The idea of living in closer proximity to Alice took on a more sinister cast. However, she'd promised Richard. "Mary, we must move to Radbourne Hall for a short time." She told Mary about Richard's plans.

"I'm glad to hear the man will make things right. But if we take Iain to Radbourne Hall, the lady may try to harm him again."

"I feel the same way. But I promised, so we must. If we do anything else, Alice might . . . We can trust no one but each other, Mary. I think that as soon as Richard returns with the king's seal on the paperwork we must leave Radbourne altogether."

Mary nodded. "Where will we go?"

"My grandmother's cottage is but a day's walk north. That is far enough away to be safe from Lady Alice and still close enough to be in touch with Richard."

"But until then we are to stay in the tower?"

"Yes. Richard said we won't be locked in, but we shall certainly lock Lady Alice out!"

Orelia placed the sleeping Iain in the cradle for a nap. He would soon outgrow the small bed, and she would not be able to rock him anymore. Mary left and Orelia sat down and rocked the cradle with her foot. The boy fussed and began to cry, and she realized the cradle was rocking in time to her agitated thoughts. Gently she pushed the cradle with her hand, soothing Iain back to sleep.

Yet her thoughts were anything but soothing. She stood up and went to the small casket where she kept the sealed parchment Ceallach had given her. *Do not open it unless you have need of me. When you read my words, you will know that I will help you no matter what your need.*

Did she need him? Was her situation desperate enough to ask Ceallach for help? No.

No matter what happened—and no matter that Orelia wanted to know what he'd written—she would never ask him to come to

England. She would not ask him to face the risk of capture, no matter what the parchment said. She put his letter back into the casket, unopened.

Orelia feared the worst was to come. She shuddered at the thought of spending the rest of her life—and Iain's—locked in a room at the top of Radbourne's tower. And if anything should happen to Richard, Orelia suspected that being locked up would be the least of her worries.

FIFTEEN

Brothers shall always travel in pairs when
outside the Order.

—from the Rule of the Templar Knights

I *have joined Bruce in another raid on England for purely
selfish reasons. I hope to get close enough to Radbourne to
obtain news about Orelia. I don't understand my feelings for
the woman. One would think that after all this time the
thought of her would not draw me so. Perhaps knowing she is
well and happy will put my fears—and my unwanted
emotions—to rest.*

*Fergus and Morrigan have joined us on this raid. I admire
Fergus and his easy way with Morrigan. She is strong enough
to wield a sword, yet I have seen her defer to Fergus with
charm and grace. This seems to be a match made in heaven.*

*Heaven is much on my mind these days. "Remember the
former things of old: for I am God, and there is none else; I am
God, and there is none like me." Isaiah 46:9*

I want to believe that God will be there when I need him.

DESPITE HER MISGIVINGS, Orelia did as Richard asked, clinging
to his assurance that he would acknowledge Iain as John's son and
the rightful heir—in spite of Alice's displeasure.

211

Perhaps, in time, Alice's health would return and her mind would be more stable. It was one thing to covet the title, a vastly different thing to actually inflict harm on a child to get it. Orelia had heard of such strange behavior before—it seemed to occur after childbirth in some women and was but a temporary condition. Once Alice had regained her health they could all live at Radbourne without the animosity and conflict her condition had wrought.

But for now, Orelia felt a terrible sense of foreboding. An undercurrent of tension between Richard and Alice permeated the castle.

Orelia established her little family in the castle's tower chamber. Mary was free to come and go, and she brought their meals and removed the tray afterward. They occupied themselves with games and storytelling, leaving the cozy room only to use the garderobe, the only other room here at the top of the steep tower stairs.

All in all the situation was bearable, but Orelia longed for their lives to be normal. Finally on the sixth day of their stay in the tower, Orelia called Mary to the window. "The guests are leaving."

"Praise be. Now we can go back to our cottage."

"Soon, I hope. I'm sure Richard will send for us when everyone has gone."

But another two days passed before they were called to come downstairs to the great hall for the evening meal. Mary went to the kitchen with Iain to eat with Alice and Richard's son and daughter.

Though Richard greeted her with warmth, Alice acted as if Orelia wasn't there, and she began to wish she'd taken her meal with the children.

Alice's eyes appeared even more glazed, and her movements were slow and dreamlike.

She leaned toward her sister-in-law. "Are you feeling well, Alice?"

Alice didn't answer.

Orelia tried again. "Alice, you don't seem yourself. Are you all right?"

Alice slowly turned her head to face Orelia. "I'm fine. I have taken some tea to calm my nerves. Perhaps I drank too much of it. I'm sure it is no concern of yours."

Richard said, "Alice, that will be enough of such talk. Orelia is our guest. Family."

"An unwelcome guest, Husband. She and her baseborn child. Our kinship to her died with John."

Orelia drew back as if she'd been slapped. She rose to her feet but Richard exploded from his chair. "That's enough, Alice. I will escort you to our chamber—you obviously are not feeling well."

Orelia picked at her food while waiting for Richard to return.

When he sat down again he said, "Please excuse Alice. I had hoped this new remedy would ease Alice's complaint, but it doesn't seem to be helping."

"Perhaps you should send for a different healer. These remedies can be helpful in proper amounts, but I fear Alice is overindulging."

Richard pushed his plate away. Servants cleared the table and brought hot tea, which Orelia sweetened with honey.

"You may be right, Orelia, about Alice. But I suspect that my decision to acknowledge Iain has somehow unhinged my wife."

So Alice knew of his decision. "Perhaps you should wait until she is better."

"I considered waiting but as I told you, I believe it is past time that the matter is taken care of. I will leave for London tomorrow for my audience with King Edward."

Richard studied her face. "You seem apprehensive. I don't believe she'll harm you, Orelia. If I did, I would take her with me."

"It's not me I'm worried about. I fear for my son."

"I'll only be gone a week."

"Yes, of course. Thank you for doing this, Richard."

Richard appeared chagrined. "I am only sorry that I didn't stand up to Alice right from the start. My brother deserved better than to be remembered as a man whose wife was unfaithful." He stood. "It's late—let me escort you to your chamber."

They said goodnight in front of her door. She entered the chamber quietly so as not to disturb Mary and Iain. Orelia felt more at peace than she had since her days at Dunstruan. The thought of her accomplished goal made her smile.

As she plaited her hair and got ready for bed, she remembered the beautiful lake at Dunstruan. And the man who lived in the castle beside it. What had become of him? Had he made peace with his memories as she had made peace with her future?

On the morrow they would move back to the cottage and when Richard returned, perhaps she would take Iain and Mary for a sojourn to Dunstruan. With her son's inheritance in order, she was free. Free to resume her life in any way she saw fit.

UPON RECEIVING a surprising invitation from Alice, Orelia, Mary, and Iain came down to the hall to break their fast and see Richard off. George of Wellsey had arrived late the night before and Orelia greeted him. "George. It is so good to see you again."

He bowed over her hand. "My lady. I was happy to learn that the report of your death was false."

She looked to Richard and he nodded. "George knows all, Orelia. He can be trusted."

They were all seated before Alice joined them, looking flushed and rain dampened.

She sat down and seemed very pleased with herself. "I've had a lovely walk this morning," she announced.

Orelia thought it beyond strange that Alice would walk before the morning meal, but said nothing. She looked better this morning, brighter; perhaps the woman was trying to make amends with Orelia by breaking their fast together. Still, Alice's long stares at Iain made Orelia shift nervously in her seat.

When the meal ended, Orelia said a quick goodbye to Richard and took Mary and her son to the safety of their room to pack the belongings they'd brought with them. By the time they'd finished, the rain had increased to a downpour and Orelia decided to wait before carrying their goods to the cottage.

Orelia busied herself dusting the room and putting it to rights before she left. But within two hours of their return to the room, Iain became acutely sick. For hours, he vomited. He could keep nothing down, not even the tea that Orelia brewed to settle his stomach.

"What ails him, my lady?" Mary asked, staring anxiously at the lad from over her shoulder.

"I don't know. Go downstairs and ask the servants if anyone else is sick."

Mary left and Orelia held Iain's listless hand. He'd emptied his stomach long ago and though he'd stopped heaving, he was not responding. What sickness was this?

Mary came back and sat down hard on a bench. She breathed heavily from climbing the stairs too quickly.

"What it is? How many are sick?"

Mary shook her head. "Only one other. The earl. His manservant brought him back slung over his horse."

Fear gripped Orelia. What pestilence was this? "Is Richard dead?"

"No. But he's worse off than poor Iain. Lady Alice is worried that her children will become sick. She wants to know if you will take care of Lord Richard here."

"Of course." Though Orelia was scared for Iain, it wouldn't hurt him to have Richard here. She could understand Alice's concern for her children. 'Twas the first rational thought Alice had had in quite some time.

Mary left again and soon returned with servants carrying Richard. They placed him on a pallet before the fireplace and made no secret of the fact they were anxious to leave him and whatever contagion consumed him.

While Mary tended Iain, Orelia sat at Richard's side, gently wiping the sweat from his face and praying. No one else had sickened, to Orelia's relief. Richard ranted and raved like he'd had too much ale between bouts of emptying his stomach. At one point he lay quiet and Orelia thought he might be getting better. He opened his eyes. "Alice," he rasped.

"'Tis Orelia, Richard."

He shook his head. "I know . . . who you are. Alice . . . poison." He grasped Orelia's hand with surprising strength. "Don't trust her."

She didn't contradict his accusation. Alice had poisoned them? Her nephew and her own husband? Surely not! Richard must save his strength and get well. *He must, for all our sakes.*

Richard's breathing became labored and Orelia nearly wept. He had been kind, was set on an honorable course to right a wrong, and now she despaired for his life. And his wife had yet to inquire of his health.

Selfishly, Orelia feared what Richard's death would mean for her and Iain. If Iain lived. Orelia fingered John's cross and prayed as she'd never prayed in her life.

IN THE DEAD OF THE NIGHT Iain awoke and managed to keep down some tea. But Richard kept slipping away.

As morning's pale light filled their chamber, Mary returned from fetching fresh water; she set the pail down and sat beside Orelia. Mary's face was pale and she trembled.

"What is it? Has someone else sickened?"

Mary shook her head. "My lady, you will remember the hound that Iain befriended?"

"Yes."

"The one that eats the crumbs the boy drops."

Orelia smiled, thinking of the bond between the boy and the dog. "The one Iain feeds most of his food to?"

"Aye." Mary paused. "The dog has been missing since Iain and the earl got sick. Cook found its carcass on the garbage heap."

Orelia could not believe the implication. Had Richard spoken the truth after all? "You think they've been poisoned?"

"Cook does. She said someone left some mushrooms on the table in the kitchen. Cook recognized them—said they were poisonous and weren't allowed in the kitchen."

Orelia's heart pounded. She didn't need more convincing. She would heed Richard's warning. "We are not staying here, Mary. Especially if Richard dies. We're leaving Radbourne as soon as Iain is well enough."

THAT AFTERNOON, Richard breathed his last. Orelia sobbed at his side, devastated that such a good man should die so young. And even more devastated that he'd gone to his grave knowing his own wife had killed him.

Orelia prayed for his speedy journey to heaven. Then she prayed for deliverance from Alice, from a woman who had apparently murdered her husband. And for what? The title? Wealth? What good were such things without faith in God and the love of your husband?

Though Orelia hated to leave the relative safety of the room, she had to tell Alice of Richard's death. When Orelia entered the great hall, she saw Alice talking to George.

Alice primped at her reddish blond hair and turning a disdainful look on Orelia, she said, "Don't bother us."

George appeared somewhat taken aback by Alice's behavior.

"I'm so glad you're here," Orelia said to him.

Alice grabbed hold of his arm. "She's not half as glad as I am, George." Alice smiled coyly.

Orelia recoiled in shock at the obvious flirtation and George shifted uncomfortably. She nearly forgot why she'd come searching for the woman. Then she blurted, "Richard is dead, Alice."

"Oh, dear. I feared he might not recover. That is why I sent for George." Alice's glazed eyes and strange behavior were even more frightening now that Richard was dead.

Orelia stared at the man who had taken Alice's arm to support her. Whose side was he on? Could Orelia trust him as Richard had assured her? Anxious to return to her son, Orelia said, "I will have the servants bring Richard's body to the hall."

Alice waved her fingers and as if she hadn't quite heard, said, "Tell them to put it in the solar." Leaning on George, Alice simply walked away.

Orelia found several servants who went with her and removed the body. When they were gone Orelia closed and barred the door. She and her loved ones were safe for now; there was only one way into or out of the room.

"Mary, I'm convinced that Lady Alice has completely lost her mind." Orelia's thoughts were spinning and her head ached. The lack of sleep, Iain's illness, and Richard's death nearly overwhelmed her ability to cope. One thing at a time. She had survived a battle and imprisonment; she could manage this situation.

"We must go to my grandmother's cottage as soon as Iain is strong enough. Then I'll find someone who will go with me to London to vouch for Iain, someone who knew John . . . George! George can vouch for Iain!"

But something about the man's behavior a few minutes ago unsettled her. Orelia wasn't sure she could trust him, not if he'd come under Alice's spell.

While Mary tended to Iain, Orelia paced the room. Would George help her? Even if he agreed, Alice had powerful friends among the nobility. Orelia doubted whether any of them would believe her story. A knock came at the door. Cautiously she opened it to find George standing there.

"My lady. For the love I held for your husband, I must warn you. Leave Radbourne. I will arrange for a wagon to take you wherever you wish to go. Be ready to leave at first light!"

And with that he strode away.

WHEN THE SCOTTISH RAIDING PARTY reached the English town of Ripon, Ceallach knew he was less than twenty miles from Radbourne Hall. The knowledge that Orelia lived so close by ate at him and he considered riding south. He would not endanger her by going to Radbourne itself, but surely the nearby villagers could give him some word of her. That's all he needed, he assured himself. Just to know she was well. And happy.

They stayed several days in Ripon, restocking their provisions and resting the horses. The days of inactivity dragged by adding to his restlessness. Finally he went to Bruce. Ceallach faced his king and foster brother in the privacy of the king's tent. They hadn't seen any English patrols and even if they had, so long as no one recognized Ceallach, the danger to him was minimal.

Robert looked at him as if he'd gone out of his mind. "You want to visit an Englishwoman?"

"No. I just want to ride a bit farther south and learn how she is faring."

"Why would you want to take such a risk? I'm not convinced you should be making social calls while we're here," Bruce said in jest.

Defensively Ceallach replied, "I don't intend to call on her. Just go into the village and see what I can learn."

"Who is she?"

Ceallach squirmed. "Lady Radbourne."

Bruce looked thoughtful. "Lady Orelia Radbourne, the woman you guarded at Dunstruan?"

Ceallach nodded.

"I see." Bruce stroked his chin, the king's eyes searching his own. There was a glint of humor in Bruce's gaze. "All right, I see no harm in your plan. We'll ride to Radbourne and you can go into the village to learn what you can about your lady."

They camped a few miles from Radbourne Hall and the next day Ceallach, Fergus, and Morrigan rode into the village. The hard rain that had plagued them for several days had given way to a dry but cloudy afternoon.

The villagers watched with suspicion as strangers rode down the main thoroughfare. Ceallach stopped his horse outside the inn and Fergus and Morrigan did the same. "You two stay with the horses. I'll go in and see what I can discover."

His comrades nodded. They did not dismount.

Ceallach pushed open the heavy oak door, went in, and sat down at one of the empty tables. After a few minutes the serving girl came over and he ordered a glass of watered wine and some meat-filled pastries to share with his companions.

When the girl brought his drink he asked, "I'm looking for Radbourne Hall. Is it close by?"

She glanced around and then leaned close to whisper, "Yes, m'lord. About a mile east of here. But ye don't want to be going there."

She started to leave and he grabbed her wrist. "I've business there. Why do you warn me off?"

Again she looked warily about. With a pleased look that told Ceallach the girl enjoyed gossiping, she said, "Some are saying the earl is dead. Poisoned, they say!"

Struggling to remain calm, Ceallach sipped his wine. "I thought the earl died at Bannockburn."

Warming to her tale, the girl leaned closer. "That would be the old earl, Lord John."

This was just the opening Ceallach had been hoping for. "Does his widow still live there?"

She shook her head. "Don't know, m'lord. Rumor had it she died of a foreign plague but I've recently heard different."

She made to walk away, giving him a shrewd glance. Much as he hated to act so interested, he decided to give the girl what she wanted in exchange for more information. He pulled out his money pouch and laid a shiny gold coin on the tabletop, far more than the cost of the meal.

The maid came back to his table and whisked the coin into her hand. "They say Lady Orelia and her son are held prisoner there." She hurried away.

Despite the girl's willingness to gossip, Ceallach still had unanswered questions. He went out to his companions and handed them each a pastry. While they ate he told them what the serving girl said.

"What do ye want to do?" Fergus asked.

"I'm not going back to Scotland without answers."

"Are we going to smuggle a message in or go in ourselves?" Fergus asked.

Ceallach had been asking himself the same question and finally came to a decision. "I think we must go in. Make it look like a raid—if Orelia is being held against her will we can take her with us and make it look as if she was forced to leave with us."

Fergus nodded. "That will make her appear innocent of conspiracy but may make them more likely to chase us."

"'Tis a chance I'm willing to take. Are you?" Ceallach asked.

Morrigan grinned and eyed Fergus. "I feel the need to go a-raiding!"

A SILVER HALF-MOON illuminated Radbourne Hall, providing a clear view of its steep walls. A swiftly flowing creek lay between the small force of Scotsmen and the south wall.

"How are you going to get inside?" Bruce asked.

Ceallach grinned. "Do you remember that summer at Lochmaben?"

Bruce laughed out loud. "Well, at least this time you're in no danger of my father's belt. You mean to cross the creek and scale the walls?"

"Just as you and I did then. Fergus and I and a half-dozen men will ford the creek. Morrigan and six others will wait for us to open the front gate and let them in."

Bruce said, "Much as I hate to miss this, I think it best that I take the rest of our men to Bolton Abbey and obtain their ransom. No use passing it up when we're so close. Meet us there and we'll head north yet tonight."

Bruce left and Morrigan and her men took up their position while Fergus and Ceallach made their way to the streambed. Although they were far enough from the castle not to be heard, Fergus kept his voice low. "I am uneasy about ye going into the keep. Ye should go with Morrigan and the reinforcements—"

"Can I assume from this that Morrigan has told you what she knows of me?"

"Not exactly. She let it slip and I hounded her until she told me all."

Ceallach nodded, not sure how he felt about Fergus knowing of his past. But he had more important worries. "I could just as easily get caught outside the walls as in. I will enter the castle and see Orelia for myself." Only then could he be assured of her well-being. Besides, there was no one here who could recognize him from Bannockburn—he'd worn a hood. The real danger—for all of them—lay in being captured as one of Bruce's raiders.

Turning to the other men who would accompany them he said, "Make sure you've sufficiently covered yourselves in soot. We must blend in with the night if we're to be successful."

After a quick inspection, Ceallach ordered everyone to retrieve their weapons, which were wrapped in sacks to prevent the moonlight from finding the polished surfaces. The cloth would also dampen any noise from metal rubbing metal. Stealth and surprise were their only hope of breaching the wall.

Ceallach ensured that ropes were tied securely around each man's waist, the weapons attached to their backs. He grinned at Fergus, smeared from head to toe in charcoal. The others matched or exceeded Fergus in height, though none equaled Ceallach's stature. They'd been chosen for their ability to swim and for being tall enough to withstand the stream's current at its deepest point. The rest of the troop awaited them near the entrance to the castle with Morrigan in command.

Clothing would hinder their ability to maneuver and might even drag them into the swift waters. They wore only tight trews of darkened material. Ceallach shivered in anticipation.

Satisfied all preparations were complete, Ceallach gestured for them to move out. They quietly made their way to the stream's bank. Goose flesh raised on bare skin, not from fear—for these were seasoned warriors—but from contact with the frigid water.

Fergus had entered the water first and the others had followed at prescribed intervals. They must not all arrive on the other side at once, or some might be forced to wait in the stream, where their strength would be sapped from the chill.

The cold water crept up his legs, then rose to chest level, slowly washing away the soot. By the time he reached the narrow strip of land at the base of the wall, Fergus and James were using a long pole to lift a knotted rope to the top. A hook attached to the rope would hold it fast and enable them to climb.

The hook held, and again Fergus went first. When Ceallach's turn came, he silently cursed his own imagination for concocting such a scheme, as first his knee and then his chest scraped the wall. Somehow this had been easier when he was seven.

After crawling over the top, and scraping tender parts not usually exposed to such abuse, he quickly hid in the shadows with the others, for now only their faces and shoulders remained blackened. Looking at his fellows, Ceallach allowed a grin to crease his face, thinking what a fright they would give the inhabitants. Just so long as Orelia recognized him.

Black-faced and barely covered—true highland warriors.

The time had come. At Ceallach's nod, the others moved to pre-arranged locations. The castle seemed unnaturally quiet and Ceallach felt goose flesh rise again on his arms.

Soon. Soon he would know if Orelia was safe or not.

A dog barked. Again, with more force this time.

"Blast." He prayed the men were in position; they must make the final move now, before the guards heeded the dog's alarm.

He gave the signal, racing across the bailey, praying all the while that Orelia was asleep in her bed and not up and about somewhere. He didn't want to waste time searching for her. As Fergus's group raced toward the gate, Ceallach systematically barged into the sleeping chambers, surprising the occupants and securing one after another with rope.

Hurrying to the next room, he heard a shout of triumph as Fergus and the others reached the portcullis and began to lower the draw-bridge to their waiting companions.

Success. Now all that remained was to secure Orelia and escape and the battle would be over. Swiftly, quietly, and with no loss of life.

Kicking in the door, aware that the occupants might have been forewarned of danger by Fergus's shout, Ceallach proceeded into the next darkened room, slowing his steps and drawing his sword.

Ceallach stopped his advance, looking all around. What foul play was this?

On the bed lay the body of a man.

Sixteen

Brothers will fast on Fridays.

—from the Rule of the Templar Knights

The danger of being captured and imprisoned is never far from my mind. Even though it's unlikely that I would be singled out, still we are deep into English territory and run the risk of being discovered. I don't think my reason would survive captivity again, especially if I were tortured. All it would take to break me this time is a simple candle flame. Yet I brave it all for Orelia's sake. She didn't ask me to come, it's true, but I must make sure she is well—I may never venture this far south again.

And if the God I pray to is a just God, he will deliver me from my enemies.

GEORGE'S WARNING SPURRED ORELIA to action. Although he hadn't been specific, Orelia feared that Alice might try to poison them all. Or maybe she planned to starve them—lock the door to their room and refuse them food and water.

Orelia tried not to let her imagination become overwrought. But she would not just sit here and wait for whatever came. "I must leave tonight, Mary." Orelia began packing the few things she would be able to take with her. Iain was barely well enough to travel, but Orelia wasn't about to stay here and find out what Alice's daft mind planned next.

"What of George? Can he be trusted?" Mary sat Iain down on a bench.

"I'd like to think so—he did warn us. But if he must choose, really choose, between Iain and his own cousin's children, then what? I won't gamble Iain's life with a man whose loyalty is so divided."

Orelia observed Mary gathering her things. "Will you go with us, Mary?"

"Am I welcome?"

Orelia rushed to her and hugged her. "Most definitely."

Mary indicated the nearly full basket. "What else shall I pack?"

Orelia peered about the room and her gaze fell upon the small chest that held Ceallach's letter. Taking the parchment from the box, she held it to her chest and closed her eyes.

"What is that, my lady?"

"A . . . letter from a friend." *Do not open it unless you have need of me. When you read my words, you will know that I will help you no matter what your need.*

Her life was about to change—in a few minutes she would leave Radbourne to seek sanctuary elsewhere. Perhaps she would write to Ceallach once she'd established her new life. Not because she needed him, she assured herself, but simply to know that he was well.

She broke the seal on the letter then hesitated. What harm could there be in reading his words? She opened the parchment and read: *There were no roses blooming when we parted. If there had been, I would have given you a cream colored one with a blush of color on its tip, a promise of the love I hold for you.*

Ceallach loved her! Memories poured over her, one after another. Dunstruan. Safety. Friendship.

"What does it say, my lady?"

Mary's query brought Orelia back to the present and the need for action. She would not send for Ceallach and endanger him, despite his declaration. But perhaps she could seek refuge in Scotland. Orelia reached up to touch the necklace around her neck, to seek reassurance with a quick prayer.

"My necklace! Where is it?" Frantically she searched her clothing, then the room, trying to remember when she'd taken the necklace off. Mary joined the search but neither of them found the precious chain and cross.

With tears in her eyes, Orelia said, "It must have fallen off and I didn't notice. I thought I'd put it on the clothing chest last night before going to bed."

Orelia sat down hard on the bed, very nearly ready to halt their flight to safety until the necklace could be found. That piece of jewelry had come to symbolize her life with John and all he had tried to teach her about God's love. Now it was gone.

"I'm sorry, my lady." Mary laid a comforting hand on Orelia's shoulder.

Orelia blew out her breath. The loss of the necklace didn't change her situation nor did it mean God loved her any less. But with its loss came the final separation from John and his home.

Yet still she doubted. "Am I doing the right thing in leaving, Mary?"

"A simple life in the country is better than a quick death at Radbourne."

Accepting that the piece of jewelry was lost forever she said, "Let's go, then."

Just before dusk, Orelia, Mary, and Iain sneaked down the tower stairs. They went into the kitchen, thankfully deserted this late in the day, and took some bread and fruit and water. Then they raced to the sheep pens in the bailey, from where they could see the gate. The gate was closed!

Orelia stifled a moan. How would they get the gate opened without being detected? Every minute in the bailey was another minute closer to discovery.

"Don't fret, my lady," Mary said. "Someone will be along and they'll be opening the gate for them, you'll see. They're always slow about closing it up again. We'll move then."

They waited for nearly an hour for an opportunity to open the gate and leave unobserved. All through those hours of waiting, Orelia repeatedly reached for the cross that should be hanging around her neck. And each time it wasn't to be found she grieved the loss. Until it dawned on her that maybe this was God's way of showing her that her future no longer lay here at Radbourne. The cross—John's cross—was part of her past; now it was time for her to look elsewhere for her future.

Well after dark, the gate was opened and left open. Orelia heard shouts and a cry of alarm, and feared they'd been discovered missing just as they were to make their escape. She touched the knife strapped to her leg, reassured by its presence. A group of horsemen entered the gate, and in the confusion, the three of them slipped out of Radbourne unnoticed.

They ran for the cover of the woods, struggling through the thick forest that lay between them and the safety of Bolton Abbey. Orelia had decided to throw herself on the mercy of the abbot and take sanctuary there for the night. They would walk to her grandmother's cottage tomorrow and there she would take the time to decide what to do next.

Iain hung like a sack of wet clothing around her neck, and her arms ached. She and Mary took turns carrying him. *We should have taken horses.* But then they would have had to stay on the road and risk being seen. She and Mary didn't talk, saving their breath to run and scramble across the rough terrain.

How much farther? *God give me strength.* The uphill climb eased and soon they crested the hill. Exhausted, she gratefully sat on an outcropping of rock that overlooked Radbourne Hall to catch her breath. Mary sat beside her.

Far below them and about a mile away, were the flickering torches from the gate and walls of the castle.

A noise in the brush sounded behind them.

Iain whimpered and she covered his mouth. "Shh," she whispered. He quieted, and Orelia gave a prayer of thanksgiving. An animal scurrying for food, nothing more.

She stood, her arms protesting as they accepted the child's weight again. Nodding to Mary, she turned for a final look at Radbourne Hall. She struggled to make sense of what she saw in the moonlight.

Smoke poured from the tower room.

WISHING HE COULD LIGHT one of the candles that lay within his reach, Ceallach cautiously approached the bed and laid his hand on the man's chest. There was no rise and fall of breath. This chamber obviously belonged to the master of the castle; the dead man must be Orelia's brother-in-law, the Earl of Radbourne.

Still a young man in his prime—what could have killed him? Ceallach saw no sign of a violent death. Had he been poisoned as the serving wench had said? And if so, by whom?

Or had the earl died of contagion? For a moment Ceallach panicked at the thought that he and his companions might be exposed to some deadly pestilence. And Orelia as well. Where was she? Had she fallen to this illness, too?

Anxious to see her again, Ceallach turned and ran back to the main hall. He smelled smoke and wondered that the fireplace drew so poorly in such an otherwise well-kept castle.

Fergus and Morrigan had rounded up some of the castle's

inhabitants. Ceallach hastily scanned the crowd but Orelia wasn't among them. Disappointed and anxious to find her, he approached a young knight. Thinking the man to be one of the castle's men-at-arms he asked, "Is this everyone?"

The man stared at Ceallach. "You!" He backed away.

Ceallach brought his sword up. "Do I know you?"

"I am Sir George of Wellsey."

"Never heard of you. How do you know me?" Ceallach asked as he menaced the man's throat with the tip of his sword.

"I was squire to Lord John Radbourne at Bannockburn. You were there. I saw you when your mask slipped."

Ah, Ceallach remembered. This must be the young man Ceallach had not killed when the hood fell off his face. Aye, the man had lived to earn his knight's spurs. And lived to be able to identify Ceallach—turn him in for Edward's bounty.

Let him. All that mattered was finding Orelia. Ceallach would worry about his own safety later. "*If* I was at Bannockburn it makes no difference tonight." He looked at the knight. "Is everyone here?"

The man didn't answer and Ceallach brought the sword back up. "I am short of patience tonight, Wellsey. Answer me."

"Everyone is here except the countess and her sister-in-law." He paused, as if judging Ceallach's threat. "What do you want? If you mean to rob us, be done with it."

Intent on his need to find Orelia, Ceallach asked, "Where are the women you mentioned?"

Hurried footsteps and shouting sounded in the entryway. Ceallach turned to look as a servant raced into the hall. "Fire! Fire in the tower! Come quickly!"

Fire!

Wellsey stood rooted to the spot. "Lady Orelia. God help us. Orelia is in the tower!"

"Orelia." Ceallach didn't even pretend not to know who she was. It no longer mattered if George or anyone knew Ceallach's true purpose for being at Radbourne. "Lead on, man!"

As Ceallach and Fergus raced after George, Ceallach asked his friend, "Did you search the tower?"

"No, I didn't see the steps."

"This way," George shouted. "I should have *made* her leave—she was supposed to leave in the morning!"

They rounded a corner and through a door to the gathering dark. Tucked onto the outside of the original castle wall was a door that led to a covered staircase. George opened the door and smoke poured out of it.

Ceallach stepped onto the first step.

Fergus pulled him back. "Ye can't go up there!"

Ceallach turned to George. "You're sure she's there?"

"She was an hour ago."

Ceallach shoved Fergus's restraining hand aside and ran up the steps, staying as low as he could. There were windows in the stairwell, open to the outside with no glass or other covering. Moonlight and fresh air streamed through them at intervals, lighting the darkness and thinning the smoke. Please God, let me get to her in time. *Not unto us, O Lord. Not for my glory, but for yours. Give me your strength that I may glorify your name.*

Ceallach ran up the narrow staircase and reached the first landing, stumbling over something in the gloom. He jerked to a stop, heart pounding, with Fergus right behind him.

A body lay at Ceallach's feet. He peered closer. Light colored hair spread in disarray around the woman's head. She lay face down, her neck at an awkward angle, and Ceallach could not force himself to turn her over. "Orelia," he whispered.

George of Wellsey came up behind them in the narrow stairway.

"What is it?" He shoved past Fergus. "Alice!" he cried. He pushed Ceallach out of the way and knelt beside the woman, righting her body and then lifting her head onto his thigh.

A smoldering torch fell from her hand and George pushed it away from her clothing. "She must have tripped coming down the stairs." George brushed the reddish blond hair off her face.

Not Orelia. Ceallach's relief was closely followed by terror— Orelia was still upstairs! Ceallach started past George and the woman when he noticed something familiar dangling from her hand. Ceallach reached down to make sure his eyes hadn't been affected by the smoke.

John of Radbourne's necklace.

Ceallach took it from the woman's lifeless fingers and placed it around his neck. Then he started up the stairs with Fergus close behind. The smoke lessened as they neared the top, and when they reached the final landing, Ceallach knew why.

The ashes of rushes gave evidence that the fire had started on the landing in front of the door. Having burned the fuel on the landing, the fire had crept under the door, igniting it. The thick oak door smoldered but had not yet burst into flames. Ceallach could hear the fire on the other side.

He tried to lift the latch. Locked! Then he saw the key dangling from the latch. Someone had locked Orelia inside and set the place on fire! Dreading what he must face, he knew that unless he opened the door and went to her, Orelia would surely die.

Stealing himself, he turned the key, lifted the latch, and opened the door to a hellish sight. The fire had spread rapidly through the floor covering to the window curtains and the bed hangings. Flames shot from the bed's canopy to the beams holding the slate roof above it.

Dry from years of protection from water, the beams snapped and popped as the fire fed on them, weakening them. Smoke swirled near the ceiling and one of the great beams made an ominous cracking sound. Burning ash and cinders rained down on the room, igniting clothing and furniture.

"Orelia!" Ceallach shouted above the fire's roar. "Orelia! Where are you?" He turned to Fergus. "We must search quickly before—"

"Look out!" Fergus screamed over the sound of wood giving way.

The beam directly over where the bed had stood came crashing toward them. Ceallach saw the flames, felt the heat, smelled the smoke, but suddenly he wasn't at Radbourne anymore. He was in the torturer's room in prison, and the flame coming toward him was a pitch-laden torch.

When the torch—in his vision—hit his chest, Ceallach came back to the present. A piece of the beam had broken off and struck Ceallach, knocking him to the floor and making his head momentarily swim. "Orelia! Answer me!"

The heat from the burning wood heated the chain and cross around his neck and Ceallach could feel the metal grow hot through his clothing. Desperate to keep the cloth from igniting, he shoved at the wood, pushing it upward while at the same time Fergus kicked it away with his foot. Fergus grabbed Ceallach and began to drag him toward the door.

Ceallach resisted, pushed against the floor but his blistered hands were so painful he had to give in. He tried to stand—how could Fergus be so strong?

They reached the door and Ceallach used the doorframe to pull himself to his feet. He stepped back into the room but Fergus held on. "No! There isn't time, Ceallach."

"I must! I must!" he cried out. Then the heavy slate roof gave way and with a roar came crashing down. Debris pelted them and Fergus pushed him to the stairs. They reached the landing where the woman's body had been as smoke billowed after them.

Ceallach turned to look but Fergus propelled him forward. They barely outraced the column of smoke to the bottom of the stairway. Coughing and staggering, the two of them came face to face with Morrigan, the silent question written on her face.

Fergus shook his head.

Ceallach sank to his knees. God had once again deserted him.

Orelia was dead.

THE WALK DOWN THE HILL had been easier to manage as the trees grew less close here and the moon's light sifted through the branches. Another small rise of ground came next, and when Orelia reached the top of it, she could see the abbey. Orelia breathed a sigh of relief as they approached the road and the bridge spanning the narrow river that laid between them and shelter.

Orelia judged that they could cross the bridge and by staying close to the river, make their way to the safety of the abbey's stable. She'd had second thoughts about contacting the abbot. Better that no one know where they'd gone. Alice might send someone looking for her.

Alice. George. The children. What would become of them all? Were they in danger, with the fire? Had the fire been laid for her? Phantom flames danced in her mind. The farther they got from Radbourne Hall this night, the better.

"Come on. 'Tis too late to disturb the abbot tonight. We can sleep with the horses." Gathering Iain to her once more, Orelia ran across the bridge with Mary close behind. Not much farther. She ran from tree to tree until all that remained was an open span of ground between them and the stable door.

A gloved hand suddenly clapped over her mouth and another came around her waist. Both she and Iain were well and truly captured in a man's strong arms. Orelia managed to twist about and stare at her attacker.

The king of Scotland grinned at her, and she nearly fainted in relief.

CEALLACH SAT WITH HIS HEAD IN HIS HANDS in the main hall of Radbourne. Morrigan instructed one of the servants to cover his blistered hands with a soothing balm. His hands didn't hurt, but he thought for sure the agony in his heart would kill him.

George of Wellsey directed the servants in putting out the fire. Soot-covered and singed, he sat down beside Ceallach. "Thank you for trying to rescue Lady Orelia, my lord."

Ceallach merely nodded. He'd failed once again to save someone he loved. Hadn't he prayed for God to spare her? "Who was the woman on the landing?"

"Lady Alice. My cousin and the Countess of Radbourne."

Orelia's sister-in-law. "Are there children?"

"Two. The new earl—a babe of one year—and his sister. I will no doubt be named their guardian."

Morrigan came over to Ceallach. "Fergus is waiting—we'd best be going, Ceallach. The fire might draw more English to the keep."

But Ceallach had more questions. "You said you warned Orelia to leave. Why? What danger was she in?"

George looked uncomfortable. "My cousin Alice wasn't well. I have reason to believe she poisoned her husband."

Shocked by such a statement, Ceallach replied, "Why would she do that?"

"Because Richard had every intention of recognizing Orelia's son as the rightful heir. Obviously Alice set the fire to kill Orelia and her son. I imagine her maid was in the room with them and is dead as well."

Morrigan looked as dumbfounded as Ceallach felt. "'Tis a good thing the woman is dead by her own doing. Otherwise I'd have had to kill her myself." Morrigan swiped her hand across her eyes in a valiant attempt to hide her tears. "Poor Orelia. If only we had arrived in time to save her and her child. She deserved so much better from life."

No one spoke.

Ceallach just wanted this nightmare to be over.

Finally Morrigan laid a hand on Ceallach's shoulder. "We must go, Ceallach. We can't stay to help . . . recover the remains."

George agreed. "No. Nor should you. You would do well to put a good distance between you and this place—there are army patrols in the area."

Ceallach heard George's warning and raised his head. "You warn me of this? You could hand me over for the ransom."

"Go with God, Ceallach. For Lady Orelia's sake, I never saw you before in my life."

But Ceallach only stared at his hands. "If Orelia is dead, I may as well stay and let you have the reward."

"You're talking like a madman. Get to your feet and let's go." Morrigan tugged at him, and Ceallach hadn't the strength to fight it. He allowed her to lead him to his horse.

They rode to their rendezvous with Bruce at Bolton Abbey. The king and his men were hidden in the woods just before the bridge that covered a fast-moving stream. Morrigan and Fergus had to lead the way—Ceallach's mind had frozen. Ceallach dismounted, tied his horse and followed Fergus to Bruce, dreading the report he must give.

Blinded by grief, barely aware of his surroundings, Ceallach didn't see whoever or whatever hit him. He staggered under the weight of the person who leaped into his arms, arms that closed automatically around the woman who clung to him, kissed him.

Kissed him? He raised his hands to push her away, but she held his face in her hands and kisses rained on his eyes, his lips, his neck.

"Orelia?" He'd lost his mind. The stress of losing Orelia and the scorching of the fire had finally destroyed him. But if this woman wasn't real, he would gladly live the rest of his life right here in this fantasy world.

He clasped her close. "Orelia." He breathed in her scent, touched her hair with his damaged hands, heard her whisper his name. "You are real. Oh God, you are real." Tears streamed down his face as he held her tight and kissed her. "Is it truly you? Or are you an apparition?"

"I am real, Ceallach. Real and alive and so glad to be seeing you again."

"I thought you were dead!"

"Dead?"

"Dead in the fire. I tried to—"

"Fire? No, no, Ceallach. I'm here. Here with you."

"God be praised—Father in heaven—he's answered my prayers. He's answered my prayers!"

She stilled in his arms. "You've been praying?"

"Aye, though I didn't think anyone was listening."

"But you changed your mind?"

"You are here—my prayer was answered." He dried his wet cheeks on the sleeve of his sark. There was no avoiding what must be done next. "Orelia . . . Alice is dead."

ORELIA SAGGED AGAINST CEALLACH, relief, guilt, and finally sadness assailing her at Ceallach's pronouncement. "Dead? How did she die?"

"Fell down the stairs after she lit the fire."

The smoke Orelia had seen coming from the tower. "She set the tower room on fire?"

"Aye. Everyone thought you were in there—you, your maid, and your child."

Orelia thanked God for George's warning and for the premonition that had sent Orelia out of the tower tonight. If she had hesitated . . . Orelia began to shake at the realization of how close she and Iain and Mary had come to a horrible death.

Ceallach drew her close. "There now, it's all right. She is gone. You can return to Radbourne."

She pulled away and eyed him, trying to gauge whether he wanted her to go back or not. "I could. George thinks I'm dead as well?"

"Aye, though he may doubt it when they don't find any bones in that room."

Should she go back and claim what was theirs? She'd already made this decision once today. Had anything changed? Radbourne held nothing for her anymore.

She looked at Ceallach and for the first time noticed he was wearing John's necklace. Orelia reached up and touched it. "I thought I lost it."

He made as if to take it off. "Lady Alice had it in her hand when we found her."

She stayed his hand. "You keep it."

Ceallach said, "Are you sure?"

Orelia nodded. "Alice had it?" How strange. What had Alice wanted with it? Then Orelia remembered that when she'd thought the necklace was lost, she saw it as an omen that God was about to change her life. That change stood here in front of her. Ceallach, who had professed his love in the letter she wasn't to open unless she needed him.

Well, she needed him, needed to leave Radbourne behind and seek her future elsewhere. Iain's too. The past was dead, gone up in the flames of the tower room. But . . .

"What would I face at Radbourne?"

"George of Wellsey seems like a honest man."

"True. But his loyalty would always be divided between his blood kin—Alice's children—and my son."

"But your son's inheritance—"

She reached up and fingered the cross hanging on Ceallach's chest. "This is Iain's inheritance. His father's faith is something Iain will be able to rely on all his life. Far more dependable than worldly goods."

"Then you will come with us?"

"With you, yes."

He took a deep breath and let it go. "I can't make you any promises, Orelia. I am still bound by my Templar vows."

What would she do if he would not or could not marry her? Was she further jeopardizing her son by following this man into an uncertain future? She glanced at John's necklace—at the cross—and thought of its promise. She would trust in God, for the believing heart was filled with surrender and trust.

"I'm not asking for promises, Ceallach. May I stay at Dunstruan with you until you find your answers?"

He enfolded her in an embrace.

Yes, she could come to love this man. From the ashes of her grief for John, God had given her a second chance for love. She was at ease with her decision to stay with Ceallach. She peered up at him, at his beloved face. "Is that a yes?"

His smile was tender. "Aye, lassie, that's a yes."

"Mount up!" Bruce ordered, pointing toward the road as a troop of horsemen cantered over the bridge toward Bolton.

"What is it?" she asked.

"The patrol George of Wellsey had warned me about. Where is your child?"

Morrigan said, "Already mounted in front of Fergus. Ceallach, mount up and I'll help Orelia to mount behind you."

"But what about my maid?"

One of the men pulled Mary up behind him.

Morrigan gave Orelia a quick hug before helping her to mount.

There was no time for a happy reunion. Once settled behind Ceallach, Orelia checked on Fergus to see how he would ride and hold fast to Iain. With relief she observed Fergus wrap his plaid around the child and tie the material snugly, binding Iain in a kind of sling.

She clung to Ceallach as he wheeled his horse and followed Bruce. Stealthily they made their way through the woods before exiting the cover of the trees. Within minutes they were on the road and racing north. Hopefully, Edward's soldiers would spend sufficient time searching the abbey to give them a good head start.

SEVENTEEN

So many times in my life I failed God with my efforts. I failed to fight in a Crusade, to use my ability as a warrior for his glory. I thought my pride and the strength of my will would save me. But pride and human strength are no match for evil. I blamed God, blamed him for abandoning me when I needed him. Because of my failure, I abandoned my faith, turned my back on God.

So why would God bless a sinner such as me? And yet he has done that very thing that all reason says he should not.

When I joined Bruce on this raid into England, I hoped to hear news of Orelia, perhaps even to see her once more. Never did I dare to hope Orelia would return to Dunstruan. That indeed would be the answer to a prayer.

So I am left with this God who blesses even the worst of sinners with his love and his promise of hope for the future. Dare I hope he will show me how to make Orelia my wife despite my Templar vows?

ORELIA'S ARMS ACHED from holding fast to Ceallach's shirt, and her thighs chafed from bumping against the saddle. They'd been riding nearly an hour when Bruce called a halt to let their sentry catch up. Ceallach reined his horse to follow Bruce off the road and into the shelter of the woods. Everyone dismounted, stretching their legs and giving the horses a rest.

Orelia gave Iain some oatcakes and water that Fergus supplied, afraid all the while that the patrol was close behind. As she fed Iain, she listened to the men's discussion.

"Report," Bruce rapped out when Fergus brought the sentry to their resting place.

"The English soldiers are following hard behind us."

Bruce stroked his chin. "The abbot no doubt told them of our visit, so the English know who their quarry is."

"The horses can't keep up this pace." Ceallach sounded grim.

Orelia studied the men in the moonlight. All looked solemn but confident. They'd followed Bruce many times and were probably used to such events. Their confidence bolstered Orelia's flagging morale.

Bruce outlined his plan. "You're right, Ceallach, the horses can't run all the way to Scotland. Especially the two with a double load. We've another full day's ride to the border." The king motioned to Fergus and Morrigan. "Sooner or later we must stand and fight. But we shall choose the time and place. We must split our forces. I'll take half the men and continue on the road."

Fergus nodded. "The moon will set soon—our pursuers aren't likely to notice there are fewer tracks. And if they do notice, they'll waste time trying to figure out where the rest of us went."

"Aye. You and your men wait here under cover of the trees. A few miles farther north the road goes through a narrow pass—do you remember?"

Fergus answered, "Aye. Steep rock on either side."

"Exactly. My men and I will be waiting for the English on the other side. You come from behind, trap them in the pass and we'll give them a good fight." He turned to Ceallach and Morrigan. "Take the lady and her son and a half dozen men and head across country. Meet us at the old ruin outside of Brough."

Orelia hid a smile as Fergus went to Morrigan and kissed her cheek before mounting his horse. How did Morrigan feel about not being part of the fighting force? She seemed to accept her king's orders to ride with Ceallach; perhaps it soothed her pride to be part of the guarding force for Orelia and her child. Iain squalled in frustration as he was quickly tied to Morrigan's chest, but Morrigan calmed him with a promise of more oatcakes for breakfast.

Orelia laid a hand on her friend's arm. "Are you sure he's not too heavy?"

"We'll be fine, Orelia. I promise."

Orelia nodded as she and Ceallach mounted up. They headed northwest, the shortest distance to the border. Ceallach kept them at a steady walk, allowing the horses to pick their way alongside the creek they followed.

Exhausted from the emotional and physical toll of the day's events, Orelia rested her head against Ceallach's back. He smelled of smoke and burned wool. He hadn't spoken of the events at Radbourne and she wondered what had transpired. And if he would tell her.

Just before dawn, Ceallach called a halt and Morrigan found a campsite not far from the stream. Ceallach threw his leg over the horse's neck and slid down, then helped Orelia dismount. He took Iain from Morrigan and brought the sleeping boy to Orelia.

Ceallach motioned to her. "We'll rest here for a few hours, then go on to meet the others."

Glad to get off the horse and seeing that Mary had already made a fast run into the bushes she said, "Could you watch Iain for a few minutes?"

His eyebrows lifted in understanding. "Aye, of course."

How good it felt to walk after the hours on horseback. She finished quickly, returning to sit by Iain. She watched as Ceallach, Morrigan, and the men unsaddled their mounts, led them to the stream for a drink, and then hobbled them so they could forage without running off.

Only after the horses were cared for did they see to their own needs, disappearing into the brush for privacy. Ceallach came back with his hands full of pine boughs. "These will do for a bed," he said as he spread the fragrant branches on the ground beside her and Mary.

"Thank you," Mary said. "I'm so tired I'd have slept right on the ground. This will be much better." She took a few of the branches and spread them out a short distance away.

Ceallach motioned to Iain. "Would you like to lay him down?"

Only then did Orelia realize the poor man knew nothing about her son. Smiling she said, "His name is Iain."

"Aye. After your husband."

"But in Gaelic, to remember you."

He stared at her, took a deep breath as if she'd shocked him. "To remember me?"

"Yes. You and Dunstruan."

He looked down at her with the same intensity as he had that night he'd told her about Peter. Then she'd only seen, only wanted to see, deep affection. Was it wishful thinking to believe that now she saw more?

Ceallach took off his gloves and went to his saddlebag. He brought a piece of brecan cloth to her. "You and the boy can wrap up in this."

She stared at the cloth, then fingered it, running her hand across the pattern. "You finished the cloth we designed."

"Aye. Didn't think I'd ever have the chance to give this to you, though."

246

In the gathering light of daybreak she noticed his fire-singed clothing. No wonder he smelled of smoke! Quickly but gently she laid Iain on the makeshift bed and stood up and covered him.

"Aren't you going to rest?" Ceallach asked.

"Not until I see how badly you are hurt."

"'Tis nothing."

Annoyed with his stubbornness, she said, "I'll be the judge of that." She took hold of his hands—the gentle hands she had watched throw a shuttle back and forth on the loom. Turning them over she saw they were blistered and red.

"Are you satisfied?" he asked lightly.

"No. How did this happen?"

"Why must you fuss—" The rest came out on a hiss of pain as Orelia let go of his hands and pulled apart the laces on his sark.

The burned edges of the shirt allowed her to see more crimson skin. "Take your shirt off so I may see the damage." When he'd done so she sucked in her breath. The burn was mild compared to what he'd suffered on his back—just redness like a burn from the sun. But the skin was not harmed underneath John's cross. It's imprint stood in white contrast to the reddened area.

Ceallach had braved fire for her! Her eyes filled with tears and she took the excess of his plaid and dried them. Idly she wondered if he'd light a fire for himself now. She smiled at the thought and hoped . . . no, best not let her thinking get too far ahead of her circumstances.

But surely God meant for them to be together. Hadn't he marked Ceallach with the cross she thought she'd lost? Yes, she would claim Ceallach and his pride and his steadfast heart as her own. Whether he would return her claim remained to be seen. Love would not be easy for either of them, but she trusted God to help them over the obstacles.

She walked to Morrigan and asked if the woman had any healing supplies. When Orelia returned to Ceallach her face must have revealed that she had a good mind to chastise him for not having his injury cared for before leaving Radbourne.

Ceallach shook his head. "Save the lecture, Orelia. Until now, I honestly haven't felt it."

"We have no salve or anything else to treat it with, Ceallach. Come to the stream. Maybe just soaking some cloth in cold water will help." She turned her back and tore a piece of material from her chemise.

WHILE MARY AND IAIN SLEPT, Ceallach and Orelia walked to the stream. Ceallach did as she ordered, leaning against a rock near the water's edge. He relaxed, enjoying the whisper soft touch of her fingers as she tended to his injuries. The cool cloth did alleviate the sting that he was now very much aware of. "I suspect this will be my last visit to England."

She wrung out the cloth and laid it on his chest again. "And mine."

Surprised, he said, "You won't return eventually to claim Iain's inheritance?"

"If he grows up to look enough like his father, perhaps he can return and try to claim what is his when he's grown. If not, I'd rather he was a poor Scotsman than a dead English earl."

Ceallach said nothing. Only now did the full realization come to him. Orelia had left her past behind and looked to Ceallach for her future. But Ceallach might never be free of his past.

She searched his face, apparently looking for reassurance. "Are you having second thoughts about taking me to Dunstruan?"

"Aye. No, I'm . . . maybe." Panic licked at him like the flames had earlier.

From the folds of her clothes Orelia pulled out the parchment, the letter he'd written. The one that said he would come for her. "Did you mean what you said on this parchment?"

He looked at the paper in her hand then at her face. "I did." He could admit that he loved her, could not deny it. But that didn't mean he could offer her marriage.

"Generally, when a man tells a woman that he loves her, it means he loves her enough to face fire and ruin to rescue her. Which you did tonight, Ceallach."

Quietly defeated he said, "I thought you were in the room. And I couldn't save you."

Orelia reached up and cupped his cheek with her hand. "I can't imagine how painful that must have been for you—to think you'd failed again. To think me dead like Peter. I wish I could take away your hurt and pain, but only God can do that, and only if you allow it."

He'd more or less come to that same conclusion himself. But old habits and thoughts were hard to part with, and Ceallach knew he was a long way from accepting God's love again.

She removed her hand from his face and paced away and back. "I dreamed of Dunstruan all the while I was gone, Ceallach. Of the lake and the castle and of the weaver's hut." She stood on tiptoe. "But mostly I dreamed of the man who lived there."

Orelia kissed him on the lips, a gentle kiss of tender promise, and Ceallach could almost hear the demon scream in defeat, deep within the far reaches of his mind.

He pulled away and looked at her with regret. How could she care for someone as undeserving as he? He looked away from her, anguished at the knowledge that his vows as a monk still held him. "I told you, I cannot make promises, Orelia."

She looked at him in confusion. "Cannot or will not?"

Until Orelia, he'd thought himself incapable of love as well as undeserving. But she had awakened him to love and desire. If it were up to him, they would marry this minute. Then his heart and hands would be free to love, to touch, to embrace with all the passion of his lonely heart.

"You must know that it is not a question of will, Orelia. I cannot marry—my vows forbid it."

"Then I will be your handfast wife."

Her statement shocked him. He struggled for words.

"Suisan and Devyn are handfast, or they were before they found a priest to bless their marriage. We can do the same."

Anxious that she understand the situation fully, certain that she did not, he grabbed hold of her arm. "We cannot do the same, Orelia. In a year and a day I will be no less bound by my Templar vows than I am now. I promised God to live a chaste and obedient life of poverty."

She swallowed and her eyes brimmed with tears. How he hated to distress her, but he couldn't give her false hope. Why had he ever written those words of love to her?

Her lip quivered before she took a deep breath and blew it out. "Then we will simply remain handfast."

Her love, her foolish love, would bring them both to ruin because he wasn't sure he was strong enough to fight it. "Why did you read the note, Orelia?"

"I needed you. But I couldn't ask you to come to England, to put yourself in danger. Especially after I knew you cared. And you came anyway."

"What have I ever done to deserve you?"

She entreated him with her hands. "You are a man of honor, loyal and brave. What more could a woman ask for in a husband?" She swiped at her tears.

He jumped up, jabbed his hand in the air and nearly shouted, trying to make her understand. "We cannot marry, Orelia. My vows are binding."

She didn't back down, this English warrior woman. Instead, she stepped toward him, her eyes earnest with a faith that just might be strong enough for them both. "If they are binding, then you evidently believe in the God you made them to, Ceallach. I assure you, God is bound to you. When you were baptized, the priest made the sign of the cross on your forehead, marking you as Christ's, did he not?"

"Aye." He shrugged his shoulders, denying her words.

But she would not be denied. "That mark is as permanent as the marks on your back, Ceallach."

He sank back down to the rock, put his head in his hands.

Orelia stood at his side, brushing her hand through his hair as she might to soothe her son. "None of us deserves God's love nor can anyone earn it. It is a gift."

He wasn't sure he believed her—all his life he'd been told he must work for his salvation. 'Twas the whole reason for becoming a Templar, to earn salvation by using his warrior's skills for Christ. He looked up at her. "Where did you learn such strange ideas?"

"From John." Her radiant smile warmed Ceallach. "John believed that God's love is freely given. I believe it too. The question is, can you?"

Ceallach closed his eyes. If he accepted this, it must come from conviction, not from convenience. Only then could he welcome the hope of a life together with her. He opened his eyes and gazed at her beautiful face. Tenderness and desire awakened in him. "I want to, Orelia. But even if I do, I cannot break one set of vows for others that now suit me better."

Gravely she said, "If you were a less honorable man I would not love you half so much. But what are we to do?"

"I don't have an answer other than prayer, Orelia. That is all I know to do."

"That is enough for now." She smiled, and he knew that some-how, this would come out right.

251

Eighteen

All things are possible to him that believeth. . . .
Lord, I believe; help thou mine unbelief.

—Mark 9:23-24

At Bannockburn, I buried my Templar surcoat and my past along with it. Though I'd proudly worn the red cross for many years, now that badge of honor could cause my death. Yet through the years many people have died defending their faith. Why did I think I was different?

The cross of Jesus always has power over death if I have faith in the God who died for me. I cannot deny my past any more than I can deny the cross of my Savior and Lord. Somehow, with God's grace, I will move on to the life and the purpose God has planned for me.

I believe; help my unbelief.

AT MIDDAY CEALLACH WOKE THE OTHERS. He was anxious to reach Brough yet today and rejoin Bruce, to have the added safety of increased numbers. And he worried about Robert. Had the man's good luck given out? Had the English patrol somehow overcome Bruce's men?

After a cold meal, they mounted up and again headed north. Iain had been well behaved, under the circumstances, but had become more and more restless as the day wore on. Everyone was glad to reach Brough that evening, and Ceallach relaxed when he saw Bruce and the others waiting there for them. Though one or two sported bruises and cuts, none of the Scots had been seriously injured in the skirmish with the English.

The campfire burned brightly as they sat around it that night. The flickering light illuminated Fergus's hands as he used them to illustrate the story. "The man's face—I wish ye could have seen the patrol commander's expression when we rode up behind him."

Fergus chuckled and continued his tale. "He and his men were no match for us. The king pushed him toward me and we fought them a bit before backing off and letting them retreat."

Morrigan said, "And I missed it all—rode all this way and never drew my sword."

"Just as well," someone called out. "Those soldiers would never live it down if they retreated from a wee Scottish lass."

The jest didn't seem to offend Morrigan—she laughed as readily as the rest at the Englishmen's expense. Ceallach supposed Morrigan was well used to such good-natured teasing.

"Orelia, we brought back a prize for ye," Fergus said. "One of George's men fell from his horse."

"He didn't fall—I knocked him off," someone boasted.

"All right then, a lovely bay palfrey lost its rider and I grabbed the reins. She'll be a perfect mount for ye."

Orelia's maid, Mary, would still have to ride double, but the men would take turns in order to ease the burden on their horses. Ceallach thought wistfully about how Orelia would no longer have her arms about his waist . . .

He mustn't let his thoughts drift there. Barring a miracle, they would not marry. Ceallach was doomed to burn again. But when the man next to him passed the flask of whiskey, Ceallach did not drink to dull his yearnings.

After a restless night's sleep, Ceallach awoke and got his and Orelia's horses ready. The saddle on Orelia's palfrey lay more flat in the front than Ceallach's war saddle, and she was able to place her son in front of her. Both she and the child seemed satisfied with the arrangement.

When they rode out, Bruce directed them off the road and into the woods in order to skirt several villages. He did not want to gain the attention of the barracks at Carlisle. Late that afternoon, Ceallach breathed a sigh of relief when they safely crossed the border into Scotland. Two days later they arrived at Dunfermline Abbey.

ORELIA WAS GRATEFUL for the little mare. After Ceallach's confession that he could not marry her now—indeed, doubted he could marry her at all—she needed to put some distance between them. She and Mary spent the days after they arrived at Dunfermline caring for Iain in the two-room suite assigned to them. Iain had completely recovered from the food poisoning and explored everything around him. More than once, Orelia was happy to have Mary's helping hand.

Every morning before she broke her fast, Orelia went to the chapel and prayed. She prayed that Richard and John were united in heaven. She tried to envision Alice there with them but couldn't quite manage it. That she would leave to God.

And Orelia prayed for Ceallach, that he would believe—truly believe—that God loved him and wanted only good for him, including love. She saw him mostly at meals, and each time she saw him wearing John's cross it renewed her hope. The memory of John and his reminder that she was not alone, no matter what happened, sustained her. Could Ceallach see his way clear to make new vows in this new chapter of his life? Vows that would honor his Lord in a different way? The solution lay between Ceallach and God. Orelia would not interfere.

A week after their arrival, Mary took Iain to the abbey garden to search for butterflies, and Orelia sought out Ceallach. She found him in the stable, repairing his saddle. She stood just inside the door and gazed at him. He sat on a bench, head bent over his task. So tall and strong, such capable hands! And a heart so tender . . .

She would follow him anywhere, if only he would allow it. But she understood that he still struggled with the dark one and his lies. She must be patient while God turned Ceallach's heart back to the light.

She smiled, thinking of Ceallach's aversion to fire. Then she walked into the aisle and he noticed her.

"Hello, Orelia." He stood up and led her to the bench he'd been occupying, but neither of them sat down. He appeared quite uncomfortable as they stood face to face.

She stared at John's necklace.

He stared at her face.

"When are—"

"How is—"

He smiled. "You first."

She chuckled. "When are we going to Dunstruan?"

His smile disappeared. "Fergus and Morrigan will leave in another day or so." He still held the tool he'd been using, and now he stared down at it in his hands. "I thought perhaps they could take you and Mary and Iain with them."

She felt her shoulders sag with disappointment. "You aren't going home?"

He bent to lay the tool on the bench, avoiding her. "I can't, Orelia. I am not strong enough to resist the temptation of taking you as a handfast wife."

"Well, at least that's something, that you find me tempting."

He straightened and stared at her, his expression full of hunger. "Never doubt my desire for you, Orelia. Or my desire to marry you."

She stared at him, awed and amazed by this declaration. "But you still seek answers."

"I do."

"And when you find these answers, what if you cannot be released from your earlier vows? Will you send me back to England?"

He shook his head. "You don't have to go back unless you want to. Dunstruan is yours. Yours and Iain's. I've had the papers drawn up."

"What? You can't do that! Dunstruan is your home, not mine."

"Orelia, I've never owned anything my whole adult life. I have no need to start now. And I will rest easier knowing that no matter what happens, you are safe and well taken care of."

She would not cry. She would not! She didn't want to accept this gift, and yet how could she refuse? She didn't want to live there without him. But she might not have a choice. How else were she and Iain to make it? To find shelter and enough land to generate an income so she wouldn't have to depend on charity? Once again she reminded herself to trust in God.

She must give Ceallach the freedom of mind to find his way back to God. For the path he had for him. She only hoped she wouldn't have to wait a lifetime. And that that path was one that joined with her own.

Resigned, she said, "I will leave with Fergus and Morrigan."

"Good. I'll come for you at Dunstruan, God willing."

She reached up and caressed the necklace. "All you need is to believe, Ceallach. Listen for his word, for his direction. God will do the rest." Orelia turned and left the stable, her sight blurred by tears, and went to the chapel to pray.

The next morning she left for Dunstruan.

CEALLACH WATCHED ORELIA LEAVE, wishing he could leave with her. But as much as he hated to see her go, he knew he needed more time. Time to attend to unfinished business. He saddled his horse and with provisions for several days, headed for Stirling and the battlefield on the Bannockburn.

He camped that night about six miles from his destination, and for the first time in years lit a fire to chase away the chill and the dark. He credited Orelia and her love for defeating this particular torment.

He arrived at Bannockburn the next day at noon and immediately headed for the spot behind Gillies Hill where they'd buried his Templar surcoat. For a time he despaired of finding the right rock, but eventually he found the one he'd marked. Pushing it aside, he used a digging tool to unearth the chest.

The material had begun to deteriorate in the dampness of the ground but the blood red cross remained in good shape. Ceallach gathered the cloth and took it to the top of Gillies Hill overlooking the battlefield. To the north lay the once great fortress of Stirling, reduced to rubble by Bruce's order.

To the east he could see the waters of the Firth of Forth whose flowing tide had decimated the English army. To the west and south the Torwood and its rocky outcrops sheltered deer and mountain lions.

Ceallach set up camp beside a wall of stone. He laid the surcoat on a log and draped John of Radbourne's cross upon the cloth. Ceallach meant to wrestle with God as Jacob had once. Maybe then God would bless him with a wife just as he'd blessed Jacob. Ceallach only hoped he wouldn't have to wait seven years.

He stayed there three days, fasting and praying and was sure of only two things when he left. He loved Orelia Radbourne with all his heart. And he knew that the cross that symbolized Christ's greatest defeat also symbolized his greatest triumph.

Orelia was right. A God who would die a miserable death on a cross was a God who loved unconditionally.

Spiritual death, or a life of faith? Accept God's love and the woman he'd given to Ceallach? Or reject them both? And what of his vows as a Templar? *I believe; Lord, help my unbelief.*

WHEN CEALLACH RETURNED to Dunfermline, the tattered surcoat lay next to his skin, folded beneath his shirt and plaid. Ceallach felt ready for whatever answer God had for him. He sought out Bruce's friend, Bishop Wishart, and they sat down together in the solar.

"What can I do for you?" the bishop asked.

Ceallach pulled the surcoat from under his shirt. The bishop's eyes widened in recognition. Ceallach confessed it all then, leaving nothing out. Talking about Peter came easier now, and telling of his love for Orelia filled him with joy.

Then came the crux of Ceallach's worries. "I made my Templar vows before God. I cannot break them just because they are no longer convenient."

The bishop stroked his beard. "I see your dilemma. However, the life that went with the vows no longer exists." The bishop pondered this for a long minute and Ceallach struggled not to fidget in his chair. "Tell me, Ceallach. In this new life God has given you, do you plan to lead a chaste life, one that is pure in conduct and intention?"

"Aye."

"So, if you were to marry, you'd be faithful to your wife, abstaining from unlawful intimate relationships?"

"Certainly." The vow of chastity would not be a burden with Orelia as his wife.

"And would you share your wealth with those less fortunate, using what blessings God may provide for the good of many?"

Ceallach smiled, seeing where this was leading. "Aye. I would give to the less fortunate from whatever wealth the Lord may bless me with."

"And while you love Orelia, your love by no means diminishes your love or faithfulness to your Lord, first, correct?"

"Nay."

"You would still die to defend him or his Word?"

"I would."

"And finally, as you move on in life, will you be obedient to the Word of God?"

"Aye, with God's help."

"Then you will still be adhering to the vows of chastity, poverty, and obedience, won't you?

Hope soared, hope for a new life with Orelia and Iain. "Yes. Yes, I will."

"Bring your lady back to Dunfermline, Ceallach. I would be glad to bless your union, and I'm sure God will too."

Six months later

ON A BEAUTIFUL SPRING DAY, Ceallach and Orelia stood in a graveyard behind what had once been the Templar stronghold outside of Paris. Posing as Peter's kinsmen, they'd made discreet inquiries until at last they'd been directed to the man's grave.

Dogwood and daffodils bloomed in the peaceful silence. A Benedictine order had taken over the buildings that had once housed the Knights of the Temple of Solomon. Honorable men who had wanted only to serve their God with the gifts he'd given them— strength of arms and courage. It seemed the perfect setting to put Ceallach's demons to rest.

The sound of monks chanting *nones* drifted on the warm afternoon air as Ceallach stared at the stone inscribed with the name of Peter the

Weaver. Orelia slid her hand into Ceallach's and he squeezed, glad for her presence. She'd been the one who urged him to come back, and he'd known he must. Before they'd left Dunstruan, Orelia had taken her scissors and removed the red cross from Ceallach's surcoat. Now it rested in his other hand, the final remnant of his past.

"God give you peace, Peter," he said as he laid the scrap of material on the headstone.

As he gazed at Peter's name and listened to the chanting of the monks, Ceallach said a silent prayer of thanks for the second chance God had given him.

He raised his head, and his gaze came to rest on the gravestone next to Peter's. Ceallach froze.

Orelia tugged at his hand. "Ceallach, what it is?"

He could only point.

Orelia gasped.

Next to Peter's grave stood another simple stone, a stone that marked the memory of Marcus of Kintyre. Staring at the name his mother had given him, Ceallach swallowed hard. "What is the meaning of this?" he whispered.

Orelia shook her head, apparently as confused as Ceallach.

Ceallach closed his eyes, opened them, and looked again. The marker was still there. Where had it come from? Who had placed it there? Jean Paul? Seven men had escaped from this place. Hurriedly Ceallach searched among the stones to see if his guess was correct.

"What are you looking for?" Orelia asked as she followed behind him.

He walked among the stones, silently counting until he found the other six markers. "I don't know how he managed it, but the man who helped us escape also made it appear as if we died here."

Together he and Orelia walked back to Peter's grave. He shook his head and smiled, then laid his hand on the grave next to it.

Orelia placed her hand over his. Beneath his fingers was cold stone. Atop them was the warm hand of his wife. "God grant you peace as well, Marcus of Kintyre," she said, looking into his eyes.

Ceallach smiled and took her hand and led her away then. As they walked toward the gate, Orelia asked, "What was the name of the man who did this?"

"Jean Paul. Why do you ask?"

"I thought perhaps we might name our son after him."

He stopped and turned to her. "We don't have . . ." One look at Orelia's grin told him all he needed to know. "God be praised!" He kissed her, his heart filled to bursting with joy. "When is the child due?"

"The middle of October."

Ceallach's journey had begun in the middle of an October night. But his long, dark walk was over—the Lord of light and life beckoned.

Ceallach pulled his wife into his embrace. "Let's go home."